A WEREWOLF, A VAMPIRE, AND A FAE WALK INTO A BAR

The Last Witch, Book 1

KARPOV KINRADE
EVAN GAUSTAD

To all the essential people who are working with the sick,
handling deliveries and providing necessary food and resources
during this crazy time: We see you and we appreciate you.

And let us all toast to an old Irish proverb:
May the best of our past be the worst of our future.

Chapter One

"So, a werewolf, a vampire and a fae walk into a bar..." Joe says, his lips pursed in exaggerated performance.

"What's a fae?" Frank asks from the end of the bar. He follows his question with a long drink of his Guinness, sloshing a bit out of his glass and onto the counter I just wiped down three seconds ago. Frank's a beefy type, with a thick body and a thick dark beard that covers his aging skin. He was a truck driver for 40 years and is now a professional barfly.

Joe shrugs, his eyes bloodshot and his beer belly hanging over his belt. "Like an elf. You know, like those movies." His alcohol habit has aged him by at least ten years. Well, that and grief. A broken heart will break your body just as fast. His 50 looks closer to 60, and his formerly brown hair is now streaked with gray.

"Nobody gives a shit about your stupid jokes, Joe," Phil says from his standard spot at a booth in the back. The youngest of them, Phil is tall and skinny, with a blond scruff of hair that dances wildly on his head, like it can hear music no one else can. He works construction, like most of the men around here, so he's always got filthy fingers wrapped around my otherwise clean pint glasses.

Joe's face falls, but he retains his optimism. "You care, don't ya, Bernie?"

I grin, rubbing a wet cotton rag over the spill Frank just made. "Sure I do, Joe. As long as you tip." I wink to take the sting out of my words, and he chuckles along with everyone else.

It's Tuesday, our slowest night of the week, and these guys are all regulars. They've been coming to Morgan's since before I was born, and will probably haunt the place long after I'm dead.

Joe takes a swig of his Smithwick's. "Okay fine. You're right. Vampires are dead. No one likes those bastards since they started to sparkle. Hold on, I've got another one. The past, present and future walked into a bar," he says, and before anyone can give him a hard time, he wraps the joke up. "It was tense."

That one actually makes me laugh out loud. What can I say? I'm a geek at heart. I just play the tough as nails Irish girl to keep the locals happy. I mean, it's not all an act. I *was* raised in a bar, my Irish heritage shines brightly in my pale skin and dark hair, and I'll absolutely punch a drunk who gets handsy. And if it weren't for these locals, I'd never have made it out of this town, even if I did end up right back where I started.

Fate is a bitch, and if she decides to walk into my bar, I'll show her ass out.

A twinge of pain flashes deep in my abdomen. I lean against the counter, exhaling quickly and holding onto my protruding belly. "Hey there, little one. What's going on? It's not time to meet yet."

Joe glances down at my stomach and is about to say something, a worry line creasing his forehead, when a loud crash sends him into full panic mode as the walls of Morgan's Irish Pub shake.

"What the hell was that?" he asks. "Is it aliens? Is this it? They've finally come for us!" He starts looking around the bar for... what? I'm not sure. A place to hide from the aliens maybe? A light saber?

I roll my eyes and make my clumsy way to the

front door. "Relax, Joe. It's probably just a tree knocked down by the storm."

That's the other reason we're so slow tonight. A wicked blizzard that's going to make driving a bitch--if it hasn't already.

When I open the door, a gust of snow and wind nearly knock me to the floor. I hold tightly to the door frame and grab my coat from the rack, shrugging into it as I trudge out into the cold to check on the damage.

I shiver against the blistering winds, and suck in my breath at the scene before me. The roads are covered in inches of thick, fluffy snow, making it look like a winter wonderland. Winters are always harsh up here, but this is something else. In fact, this might be the worst we've had since I've been alive.

It will take out power for at least a few days, and I shudder to think what the homeless will do, but I can't help but marvel at the temporary beauty it's inspired.

I stand there so long my eyelashes begin to freeze shut. Blinking, I trudge through the inches of snow to the right, where the crashing sound came from.

I'm expecting a downed tree or power line, but I

don't see anything unusual at first. Then I notice a hole in my wall the size of a grapefruit. I scoot closer, tugging my coat around my belly as best I can—I was too cheap to spring for a maternity coat and am really regretting that act of frugality right now—and peer into the hole looking for evidence of what caused it.

Something is stuck deep in the crumbling brick, but it's not a tree or a branch.

I reach in, my fingers numb from the cold, and feel around, hoping I'm not about to get bitten by a radioactive spider or feral chipmunk.

Nothing bites me, but I do feel the smooth edges of a rock. It's a little warm, but not hot enough to burn. Gripping the ridges, I nudge it out inch by inch as the brick crumbles around my hand into dust.

With one final tug, I pry the object free and hold it in my hand. Before I can get a good look, the light above flickers out. I turn to the road and watch the street lights do the same.

Awesome.

I take the rock with me, my thoughts bouncing between what category storm can toss around small boulders and how strong the generators at the maternity wing of the hospital are.

I hurry back to the warmth of the bar as fast as I can without slipping on the ice and falling on my ass. Heat blasts me as I step inside. Naturally, my alcoholic patrons have already started lighting candles so I won't kick them out. I love them, even with all their problems.

I take a moment to look at this rock. It's metallic gray with copper veins running through it. Veins that seem to glow, though I'm sure that's just a trick of the light. I shrug off my jacket and tuck the rock away on a shelf behind the bar.

"What you got there?" Joe asks, his voice slightly slurred because even I've lost track of how many Smithwick's he's had.

I look at it and shrug. "A rock, I guess. A bit unusual looking. You guys ever seen the wind throw stones before?"

I look around at Frank, Joe and Phil, the only patrons of our fine establishment tonight. Well, except Karl, but he's passed out in the back booth as always. There are stories that he has never moved, and he's actually a well-preserved corpse. I can neither confirm nor deny this. But his tab gets paid and he doesn't smell any worse than these other bastards. So we're good.

"It's bad out there, guys. One last round? Then I'm closing shop before you're stuck here all week."

There's a collective groan at being kicked out before nine (on a Tuesday, God forbid), but I shrug and top off drinks. They'll thank me in the morning when they wake up in their own beds rather than the floor of my bar. I'm just serving the last beer when the bell over the door dings, and I look up in surprise as a flurry of snow chases three men into my bar.

And by three men, I mean three absolute specimens. These are, hands down, the sexiest guys I've ever seen. It takes me all of two seconds to make that assessment.

I place a hand over my baby bump to remind myself what happens when I let a pretty face and a hot body talk me into bad decisions--and these guys look like a lot of bad decisions wrapped in a delicious bow.

Settle yourself, woman. You don't need more complications with a baby on the way.

"Close the door," Frank shouts. "You're letting in the storm and Bernie ain't mopping that shit in her condition."

A smile tugs at the corner of my lips. This town takes care of its own, that's for sure. And by the looks of these newcomers, they're definitely not from around here.

Though they came in together, I get the distinct impression they're not exactly friends as they glare at each other suspiciously.

What they're doing in my pub on a weeknight during a blizzard is beyond me.

They each choose separate tables near the back, though they don't take their eyes off each other. Strange. As I walk over to take their order, I also study them.

I may have sworn off men for the foreseeable future… like, until my kid is in college… but that doesn't mean I can't enjoy some eye candy when it walks into my bar.

"Hey guys, we just called last round, so I can get you something, but then we're closing up early on account of the storm."

"A whiskey on the rocks," Mr. Sexy #1 says, in an accent that sounds vaguely British. He is a tall drink of water and I am thirsty for it. I haven't had sex since the night this baby happened, but again, that's beside the point. His skin is pale, like moonlight, and his hair is as dark as midnight and matches the deep, dark depths of his eyes. He has a face chiseled from marble and full lips that are currently pinched in annoyance. He's dressed unusually--in fact, all three of them are. Like they've just come from a cosplay convention, though no cosplay convention would ever come to Rowley. This guy has a long black cloak and wears fitted leather pants and a black silk shirt underneath.

It takes all my will power to pry my eyes off of him and train them on Mr. Sexy #2. This boy is all wild energy--like an untamed forest, with eyes the color of deep green leaves, coppery brown hair that's tussled in that just-had-sex way, and a matching stubble that accentuates his rugged good looks. He's dressed in neutral colors and natural fabrics, and looks ready to lead a hike through the woods at night.

"What'll it be?" I ask, trying to sound like the hardened bar owner I should be and not the swoony undersexed pregnant lady I currently am. "And are these on the same tab?"

"An ale," he says, his voice deep and resonant, with a sexy lilt that's almost Irish. "And no."

"Alright, what about you?" I ask Mr. Sexy #3, whose eyes are the lightest blue I've ever seen. He has long, pale blond hair that only adds to his sex appeal, and wears a rich, velvet cloak pinned with a silver broach.

He looks unsure about his choices, so I size him up and suggest a Vesper Martini, even though it means more work for me.

"Very well," he says, and I can't place his accent, but it's definitely not American.

"What brings you boys to town?" I ask, keenly aware that everyone is watching this interaction.

The three Sexies silently glare at each other for a long moment before Sexy #2 finally answers. "A family errand," he says vaguely.

"Huh. Well, I hope you didn't drive. It's going to be a rough night on those roads."

When none of them reply, I turn and head back to the bar to get their drinks.

Joe wags his eyebrows as I work. "What's their deal?"

"I don't know. Never seen them before."

"You gonna bag one of 'em?" he asks with a dumb grin.

I roll my eyes. "You know I'm not interested in guys right now," I say, trying to hide the fact that I'm extremely interested in all three.

He sighs. "You deserve a nice guy to settle down with."

Before I can reply, another wave of pain grips me, and I lean against the bar to catch my breath.

Joe stands, clutching his beer as he does. "Bern, you okay?" He looks around, a panicked expression on his face. "Hey guys, Bernie's baby's coming. We got to get her help!"

"I'm fine. Relax. It's just Braxton Hicks. Totally normal."

Frank and Phil stand and drop some bills in front of them. "You sure you're okay?" Phil asks.

I nod, loading drinks on a tray to take to the newcomers.

"Alright then. Take care, Bernie. See you tomorrow," Phil says as he teeters out on slightly drunk legs.

Frank hesitates by the door, glancing at Joe then back at me. "You gonna be okay, kid?" he asks. I wince at the kid part, but he's been calling me that since I was born so it's hard to expect different.

"Yeah, it's fine. I'll be closing up soon anyways. Get home safe. Say hi to Alice and the kids."

He grimaces at the thought of his family. "Will do."

When the door opens, a flurry of snow and cold air blows in. Frank and Phil leave quickly, shivering as they step outside.

I hold the tray carefully and serve the new guys, studying them as I do. None of them speaks, but their simmering glares speak volumes.

"You three look like you're having fun," I say. "Bachelor party?"

Sexy #1 raises an eyebrow. "Are you Bernadette Morgan?" he asks.

It's my turn to raise an eyebrow in return. "Who's asking?"

"Hey Bern, one more drink, pretty please?" Joe asks, interrupting whatever Sexy #1 was about to say, if he was about to say anything at all. "I've only had… a couple? A few."

"Joe, you know that's not a good idea. You're drunk enough for a night like this."

I head back to the bar and start running through my closing check list when another pain grips my belly and I brace myself against the counter, taking quick breaths that sound a little too much like I'm in labor.

I'm not.

I can't be.

It's too soon and I'm snowed in. There would be no way to get to a hospital tonight.

I grab my phone to Google Braxton Hicks contractions. I mean, I've read all the damn books and I know what I'll find, but I need Dr. Google to make me feel better—or convince me I'm dying of a rare disease. Either way, as long as this baby doesn't make her debut today, I'm good.

I open my browser, but it lags. Shit. No service.

Joe is sweating profusely and cursing under his breath. "You okay there, buddy?" I ask through my own gritted teeth.

He looks up, his eyes widening. "Uh, yeah. It's just. You know. You look like shit."

I grimace. "Thanks. Every woman's dream compliment."

"Oh I didn't mean that, Bernie." He tugs at his overgrown facial hair nervously, his gray bushy eyebrows dancing atop his eyes like agitated caterpillars.

As the cramps in my belly ease, I take a relieved breath and smile. "There ya go. All better. I told you, false alarm."

He scoots himself back onto the barstool in front of me and grabs the remains of the drink Frank left, downing it in one long gulp that only seasoned alcoholics can manage with such aplomb.

I crack a wry grin, raising an eyebrow. "You good now?"

He swipes his forehead with the back of his

hand. "Yeah. Sorry. I'm… not great in medical emergencies," he says shyly. "My wife always handled that shit… when… "

I pat his hand. " I know Joe, it's okay."

Outside the storm intensifies, the howling of the wind sending a shiver down my spine. "How long has it been now? Two years?"

He nods. "Last week marked two years since cancer stole my Betty." He sniffs, looking around for another drink.

"Did you drive here?" I ask.

"Nope. Walked."

I nod and pull out a clean tumbler. Normally on a night like tonight I'd pour two and share in the drink, but with this little one riding shotgun on my bladder, my drinking days are on pause. I pour two fingers of whiskey and scoot the glass to Joe, caving on my earlier resolution to cut him off.

"On the house," I say, pouring myself a club soda. I hold my glass up in toast. "To Betty."

Joe's eyes moisten as he raises his to clink against mine. "To Betty."

He throws back his whiskey, draining his glass before I've even brought mine to my lips. It's one of those nights, it seems, which, honestly, is a mood.

One I'm looking forward to giving into once I'm

no longer an incubator to this little leech I already love more than is proper or right.

"Are you ready for motherhood?" Joe asks, leaning back as the whiskey relaxes him.

"Nope," I say, wiping down the already clean bar and throwing a glance at the Sexies to make sure they're still sexy. None of them have touched their drinks, but they are still sexy. I look back to Joe. "But is anyone ever really ready?"

He shrugs. "Betty was. She was born to it."

I don't bother telling him about the times she was in this very bar crying her heart out over a pint while bemoaning her mothering skills. I was a kid then, working the bar with my grandmother. We're a tight-knit community, so everyone turned a blind eye to my underage service. Even the cops who occasionally came by.

Betty is gone and he's all alone. Well, he's got a son, Alex, but he just reminds Joe of the life that got away so they don't really talk or see each other much. So I won't disabuse him of the notion that things were effortless for his wife. But dear god in heaven can we please stop acting like this shit isn't hard?

Cuz from what I've seen and heard—and

growing up in a family-owned Irish pub, I've seen and heard a lot—this shit is the hardest.

"You know we just want you to be happy," he says, glancing at the three strangers nursing their drinks.

"I know... but guys are too much work, and I'm all full up with work at the moment." I glance at my protruding stomach and the bar that is now my full-time job since my grandfather died and my grandmother was put in a home.

Guys are the very last thing on my mind.

Especially since my grandfather ran this place into the red when my grandmother was no longer around to keep the books. Now I've got to salvage my family legacy if I have half a chance of supporting myself and my baby and keeping a roof over our heads.

Joe finishes up everyone's drinks that were left on the bar, and I check the time. 11:14 p.m.

"Okay, guys, wrap it up," I say as I wipe down all the tables, hobbling through the pub like that girl in Willy Wonka who eats the wrong candy and inflates into a ball. Most of the dishes are already washed, and I'm half tempted to leave the rest for the morning.

Joe stands and wobbles to the door, grabbing his

coat from the rack. "I hate leaving ya like this, Bern. Want me to stay? I could sleep in one of the booths."

I yawn, suddenly feeling the weight of the day bear down on me. "Nah, I'm good. Get home before you can't."

"What about your Partner in Crime? Can she come?" he asks.

"Joe, I'm fine. AJ will be helping out with the bar and everything else nonstop once the baby arrives. I don't want to bother her till then. You know how things are there."

Joe shakes his head, and I know what he's thinking. AJ was my best friend growing up, but she never left town like I did. She married her high school boyfriend, a guy none of us like. But...we can't live her life for her. That's something she's got to figure out.

"Go on now. It's getting worse out there."

Finally, Joe nods, casting one last glance at the silent strangers, and leaves.

I want to go to bed, to get off my feet and zone out to Netflix, but I know if I leave the bar a mess, my future self won't be happy with me.

Begrudgingly, I grab a broom and start sweeping, but before I can get even half the job done, another contraction grips my belly, and for the first time tonight real fear worms its way into my heart.

It's easy to stay out of my head when I'm busy working, but in the silence of the night, I start to question all of my life choices.

Especially the one that landed me knocked up and single just as I was about to live my dream.

Tears burn my eyes as I take a seat on the piano bench, my hands cupping my belly, and I remind myself it wouldn't have mattered. Pregnant or not, my grandfather would still be dead, and I would still be the only Morgan left to carry on our family business.

There was no choice then, and there's no choice now. I can do this. I have to do this. It's no longer just my life on the line anymore.

I smile through my tears as my baby kicks out, already asserting her right to be here in my life.

Through gritted teeth and with steely determination, I stand and keep cleaning, though I have to stop regularly to let the contractions pass.

I'm still telling myself it's not the real deal when I feel a gush of liquid run down my legs.

Shit.

My water broke.

I'm having this baby. Right here. In the middle of the night. In the middle of a storm.

"Guys, um... I don't suppose any of you is a doctor?"

Instead of a hospital with an OBGYN, I'm stuck in my bar with three strangers, and I'm definitely going into labor.

I can no longer stand, so I slide to the floor, clutching my stomach, not sure what I'm going to do now. How can I have a baby alone? They don't teach this in the pregnancy books.

I can no longer keep my pain in, and as my muscles squeeze and my back spasms, I scream.

I fleetingly wonder if I can make it upstairs to my apartment. I could run a bath, get undressed, and give birth in the water. That wouldn't be too hard, would it?

Knowing I absolutely cannot do this on the floor of a bar, I attempt to pull myself up, but lose my grip and slide back down as my contractions quicken.

Shit.

Shit. Shit. Shit.

Terror latches onto me but I grit my teeth and wipe away the tears. I will do this. If not for me, for my child.

When the men all walk over to me, I suddenly feel terror of another sort. I have no idea who these guys are, and I'm completely vulnerable. I curse myself for kicking Joe out, but what would an old drunk do against these guys, who look made of pure muscles?

"In point of fact," Sexy #2 says. "I'm a healer. A doctor, if you like."

A doctor *if I like*. What the blazes does that mean?

"Have you ever delivered a baby?" I ask.

He nods. "Many."

"Good, cuz you're about to deliver mine."

Chapter Two

I can't describe this kind of pain. Blinding comes to mind, but that might just be because my eyes are slammed shut while I wait for either the pain to pass or my life to end. In any case, the feeling of a baby wedging its way out of my uterus makes it hard to focus on anything else, even the outrageously sexy man propped between my legs barking orders at the other two.

"Get water boiling," he tells Sexy #1. "And you," he says to Sexy #3, "get me clean rags and the sharpest knife you can find."

"No," I say, trying to sit up. "Take me upsta-AAAIIIIRRS... I need to LLLLLIIIIIIIEEEEEE down."

Sexy #2 shakes his head. "No, you'll stay down

here. You're in no condition to be moved right now." He locks eyes with me, and the pain ripping through me ceases momentarily as I get lost in his forest green gaze.

"Who are you?" I ask, panting through another contraction.

"My name is Zev, Bernadette. I'll make sure you deliver the child safely."

The brutal contractions fade again as my head spins. Zev? A doctor I've never met who knows my name and waltzed into my bar moments before I went into labor?

"No one calls me Bernadette unless they're trying to piiIIIIIIIIIIIIIIISSSSSSS... me off. And I don't think you want to doOOOOOOOOOOOOOOOOO... that."

"Anger won't help, but a charge of adrenaline can't hurt," Zev says, as he directs Sexy #1. "Get behind her and support her back."

I feel strong arms slip around my waist and I lean into his chest. I have no shits left to give. "What's your name, then?" I ask when I can speak again.

"Darius," he says, his lips brushing against my ear with his words.

"Zev and Darius," I repeat, mostly to make sure

I heard right the first time. "And how about yooo-OOUUUUUUUU?!" I say to Sexy #3 right as another contraction hits. This labor is progressing much more quickly than what the lady in my birthing class described.

Before the third mystery man can answer, Darius chimes in again. "Rune, take her other arm, even out the support." Okay, I guess Sexy #3 goes by Rune. It also seems as though these guys know each other, even if they like to sit at different tables when they go out.

The pain dulls enough for me to do some quick math. Outside, the storm's getting worse. Inside, I'm going into labor a week early. Most importantly, three oddly-named, unconscionably sexy men are helping deliver my baby with a calm very few men show in the labor ward. So… WTF?

"I'm surprised we all arrived at the same time," Rune says to the others. "I was sure I had a head start."

"We work off the same prophecy, old friend," Zev responds in his gruff baritone. "There's only one star to guide us."

"The only surprise," Darius says, "is that we never had a discussion as to what we'd do when it came time to take the child."

My head cranks toward Darius at these words. Is he talking about *my* child? I'd ask him directly but another contraction wracks my body and I scream, clutching Darius and Rune's hands with all my strength. Neither even flinches.

Meanwhile, with my eyes clamped shut, I feel a firm tugging at my pants. "You cannot deliver this child while wearing these," Zev says calmly.

Oh God, I hadn't thought about this part. Shit.

"Someone get me a blanket at least," I say through clenched teeth.

Darius and Zev look to Rune, who swiftly pops up and moves to the kitchen.

"He's good at finding things," Zev explains.

As advertised, Rune promptly returns with an armful of large towels

"Will this do?" he asks, suggesting he could go back into *my* kitchen and find more, somehow better towels.

"Those are fine."

He drapes the cover over my abdomen, as Zev gets me half naked.

"I will be watching you, dog," Darius says with an unfriendly bite to his voice. "Don't think for a second you're quick enough to catch the baby and escape."

Zev barks out a short laugh. "Oh, Darius, how I've missed your playful name calling. And don't expect me to run, I wouldn't want to deprive myself of tearing you apart."

"Now's not the time to revisit old wounds," Rune says in a condescending tone, like a bored professor explaining something simple to his students for the tenth time. "You can carry on with your bickering when the prophecy is fulfilled and the fae flourish once again."

"Cocky as ever," Darius mutters.

As fascinating as this exchange is, the language terrifies me. If I wasn't so actively birthing a child, I would absolutely sprint into a deadly storm to get away from these men.

"Who the hell are you people? How did you know my name? Why...aaaAAAAAAHHHHHH!" I can't even finish the question, which is for the best because I didn't really know what to ask. Everything about this situation needs answers, but for now I'm just going to hope these men keep helping since I've got nowhere else to go.

"Hold my hands, Bernadette," Darius says from behind me. "Squeeze when you feel a contraction and focus on pushing."

"You three stop acting like psychopaths and I

will." My face probably shows that I'm terrified, but I don't let on with my words. Growing up in a Massachusetts bar, I learned to talk tougher than I felt at a very early age.

Rune lowers himself to the floor, pressing gently against my knee, spreading my legs a little further and bringing back a shade of self-consciousness. He catches my eye and clearly sees a discomfort that goes beyond just the physical.

"When you feel a contraction, push your leg against my hand. That will activate the muscles you need to move the baby along."

I'm about to throw out another verbal lashing when I see Zev nod. "He's right. I'll keep my hand on the other knee."

I'm surrounded by men who might all be murderers, but without any other options I've landed on implicitly trusting Zev based on his word that he's a doctor...*if I like*. I hope it's the doctor claim that got Zev in my good graces and not the ruggedly handsome face, which has always been a weakness of mine.

Whatever the case, the new position helps. I scream and push between breaths, barely aware that Darius has put a wet washcloth over my forehead. I trust he grabbed a clean one and not the towel I'd been using to mop up Joe's beer.

Everything about this birth has gone wrong, and yet I find the situation strangely empowering. I'd planned on a very sterile, clinical, hospital bed delivery, none of that froufrou home or water birth stuff that the neighborhood midwives tried to sell me on. But now, sitting at an incline against a guy named Darius, two dudes named Zev and Rune side by side between my wide open legs, naked butt on the cold floor of an empty bar, I feel a small rush of pride over my natural birth. Who needs an epidural when you've got creepy intruders?

"The head is emerging," Zev says without a trace of happiness in his voice, casually explaining that my labor pains might soon come to an end. "Push harder with the next feeling of contraction."

"Oh, I'm sorry, have I not been pushing hard enough for you?"

Zev gives me a confused look, clearly not a sarcasm buff. This will make my feisty tone less effective.

As another wave of agony ripples through my torso, my legs start to close as my muscles flex. The pressure from Zev and Rune's hands gives me a little extra oomph in my push and suddenly the pain, while still incomprehensibly awful, takes on a new burn.

"She's out," Rune says, a look of awe on his face, just as the old clock behind the bar strikes midnight. I open my eyes, which have long been soaked with tears but now get a fresh coating. Just a few feet away, after growing inside me for the better part of a year, I see my baby. She's crying, bloody, and perfect. I'm a broken vessel, torn and sweaty and surrounded by demented intruders, but I don't care. I've never felt love like this.

"Rain…" I murmur, saying my baby's name out loud for the first time. She was always going to have that name, but I promised myself I wouldn't speak it until she arrived.

Rune holds the baby with great care, which at first puts me at ease before giving me a funny feeling. He stares at Rain with a kind of reverence that has my hackles up, and he's not making any move to hand her over my way.

"Give her to me," I say in a steady voice, my body absolutely giddy about being done with the throws of labor.

He hesitates. His eyes shift from me to Darius to Zev, and there's a palpable tension between the three. It pisses me off because... because give me my freaking baby.

He's still cradling my daughter when Zev stands, his impressive stature becoming apparent. Darius rises as well, also a taller-than-average man.

"Give the child to her mother," Zev says in a voice that's both calm and terrifying. "I know what you're doing, I know the impulse you feel, and neither Darius nor myself will let you move an inch from where you stand while you hold that baby."

Maybe it's that I'm still in agony and sitting in afterbirth, but these guys strike me as a special kind of crazy. Nevertheless, Rune seems to catch Zev's drift and he carefully leans over with Rain. I'm about to hold the baby I've been waiting so long to meet.

"Do you wrap the placenta around the child now or later?"

Rune's question feels like a mix of the right words in the wrong order. Wrap the baby in the placenta?

"Do I what now?"

"Or is that something the elders do while your body mends?"

It's late and I've labored, so I've got zero brain

space for these weird questions. Fortunately, Zev steps in.

"She doesn't share your rituals. Here they eat the placenta. Just pass the child, Rune."

While I have no intention of eating the placenta, Zev's suggestion is less bonkers than the previous one. Rune does as he's told, with a mild look of disgust on his beautiful face.

As I take her into my arms, I feel my shirt being lifted. Darius, in the most forward and inappropriate move ever, is taking off my clothes while I'm incapacitated. My bar-owner instinct is to swing the baby at him like the bat I keep behind the counter to scare off the occasional drunk who has one too many. Fortunately, my maternal instinct steps in and stops me.

Darius manages to read the room and explains himself. "She needs to feel your skin." Of course I know about skin-to-skin time and how important it is, but this delivery and my new company has thrown me off my game. I drop a little of the tension and let Darius resume with the unprompted disrobing.

Finally, naked as a jaybird, I get to hold my baby. As soon as I press her up to my breast, she stops crying and my heart melts all over again. Her little lips inch along my skin, searching for a nipple, and it's absolutely the cutest thing that's ever happened in the world.

As she starts to nurse, a hand cups the underside of my breast to make the feeding angle easier. I honestly don't know which weirdo's weird hand it is, I'm too absorbed watching my sweet girl. While my eyes stay locked on Rain, I half-listen to more outlandish conversation from these men who should feel free to leave at any time.

"When did you notice the approach of the star?" Darius questions the other two, his calm voice floating over my head.

"We started watching the sky two weeks ago," Rune answers. "Violence in the realm had escalated, and the Readers announced the nearing of the date."

"I arrived last night," Zev adds. "Waited in the woods until the moment arrived. And you, Darius? Surely your kingdom knew of this day well in advance."

There's a tense moment between the two men, neither speaking, breathing or blinking.

Darius finally responds, "Of course. We've known for months."

While every inch of my being wants to scream,

what the hell is going on?!, I resist. I'll learn more by listening, and I don't want to do anything that might startle Rain. She's lost the nipple and is making the softest little murmuring sounds.

"What now?" Rune asks, his voice quieter than before. "We've arrived at the moment we all expected but never spoke about. There's only one child, and I see only one way out."

Whatever Rune is saying makes Zev tense, as I feel his hand squeeze my thigh more tightly, and it sounds like he's... growling? Lack of sleep and an exhaustive labor have worn me out. I'm sure the growl was just in my head.

Darius puts his hands on my shoulders, sending a shiver down my spine that's both exhilarating and terrifying. "It may come to that, Rune, but you'll be up against Zev and myself if you make a false move. We all want the child, but she's of no use dead or unhealthy."

Now I've heard enough to pipe in. "I'm sorry, 'you want the child'? I don't know who you are or where-"

My voice stops. It's the craziest sensation, because I know what I wanted to say and now I'm silent, my brain's in a fog, and all I can do is stare into Darius' eyes, like I'm in a trance.

"Let her go," Zev says, though the words don't really register in my clouded head. "She needs her wits about her."

"Let's get her up to her bed," Rune says. "The baby is asleep so the mother should rest as well."

Maybe it's the mention of rest, but my mind suddenly becomes mine again and my voice returns. "Yes, please. And someone call a real doctor, I think I need actual help-"

"You'll be fine," Zev cuts me off. "Darius, carry her up. I'll clean the baby and then come up to tend to the mother's wounds."

"I'll tidy up down here," Rune says. "Needn't create a scene that garners unnecessary attention."

Zev gently pulls Rain away from me, which I allow because I'm not sure I have another option. As Darius lifts me from the ground and starts carrying me upstairs, my emotions overwhelm me. I'm scared shitless, utterly confused, and deeply in love with my newborn baby. And, while this situation makes me feel incredibly uneasy to say the least, it's not lost on me that I've currently got three dashing men waiting on me hand and foot. Unfortunately, from what I've gathered, they came to steal my baby, and the only way that'll happen is if they kill me and rip her from my cold, dead hands.

Chapter Three

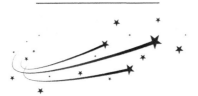

L ying in bed, Rain asleep in her crib in the corner, I slowly come to. I can't have slept much, my body and brain ache for rest... but it's impossible to ignore the conversation going on right outside my bedroom.

I still don't have a concrete idea of who - or what - Darius, Zev, and Rune are, but I know they are different. Not just in the obvious ways, like being grossly good-looking and able to help a first-time mother safely deliver a baby on the floor of her bar, but in larger, more cataclysmic ways.

For starters, they're not from America. If I had enough to drink, I'd very quickly tell you they aren't from Earth, but my brain still isn't ready to make that leap. Nevertheless, they talk of places I've never heard of before and know things they should have no way of knowing. And while those particulars could be explained with a little con artistry, other things seem… magical.

It takes a lot of effort to get past my cynicism. On more than one occasion I've made a magician cry by yelling "bullshit!" until he or she pulled back the curtain to show me how the trick worked. Mysterious men, hot as they may be, don't immediately have me believing in the paranormal.

And yet, things just seem… otherworldly. Everything from the timing of their arrival to the ways they dress, talk, and move makes me feel like these men can't be explained using traditional terms and ideas.

I nodded off a lot during birthing classes because I didn't think I was learning anything, but I'm starting to wonder if I slept through the part where they tell you that the pain of labor causes the most vivid hallucinations imaginable. Though, if that were the case, wouldn't other women be talking about how they thought their doctors and nurses morphed into exceedingly sexy strangers?

These thoughts are keeping me awake, as well as the conversation my possibly hallucinated companions are having.

"Of course we can't arrange a deal, Darius," Zev says in a hushed tone. "We all want the child for the same reason. What are you prepared to offer that's equal in value to being eternally allied with the Fates and saving your people from extinction?"

"I haven't thought that far, friend," Darius responds. It's getting easier to distinguish their voices, and I'm still solidly pretending I'm asleep.

Growing up above a bar with very little privacy in our tiny two-room apartment, I learned the best way to get information the grown-ups didn't want you to have was to fake sleep. I'm a pro.

"There must be something in the prophecy to use as a guide," Rune says. "An impartial detail to determine who is the rightful courier."

"Don't be foolish." The condescension in his tone lets me know this is Darius. "The entire point of the prophecy is that this last step is undecided. We, in this room, are the final sentence of the scroll."

"Our version wasn't written, only spoken amongst elders and royals." Zev speaks with a tone that's calm, sophisticated, and gruff. His voice alone gives me goosebumps.

"You relied on an oral translation of the Fate's declaration?" Darius says snidely.

"Got me here at the same time as you, *friend.*"

I know I need sleep, but I can't stop listening, and I don't want them to stop talking. Also, for three beings who may or may not have superpowers, they are doing a crap job at noticing how loud they are and how nearby I am. Or maybe they just recognize that I'm vulnerable and powerless and they don't really care what I hear.

I shift slightly on account of the ever-present throbbing throughout my body, and the movement immediately shushes the conversation. This is as good a time as any to join in on the Sexies' little pow wow.

"What are you three talking about?"

There's a beat of silence, then the Sexies slowly shuffle into my doorway, looking like teens caught coming home after curfew. Look at me, only a few hours into motherhood and already commanding respect.

"You should keep resting, Bern-"

"Neeee," I jump in, knowing Zev is about to go with the full name. I've hated it since I was a kid and I'm not about to change my tune. Zev can deliver as many of my babies as he pleases, we're still not going full Bernadette.

"Yeah, I know I need rest. Thing is, there are

three guys in my house that I don't remember asking to stay, and it's making it a little hard to sleep."

"We're only keeping an eye on you and the baby... Bern-E." I applaud Darius for the awkward attempt, even if his face looks ridiculous while he tries to make an E sound.

"Your health and safety is our chief concern," Rune picks up where Darius left off. "We can assure you of that."

Whether it's the constant chatter or it's actually feeding time, Rain starts to fuss. I'm sure she's hungry, but I'll use this as an opportunity to shame my trio of midwives.

"Well, you seem to be overlooking the importance of the baby sleeping, so maybe you can take the conversation to the living room while I feed her?"

I may have scored a small victory here, as the three turn to leave. Each moves differently, yet all possess the same silent grace that makes them so hard to look away from. A growing cry from my baby finally breaks my trance and I shuffle over to her.

Walking doesn't hurt the way I'd expect it to, and I take a moment to examine my nether regions.

Jesus, Mary and Joseph... which one of them stitched me up? And when? Maybe that happened while I was first holding Rain, but you'd think I'd remember a hulking man running a needle and thread through my... you know. Again, I push thoughts of my visitors aside as my gaze lands on Rain.

She was perfect the first time I saw her and she's somehow even more incredible now, all swaddled up and clean. She's so beautiful in her little crib, more precious than I ever could have imagined.

"Come here, sweet little peanut. Momma's got you."

Her cries taper off as I pick her up and move her to my breast. I'm still scared of feeding, no real idea if I'm doing it right and no real advisor other than some of the wives of my drunken regulars. Still, she looks like she's eating, so I'll keep doing what I'm doing.

I ease into the rocker by the crib, going as slowly as possible because I'm still a little suspect of the stitch job downstairs. Just as I lean my back into the chair, three figures careen through the room, moving at a pace that makes them a literal blur.

In my state, I can't confidently describe what happens, but I'll swear on my mother's grave it didn't involve humans. Rune comes into the room first, but he doesn't enter, he *appears*. Like, out of thin air.

Before my brain processes that, a shadow travels along the ceiling, though nothing's there to cast it. The shadow is flying solo, and I know that's not how shadows work.

Just as this dark enigma is landing by my side, Zev explodes next to me. Explode doesn't sound right, but neither does the manner in which he arrives, because all I see out of the corner of my eye is a mix of fur and legs and face.

As fast as the dizzying movement starts, it ends, and now the guests I kicked out of my room thirty seconds ago are back.

"What in the flying f-"

"Move an inch and I'll rip your heart out through your back."

I'm *sure* Zev's not talking to me, but I still glance his way to see where his eyes are trained. He's clearly locked in on Darius, and he's got one of his enormous hands hovering centimeters from Rain's head. It scares the breath from my lungs, but that's as much as I dare to move.

"I'm standing between the fae and the baby, fool," Darius spits back. "He moved to come back in here the second he stepped into the living room."

"The wolf flinched first, not I," Rune hisses defensively.

"I smelled aggression on one of you, and clearly, I was right," Zev says, a low growl in his throat.

Wolf? Fae? The little corner of my brain that's been warning me we're no longer in Kansas finally has the microphone. This shit is *different*.

"Move your paw away from the baby, Zev." Rune speaks in a tone that seems less about commanding Zev and more about protecting Rain, which is finally something I can appreciate in this excruciating standoff.

The three men say nothing, each tense from teeth to toes as they wait to see if the other might move. I finally decide to speak, though I'm half expecting I'll startle Zev and get swallowed whole.

"Each of you," I start, talking as quietly and slowly as possible, "step to the center of the room and sit in front of me. Do it now, or I'll find a way to murder all of you, so help me God."

I feel their eyes on me as they consider my pitch. While I know they don't fear for their physical safety, it does seem they either respect me or need me for something, so my words carry a little weight.

After a few more seconds of stillness, they do as directed, and the feeling of getting these three to follow instructions is borderline orgasmic.

As he moves to sit, I notice a small smirk on Rune's face. It might be the first emotion I've seen other than indifference and white-hot anger.

"Something funny, Runey Toons?" When in doubt, go schoolyard nicknames.

"Funny? I suppose, in its way. You say God. Singular. I always forget the simplicity of the earthly deities." His answer elicits a slight nod from Zev.

"Simplicity?" I respond, a little incredulous. "If religion here is simple, I'd hate to see the complex version. How do things work where you're from, pal?"

Rune stays silent. So do the others. It seems like my prying questions are going to get a little resistance, so I opt to go all in. It helps my confidence that they are sitting criss cross applesauce like children in front of me, all lined up in a row. I smirk at that and straighten my spine as I speak.

"You clearly need something from me, and none of you are happy with the others being here. So, if you want to get on my good side, one of you assholes better tell me what the bloody hell is going on."

I notice a feeling of safety creeping in, like my body trusts the people nearby and has released some tension. It's probably just the oxytocin from nursing flooding me with a happy hormone cocktail, but it's giving me the self-assurance to make demands, and hopefully that will help me keep a little control in a life that otherwise has gone way the hell off the rails in the last few hours.

Darius clears his throat, the first to man up and answer my damn question. Rune and Zev both look at him, apparently as eager to hear what he's got to say as I am.

"There's a prophecy, one you know not of, though it exists in your world."

"Great stopping point," I barge right in, needing clear answers in a hurry. "If this is my world, where are you from?"

"A different realm, I'm not sure you can understand it." His dark eyes flick away, like he's already bored with this conversation.

I narrow my eyes at his condescending tone. "Try me."

"We're in the same spheres of time, but a different world altogether," he says, and then adds under his breath, "One safe from the plague of humanity."

I'll unpack that plague of humanity bit in a minute. "Zev, Rune, this is true?" I ask for confirmation like I'm cross-checking the alibis of three kids who cut school. Talking like a principal is one of the few ways I can fake authority when I don't feel like I've really got it. The others nod and don't offer anything new, so I look back to Darius, prompting him to continue.

"The prophecy speaks of your child: when it would be born, the star that would guide its spirit, and the incomparable importance of its soul."

He lets those words hang as though they mean something, and clearly they do, but only to a person who's in league with these whackjobs.

"Okay," I shrug. "And?"

This time Zev butts in before Darius can continue. He seems to read the room a little better than his counterpart.

"Rain must leave this realm. Her soul is needed in another kingdom, for a purpose you're not ready to hear."

"Yeah, well, that's fine, because we're not going anywhere so it doesn't matter if I hear it or not." To punctuate my sentence, I quickly move my nursing child from one breast to the next, immediately regretting the decision as she nearly rips a nipple clean off.

When I get her settled and look back up, I'm met with three very serious, very stern sets of eyes.

"No, *you're* not going anywhere, that is true," Darius says. "Rain must come alone to the vampire's kingdom."

Zev snorts. "The vampires are at the root of these problems, dear Darius."

"Don't act as though the wolves are innocent, *dear Zev*," Rune interrupts. "Only the fae, with our connection to nature, can truly right this."

"Hold up, so Darius, you're a vampire?"

I'm waiting for someone to pop out of a corner and tell me I'm being pranked. But when no one does and Darius gives an imperceptible nod, I shift my gaze to Zev. "And you?"

"Werewolf, or wolf spirit, or wolf shifter, we have many names," he says, as if explaining his dad's half German.

"And I am fae," Rune says with a lofty pride the other two clearly don't care for.

I'm about three seconds from unleashing some serious mother bear energy on these three psychos, when a knock at the front door interrupts me.

All three guys turn their attention to the intrusion, and I stand with Rain clutched to my chest. Who could possibly be coming for the visit right now?

Darius looks unwilling to let me pass, but the pounding on the door gets louder.

"Bernie? You in there?" a voice calls from outside. "Joe called the station, said you might be in labor. I got here as soon as I could."

I glare at Darius, then share the glare with the others. "That would be the Chief of Police and a longtime family friend. If you don't let me answer that, you're going to have a much bigger problem to deal with very soon."

I mean what I say--if he thinks I'm in trouble, Chief Roland will try to give these guys hell without regard for his own safety. The question then becomes, what will these strangers do to him? And after that, what will they do to me?

Chapter Four

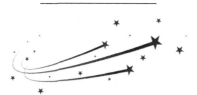

"**B**ernie?" The banging on the door becomes more aggressive and Rain hiccups and begins to cry. "I'm coming in one way or another, hon. Answer me, please?"

"What's it gonna be?" I ask the trio before me as I gently rock Rain, patting her back to soothe her.

This only seems to make her cry more loudly, and her screams echo through my small apartment.

"Bernadette!" Now the chief sounds panicked.

"He's using my full name. That's not a good sign," I say.

Darius steps aside. "Go. But watch what you say. We are not the ones who would be at risk were you to speak out of turn."

I narrow my eyes at the implied threat, but I hold my tongue when I see the unbridled violence simmering in his pitch black eyes. Turning away from his glare, I weave through the three guys towards my front door. When I yank it open, the chief--who was mid-knock--pulls his hand back, startled.

"My God, Bernie, you gave me a real scare." His gaze drops to the screaming bundle in my arms and his eyes widen. "So it's true. You had your baby."

"I certainly didn't steal this one from someone else," I joke.

He chuckles and runs a hand through his slightly balding hair. "You had us all worried," he says as he cranes his neck to scope out my apartment. "Who helped you?"

I glance back at the men crowding the entrance to my bedroom, wondering how much I should say. Could Chief Roland help me get rid of these guys? From what I've seen, I'm not sure, but it doesn't mean I'm not gonna try. "Why don't you come in and meet my knights in shining armor," I say with a saccharine smile.

The chief blinks, likely unused to me acting this

way when I'm not on bar duty. "Uh, sure. Yeah, I'd like that."

He's dressed in street clothes, but he shifts his coat just enough to reveal the gun holstered at his hip. I nod in approval and lead him into my apartment, which--to be honest, has seen better days. The hardwood floor is pretty timeless--if scuffed in places, but the couch is threadbare and sagging; the recliner is a relic from a different epoch, and not in a cool antique kind of way; the kitchen is littered with dated dishes and appliances that scream 60s yard sale rejects; and the wallpaper is peeling. And this wallpaper...yeah, not the trend. Still, it's been home since my mom died and my grandparents took me in.

The chief looks a little misty-eyed as he studies the place. "I haven't been in here since...."

"Since my grandfather died," I say. "Well, you're always welcome. Grandpa would love to know his old friends were still coming by."

Rain has finally settled down and, though she doesn't fall back asleep, is enjoying snuggling against my chest. "Would you like to hold her?" I ask, though I'm reluctant to let go of my baby.

The chief's eyes widen. "Yes. I would."

He has four of his own kids and a handful of

grandbabies, so he knows how to support her head, but as he takes her, the three men hiding out near my bedroom appear, their predatory instincts on high alert.

"Who might you be?" The chief asks, one hand dropping back to his gun as he clutches my child carefully with his other.

"These are the fine gentlemen who came to my rescue," I say, introducing them. "Zev here is a doctor *of sorts*, and he delivered little Rain with the help of his friends. They stayed to make sure I was okay. But your timing is perfect. They were looking for a place to stay in town. Maybe you could take them to Nancy's Bed and Breakfast and convince her to give them a room until the roads are clear enough for them to continue on their way?"

The chief frowns. "I'm sure Nancy could find you boys something."

Darius glares at me. "We are not in need of accommodations at this time."

"You're going to need somewhere to stay until the power comes back and the roads are safe for driving," I say sweetly.

The chief, sensing the tension, hands Rain back to me. "Why don't you boys come with me. We'll get you sorted. I'm sure Nancy will comp your stay for helping out our Bernie, here."

"Thanks, Chief," I say, nuzzling my baby. Why does she smell so good? How'd she get so perfect so fast?

When the guys don't move to follow him, the chief unsnaps his holster and pulls at his gun. "Do we have a problem here?"

Darius steps forward, his dark-as-sin eyes locked on the chief. "There is no problem here. You can leave. Bern--EE," he says, stumbling on my name, "is safe. We are friends here to help her. You will spread the word that we are staying with Bernie and everything is fine."

"Hey, hold up!" I say, turning to the chief, but his pupils are dilated and he nods.

"Of course. So glad you boys are here to take care of her. If you need anything, call." And then he walks out and closes the door behind him, leaving me speechless with the three Sexies--who might need a new nickname at this point. The three irritants perhaps. Or the three pains in my ass, maybe.

"What did you do to him?" I ask, poking Darius in his rock hard chest. I swear I nearly sprain my finger. But he doesn't even flinch.

"What had to be done. This child is too valuable to leave unprotected," he says.

"Um, excuse me? I'm the mother, in case you assholes forgot that tiny detail. I can protect my baby just fine. And I think it's past time the three of you left."

Darius sinks into my couch, frowning in discomfort. "I won't be going anywhere. Not without the child."

I look to Rune and Zev but they each shrug. "I'm afraid you're stuck with us," Zev says with a flirty grin and a wink. "You get free postpartum medical support, if that's any consolation."

I hesitate, because that is actually the best argument they've had so far given my shit insurance. I had no idea how I was going to cover the cost of giving birth to Rain, and yet here I am, in the clear. However, Zev fails to mention the part about them all wanting to steal my baby. "Yeah, that's great, right up until one of you tries to snatch my kid. Also, come on, you can't all expect to stay in my tiny apartment. Where will you sleep?"

They each glance at the second bedroom, the one my grandparents shared for fifty years. "All three of you will share a queen bed?" I ask, bemused.

Rune frowns. "I believe our sleeping needs are different."

"Is this seriously happening?" I ask, frustrated beyond measure and suddenly completely exhausted. I hobble to the recliner as Rain starts to fuss again and begin nursing her just as my stomach rumbles.

"When was the last time you ate?" Rune asks, casting a sideways glance at my sad kitchen.

I shrug. "It's been a while," I admit.

Rune heads to my kitchen and begins rummaging through cupboards. "When was the last time you acquired food?"

I shrug again. "Look, it's been a busy third trimester."

Rune looks to Darius and Mr. Tall, Dark and Sexy sighs in annoyance, then in a blink disappears through my window.

What the-- "Listen," I say, pulling my gaze from the window to the remaining two Sexies. "You guys need to start acting like normal human beings if you plan on staying here, or this isn't going to work."

Sadly, my point is undermined when I yawn, exhaustion overtaking me.

Zev saunters over, his gait like a wild animal,

sleek and fluid. "Come. Get some rest. Your body is still healing."

Another yawn takes control of my face and I don't argue as he helps me up. I burp Rain while making my way to the bedroom. I have no energy left for arguing, and it's clear it won't do any good anyways. Maybe with some sleep I'll have a better idea how to get these guys out of my life for good.

Not wanting to let go of Rain, I take her to bed with me, and the moment my head hits the pillow, I pass out.

My dreams are feverish in nature, full of strange beasts and haunting images that blend my life in New York with other realms, and monsters chasing me. When I wake, I am covered in a sheen of sweat that makes my sheets stick to me.

I'm groggy as I try to figure out what woke me, and realize my breasts are painfully swollen and leaking milk all over my bed. Rain still sleeps, and my bladder feels ready to burst. Oh the joys of motherhood.

As I sit up and prepare to secure Rain with pillows while I head to the bathroom, I gasp.

This is my room, but it isn't. The wallpaper has been replaced with a pale blue paint and elaborate moulding. My bed is no longer the ancient mattress with springs that poke and prod, but instead seems to be made of clouds with a new four-poster rosewood canopy draped with shimmering silver silk. My sheets are luxuriously soft and match the walls, with a thick velvet white comforter embroidered with small flowers. New art hangs on my walls, and new furniture has replaced what I once had.

My urgent need to pee propels me forward despite my confusion, and I find the bathroom has also been redone with scented hand-carved soaps, new paint and light fixtures, and a thick carpet. Even the sink, toilet and bathtub have been replaced. What the actual hell?

Once I relieve myself, I head to the living room to find out what's going on. Am I hallucinating? Have I lost my damn mind?

Rune is in my kitchen plating food--a kitchen that now boasts new cabinets, new tile flooring, and state of the art appliances. Darius is sitting on an exquisite love seat, and Zev is stoking a fire in a fireplace I didn't have a few hours ago. My rickety upright out of tune piano has been replaced with a Steinway that easily cost $200,000. My fingers itch to play it, so much that my eyes burn with tears at the thought. It's been awhile since I've had one of those babies under my fingers.

"Could someone please explain to me how my entire apartment has changed while I slept?" I ask. "Wait, is this paranormal thing a bit, and you're actually part of an HGTV remodeling show?"

"H...G... what?" Leave it to Rune to be confused by everything and confirm that, no, I'm not on a reality show.

Darius looks up from a book he's reading. "The chosen one needed better accommodations," he says, simply, as if that explains everything.

Rune approaches with a plate--bone china, mind you--filled with chicken, a fresh salad and a side of grilled vegetables. "You must eat and replenish your strength."

"How'd you cook without power?" I ask, my stomach rumbling as I take a seat on the new couch and sigh at how comfortable it is.

"You now have a barbeque on your balcony," Rune says. "And you have a balcony."

I raise an eyebrow, and glance out the new door leading to said balcony. This isn't possible. "Where did all this stuff come from?" I ask, studying my surroundings.

"It wasn't easy," Zev says, "but we're resourceful."

"How did I not hear this? How did you add a

balcony and change wallpaper and redo my floors in just a few hours while my baby and I slept through it all?"

"We have our ways," Rune says. "Ways that would not be comprehensible to your kind."

I shake my head, entirely bemused and befuddled, but also slightly ravenous.

The food is delicious and I make quick work of it. Rune is on hand to take my plate back to my entirely renovated kitchen. The apartment is still small, but it no longer feels that way. Everything is high quality and top of the line. I feel... pampered. It's a strange sensation and I don't know how to respond.

"What happened to my personal stuff?" I ask, looking around, my eyes landing on my family portrait with relief. I walk over, still careful with my stiff and fragile body, and study the four of us. "This was the last picture taken of us before my mom died," I say to the room, not really caring who's listening. "The day we had it done she and I had gotten into a huge fight. I don't even remember what about, just that I was still in a pissy mood when the photographer showed up."

I study my young face, all tween angst and drama. But my mom, she's glancing down at me with such fierce love. Sometimes this image is the only one I can clearly remember of her, the way the right side of her lip curls higher than the left when she smiles, and the tiny scar on her forehead that had a different story to it every time I asked her how she got it. She and I share the same bright blue eyes and dark hair, the same pale complexion. We both take after my grandmother, who is clutching my grandfather's hand in the portrait. "My grandparents raised me after my mom died," I say. I'll need to visit my grandmother soon. Introduce her to Rain. She may not remember us, but I want her to know her great-granddaughter nonetheless.

"Anything personal was kept," Zev says. "The rest was tossed."

Right. I really hope these guys know how to tell the difference between what's personal and what's not.

Now that I've eaten my fill, I can no longer resist the temptation of that piano, regardless of how they acquired all this shit in a black out snow storm.

"You didn't rob anyone, did you?" I ask, suddenly worried as I make my way to the piano bench.

Darius chuckles. "No. We have no need for that. Everyone was well compensated."

"Much of this was accomplished by magic," Rune says with a shrug, as if that explains it all.

As long as they didn't steal it, I'm satisfied enough to enjoy it for now. I let my fingers run over the ivory keys, closing my eyes as my memories drift back to my time in New York, to the life that could have been… if I hadn't gotten pregnant. If my grandfather hadn't died. If…if…if.

Too many ifs. I shove them away and begin to play. I start with something easy to warm up. I haven't had much time for this since I've been back. But as muscle memory kicks in, I move to more complicated pieces, finally landing on Ravel's *Gaspard de la Nuit*, one of the hardest piano pieces ever written. Everything disappears and I lose myself in the complex notes, reveling in the way my body feels, the way the music fills the apartment, the way I connect to the instrument like I am one with it.

When I finish, there is a profound silence in the room, and I turn to see all three guys staring at me in wonder.

Darius exhales a breath he seems to have been holding in. "I have never in my significantly long life heard anything so beautiful." His voice is soft, almost a breath against my mind, and his praise fills something in me that has been empty for far too long. I fall into the feeling, wishing I could have had the life that was once promised to me.

Before.

The mood is broken by the sound of someone knocking at the door.

Who's here now? I don't get this many visitors on a normal day, let alone in the middle of a freaking blizzard.

The guys exchange worried glances, and I sigh and go to answer.

My childhood bestie stands at the threshold, mascara running down her cheeks, long blond hair pulled into a messy bun, her clothing disheveled.

"AJ?" My gaze falls to the blood seeping through a bandage tied haphazardly around her arm. "What the hell?"

"Can I stay here for a few days?" she asks, sniffling. "John shot me."

Chapter Five

"Jesus Christ, AJ!" I guide her out of the cold, trembling with fear and rage. I disliked John when they started dating, loathed him a year into their marriage, and now I finally get to kill him.

We move toward the loveseat, and my sexy, irritating, home remodelers all gather round. I'm too focused on AJ's wound to consider the scene she finds herself walking into.

"Sweet Lord have mercy," AJ mutters under her breath, her head on a swivel as she looks between my gorgeous guests. "Shit, Bernie, did you win the lottery?"

AJ's the best. The bullet wound could be in her head and she'd still crack wise. I get her seated and, before I can make the request, Zev is there with a towel and some unmarked glass bottles. Those weren't here a day ago, so I guess he found an apothecary while he was piano shopping.

"Hi…" AJ manages to say as she falls into the wilderness that lives in Zev's green eyes.

"Good morning," Zev replies in his gruff but soothing voice. "I'm sorry, I didn't catch your name."

"I'm Anna Jane," she says softly, with an obvious subtext of "please ravage me."

Hearing AJ use her full name throws me. She *hates* her name, even more than I hate Bernadette. Clearly, she's overwhelmed by the magnitude of hotness in my apartment. Hell, she hasn't even noticed the million-dollar renovation yet--or my freaking baby!

Rune walks over with a glass of water for her. The manners on these intruders consistently surprise me. As he hands her the glass, he pours a single drop of something from another unmarked bottle.

"Here, this will help with the pain."

I stifle a laugh. Since walking in and laying eyes on Darius, Zev, and Rune, I don't think AJ's felt a thing.

"Thank you, I--oh my."

Her reaction to Zev ripping the sleeve off her undershirt is ridiculously muted. *Oh my?* This girl normally swears like a sailor, and now she's trying to pull off the demure act while my Sexies tend to her gunshot wound? I catch myself getting possessive and try to dial it back. *These uber-hot creeps are here to steal your baby, Bernie. Don't forget that.*

"It's a deep cut, but the instrument passed through surface tissue and didn't hit the bone," Zev explains, his words entirely lost on AJ as she studies his woodland god-like face.

"AJ," I say firmly, kneeling down and putting my hands on her knees. God, it feels good to kneel again. That's something you take for granted until you're eight months pregnant and trying to put on a shoe. "AJ, what happened? And where is that son of a bitch?"

She finally turns away from Zev and looks at me, a sadness settling in behind her big brown eyes.

"He was drunk and mad, because, you know, that's just his natural state of being," she starts, and I can see there's more anger than sadness in her look. It's a hard shift to notice, but after a few thousand heart-to-hearts with this girl, I pick up on her mood pretty fast.

"Then the power went out and he started

getting drunker, and that made him madder. We yelled at each other a little last night and then he passed out, so I thought that was the end of it. But the bastard started drinking first thing this morning. I called him a deadbeat loser and may have said a thing or two about his mother, then I got shot."

She's a little too casual in her storytelling for my taste, but I know she's trying to keep her rage at bay. John started making life more difficult the day he and AJ met when he transferred to our high school senior year, but she always thought she could fix him. I wonder if this will be her breaking point.

"I'm so sorry. Of course you can stay--"

I'm interrupted by a cry from the bedroom, which serves as a great reminder that I have a baby. It also alerts AJ to a few of the changes.

"Holy shit! Bern! You're not pregnant!"

That was the obvious one. I'll give her time to catch up on the other tweaks as the day goes on.

She bursts to her feet and pulls me into a strong embrace, thwarting Zev's efforts to clean her wound.

"Where is she?" AJ asks, happy tears in her eyes. "I have to meet her."

"Stay right here, I'll bring her in," I say, giving AJ a gentle squeeze on her un-shot arm as I go.

Just as I disappear into the bedroom, I hear my friend sounding a bit more like herself and not an overwhelmed schoolgirl as she addresses the unexpected guests.

"So, in the name of all that is good and holy, who the hell are you three?"

When I get to Rain, I can tell it's time for a diaper change and a feeding. I feel a little uncomfortable leaving AJ alone with the sexy stranger brigade, but she can stand up for herself as well as anyone, and I know they don't want any extra trouble.

I move Rain to her changing table and try to listen to the conversation in the front room in between the sobs. I can't hear much, just the occasional mention of countries as AJ tries to guess where everyone is from.

"Like, Paraguay? No, Portugal. Which one's in Europe? No, never mind, your hair's too light."

I love this girl so much. Her knowledge of the world outside of Massachusetts has, let's say, some gaps. That doesn't stop her from talking like she knows shit.

Their conversation makes me wonder--what *do* I tell AJ? Do I bring her into the loop? Will she believe me if I try? And what will these guys do, to me or her, if someone else knows what's going on? It might not be worth the risk.

I haven't quite decided on a plan of action as I head back out with Rain. AJ stands with the men in a circle around her, and I'm quite sure she orchestrated this positioning. Don't get me wrong, she's never been unfaithful, but she recognizes a thing--or three things--of beauty when she sees it. Plus, with John being the world's biggest piece of shit, I hope she takes all the time she wants to enjoy the view.

Still, she knows what's important and abandons the Sexies when she sees her goddaughter coming her way.

"She still needs to eat, so don't be offended if she screams the whole time you hold her," I say, like I'm a total expert on babies as I gently hand Rain to her.

"She can cry all she wants and I'll still love her forever," AJ says, and I know it's true. "My God, Bern, she's gorgeous. What's her name?"

"Rain," I answer, knowing full well--

"You and your weird hippie shit."

For being best friends since we were kids, AJ and I don't have a lot in common. It's why I left Rowley and she never did, nor did she ever plan to. Our differences have helped strengthen our bond over time, forcing us to appreciate and overlook traits we might not have had patience for if it weren't for the depth of our friendship.

I love seeing her hold Rain, and look forward to years of them spending time together, but she's still bleeding from a small hole on her upper arm.

"AJ, you need more time with my medics," I say, reaching for Rain. "You can play with the baby after you're stitched up."

She looks down at her arm, remembering the reason she came here.

"Right…" her voice trails off as she looks over her shoulder at the flawless men, quietly observing our every move. "Bernie, what's happening? When was she born? Who are these guys? Why… I don't know, why everything?"

Before I can start to respond, Zev comes over and gently guides AJ back to the loveseat. The moment he touches her, she's lost again in a sexy fog.

"I'm going to numb your arm then suture the wound," Zev explains as he sits AJ down, her eyes never leaving his face. "My thread will help you to heal."

AJ offers a slight nod to Zev, then looks at me questioningly.

"Wait, Bernie, for real, who are these guys? I appreciate the medical attention and all, but this is too weird to ignore."

Well. Shit. Now I've got half a second to decide how to play this. I don't know what to do, what's going to happen, or how much danger any of us are in, but my gut tells me to keep up the ruse. If nothing else, that might give me more time to figure something out.

"Um, where do I start? This is Zev, Rune, and Darius." All male eyes are glued to me, also interested in how my introduction will go. "They showed up at my bar last night, on their way to... Montreal. Got stuck here when the power went out, and that's pretty much why Rain and I are alive."

AJ's eyes go wide. "Are you serious?"

I nod, and it dawns on me that I mostly told the truth. A little fib about where they're headed, but I don't know what would have happened if these men didn't have some insane prophecy guiding them to my doorstep. As for that final part, I'll fill AJ in after I figure out how we're going to survive.

"I mean... that's insane," AJ very astutely observes. "And you're all doctors?"

There's a momentary silence as the men figure

out who will field questions addressing the group. Darius takes the lead.

"We all have medical training, if not the actual title of doctor."

"And what's in Montreal?" AJ's always been a talker, especially around cute guys. With so many years lost to a loveless marriage, I imagine it's only going to be worse now. "Are you all going to a medical conference or something?"

Another beat. So handsome, smart, and strong, but the quick wit is severely lacking. They look between one another, hoping someone will speak. Naturally, AJ fills the dead air.

"What's up, fellas? No one remembers why they're going to Montreal?"

"Yes," Rune blurts out, clearly an unskilled liar. "A medical conference or something."

Zev and Darius nod, trying to show how they're all on the same page. AJ just stares--then starts to laugh.

"Okay, whatever. You guys are lying through your teeth, but you're fixing my arm so I'll let it slide." Her ability to brush things off has always astounded me. It's probably made her a little complacent at times, but right now it's really bene-fiting us all.

"So, um, Bernie," AJ says, changing the subject. "When did you get all this amazing shit?"

Goddammit. And I thought explaining the hottest men in the universe being in my house would be the biggest challenge. This is definitely going to be harder.

"Oh, yeah, I forgot you hadn't seen the place yet," I gesture around, trying to buy myself some thinking time. Won the lottery? Took out a loan? Lie and say nothing's changed? None of those will fly. Gotta go random.

"I... inherited everything," I start, having no trouble sounding surprised because I'm not entirely sure what'll come out of my mouth next. "An older cousin on my mom's side left a bunch of stuff to my mom. I guess he's got no next of kin and somehow didn't know my mom was dead. Honestly, I keep waiting for someone to come back and reclaim it all. A truck showed up a few days ago and now I'm wicked fancy."

AJ stares at me, her right eyebrow cocked in a very disbelieving fashion. The Sexies all stare at me as well, none of them with a clue as to what I said.

"Clearly," AJ says, and I'm half-sure she's about to call out my bullshit. But then she goes on, "this is the universe trying to get you to live in Rowley forever. And I appreciate it, powers that be," she says, looking up and doing a kind of cross thing over her chest that I'm pretty sure is made up, "but I won't allow it. Bernie's too good for this dumb town, so she's back to playing concert halls and shit as soon as Baby Rain's old enough to stay with her auntie."

If she's moved on to taking shots at our hometown, she's good with my story. AJ will kill a bitch who bad mouths Rowley if they're not from here, but when it comes to me and pursuing my dreams, she thinks this town can "get bent." I'd never felt like AJ was truly mad at me about anything until I moved back. That's something we're still working out.

"Finished," Zev cuts in, having swiftly tended to AJ's arm while we talked it out.

"Oh. Whoa." AJ looks at her wound and isn't sure how to react. It's so tightly stitched the gash is only barely noticeable. And yet, from a few feet away, I can hardly see the thread.

"What kind of invisible synthetic shit is this?" AJ asks.

"It's… not a material you would know about," Zev offers, and I'm curious to hear how he handles a barrage of follow-up questions. Before he can continue, Darius' voice interrupts. But the words don't come from his mouth, instead they go straight into my freaking head.

The thread is made of his own hair, Bernadette.

I make eye contact with Darius, and I know he's talking directly with me, but doing it so AJ can't hear him. It gives me the funniest feeling, like I'm having a casual conversation against my will. He's overpowering my mind and, frankly, I wish I didn't like it so much.

It's what he used to stitch the tearing after Rain was born. You have werewolf hair sewn throughout your va--

"Get out!" I scream to make Darius leave my mind, but unlike his words, mine resound loudly throughout the room. Everyone looks up, worried. Sticking with the theme of the day, I improvise.

"Get out... of here with those medical stories, Zev! We don't have time to learn the history of medicine from wherever you're from. I've got a baby to tend to, AJ needs to decide how many charges she wants to press against her husband, and you three need to learn how to tend bar."

I pulled that last one out of my ass, and couldn't be happier with myself.

"Oh yeah, I forgot to mention," I say to AJ, though my words are mostly meant for the men I'm going to try like hell to turn into my sexy slaves. "Since I'm on mom duty, these guys are going to handle the business downstairs for a day or two while they're stranded. Win win, am I right?"

AJ smiles, because I am right. The three men frown, because they don't necessarily agree.

"If you don't mind, maybe you can teach them some tricks of the trade? Start by showing Rune where the kegs are and how to change a tap?"

"Of course I don't mind," AJ answers, giving my arm a squeeze and Rain's head a tiny kiss. "Rune is... blondie, right? Follow me."

I watch them head out the door, and I'm thrilled to death that AJ is here, even if it does complicate my living arrangements even more than they already were. My immediate future is still incredibly vague, but she brings a burst of hope and happiness into my life that I'm grateful for, especially now.

After they leave, I turn to Darius and Zev.

"First off, don't pull that shit again, Darius. Stay out of my head."

He offers a curt nod, but I'm not sure he's going to follow my order. Then I turn to Zev.

"And you--did you really stitch me up downstairs with your own hair?"

"Downstairs? No, you were up in your bedroom-"

"You know what I mean. The wounds *below my waist.*"

"Ah," Zev says, finally catching on. "Yes. You'll find no thread as strong or as sterile as the hair of a wolf. Not an Earth wolf, of course, but from-"

"Got it, thank you," I cut him off, my brain not needing any more information to process. I head for the hallway, taking Rain to the comfort of our own bedroom.

"You two can join Rune, down in the walk-in fridge," I say as I reach the door. "This is a small town, where everyone knows me and everyone talks. If people don't think you should be here, they'll make their feelings clear."

I look at Rain and her beautiful little face. We just met, but I'd die for her in an instant.

"You might have powers we don't," I say with renewed passion, "but a town of angry Massholes looking out for their own isn't something you want to reckon with."

"Be that as it may," Darius says, stepping forward, his dark eyes mesmerizing me into temporary silence, "we cannot leave the child unprotected." He glances at Zev then back at me. "While you slept, we agreed that at least two of us would stay near her at all times."

I glare at the man before me. "First, she's not unprotected. She's with me, and I will not let anything happen to her. Second, you three don't get to make decisions about my baby. You don't get to make any decisions about--"

But before I can finish, the sound of a gunshot coming from outside my door interrupts me.

Rain screams bloody murder in my arms, my breasts pulse in pain from the pressure of the milk, and Zev growls like a wild animal.

My front door crashes in and slams to the floor, a hulk of man on the other side, his dirty blond hair a greasy mess, his wife-beater shirt stained with dirt and beer, his brown eyes wild with fury, and a double-barreled shotgun cocked in his hands.

It's John, AJ's good for nothing husband.

"I know she's here you dumb bitch. Give me back my wife or you and that brat of yours are gonna get shot."

Chapter Six

I t's not an exaggeration to say that having a gun pointed at you and your newborn child is one of the most terrifying things that can happen to a person.

But my terror is short lived.

As short lived as that asshole's life in my apartment.

Several things happen at once, and I only have time to step back and tighten my arms around my irate child as a scene straight out of a horror movie unfolds before me.

First, Zev's body shifts from man to wolf in one astounding moment. It's like a controlled burst of energy--he takes in a breath, then his features and limbs transform in a smooth, exotic motion, his bones reshaping as white fur grows over skin. He lands gracefully on all fours, majestic and intimidating. I've seen a couple wolves in my life, and Zev's at least twice as big as any of them.

Before I can even unpack that transition, Darius moves with lightning speed, disarming John just as the gun goes off, blowing a hole in my ceiling and traumatizing my eardrums.

Next, Zev leaps into the fray, his claws digging into John's chest and tearing through flesh, muscle and bone like the bastard is made of butter.

And finally, Darius's teeth sharpen into knives, and he twists John's neck to the side, sinking his fangs into John's pulsing vein.

I don't know what kills him. The wolf mauling or the vampire draining, but within seconds, his lifeless form is dropped to my floor like a bag of flour.

The thunk he makes is slightly wet, like a splat, and I swallow back vomit and shield Rain's eyes from the gore, even though I know she technically can't see that far yet.

"What the f--" I can't even finish my thoughts before Rune appears, his body blocking what remains of the door frame as his sharp blue eyes take in the scene.

Darius glances at him. "There was a situation,"

he says before looking down at the body and then back to Rune. "It's been resolved."

I nearly choke on his casual tone.

Rune nods. "Good. AJ is in the bar. You might need to..."

Darius nods. "Understood." He disappears downstairs, while Zev remains a wolf, sitting by the door like a guard dog.

"And the child?" Rune locks his gaze with mine, and in four long strides is by my side, assessing both Rain and me. "You are shaking. It's shock. Come."

He guides me out of the living room and into my bedroom, then sits me on the bed and gently removes the screaming child from my arms. "She is hungry but safe." He looks at me with more compassion than I've ever seen from any of them. "If you cannot feed her, I can make her a formula that will satisfy."

My mind is having trouble translating sound to words, but it clicks into place when he starts to leave with her.

"No. Give her to me. I can do it."

He nods and hands Rain back, and without regard for modesty--as that ship has long since sailed--I pull out a breast and let my baby latch on.

Rune watches, his eyes mostly locked on Rain, I'm sure to confirm she's okay after everything that transpired. Still, his eyes spend a little more time on me than they have in the past. His gaze trails over my naked breast, then along my neck and up to my eyes. A hint of modesty creeps back into my psyche, as I realize how disheveled and generally disgusting I must look. I know I certainly feel beyond gross after a day of work, childbirth, intermittent sleep and no bathing.

I break eye contact before he does, checking on Rain to make sure she's drinking all right. She's chugging away, blissfully unaware of everything. I wonder how old she'll be when I can finally tell her the story of her birth. Right now, it seems like it would be too traumatic at any age. I smile to myself as I think of getting a picture of the three Sexies holding Rain, each looking deathly serious, to put in her baby book. Then I laugh out loud when I imagine Darius not showing up in the picture--if that adage about vampires is true.

"What? What's wrong?" Rune asks.

Is laughter a sign of distress where he's from?

"Do vampires show up in mirrors or pictures?" I ask.

Rune frowns. "Is there a reason they wouldn't?"

I shrug. "Just trying to figure out how much of what I think I know is real."

He sniffs. "Well, I wouldn't put a lot of stock in what most humans imagine any of us to be like. Honestly, I have no idea where they come up with some of it."

"Right. Well. You'll have to fill me in on what's real and what's not." I switch Rain to my other breast. "In the meantime, I'm going to finish feeding and change her, you should go see--"

"What the actual mother-loving hell is this?"

It would appear AJ has seen the body of her now-dead husband.

I hear one of the guys saying something to her, but she comes busting into my room, her eyes wide, blood drained from her skin. "Oh my Lord, woman, you scared the shit out of me. I thought that bastard…"

She rushes me and the baby, evading Rune who tries to stop her as she sits next to me on the bed and wraps her arms awkwardly around me as Rain continues to feed.

"Are you okay? Is my god-baby okay?" she asks, tears now streaming down her face.

I lean my head against her forehead, the way we used to do, like cats headbutting each other.

"We're safe. But...I'm sorry? About... you know." It's a pretty weak apology for, I don't know, being an accessory to murder? Not really sure what my role was so I can't figure out the appropriate response. Hallmark doesn't make cards for 'sorry the three supernatural beings who came here to kidnap my kid killed your abusive asshole husband in the most violent way possible.' I'm guessing the demand isn't high for that sort of thing. Very niche market.

But AJ just shakes her head. "Girl, there's a lot you need to explain, but right now I'm just relieved you and cutie-pie here are okay. That asswipe can burn in hell for all I care."

"You're not mad?" I ask. I mean, I'm not mad he's dead. I'm mad there's blood all over my newly refurbished apartment, but John can rot, as she said. Still, AJ has had a complicated relationship with him since high school. I know this can't be easy, even if he was an animated piece of evil dog shit.

She shakes her head, letting blond curls spill in front of her eyes. "Listen, this marriage has been dead for a long time. It was just...living in a small town, with nowhere else to go, it always felt too hard to get out." AJ wipes her eyes, then smiles.

"Now the marriage is literally dead, and I didn't have to do the murdering, so I guess--"

Rain interrupts our heart to heart by pulling off my nipple, satisfied with a full tummy. Before I can burp her, Rune--who I nearly forgot was there, that boy is stealth--holds his hands out for her. "I'd like to check her ears, if that's okay?"

When I frown, confused, he adds. "From the gunshot? And I can burp her and get her back to sleep."

Shit. What kind of mother am I that I didn't even consider the effect a gunshot so close to her head would have? I nod and hand her to Rain.

Zev, who is still a giant white wolf, appears at the door and hovers near Rune as they leave my room. The wolf glances at me briefly, then walks away.

I gracelessly shove my breast back into my shirt and sigh as AJ narrows her eyes. "You gonna tell me what the hell is going on now? For real? Who are these guys?"

I inwardly wince, not wanting to lie, but knowing I must. For reasons. "I already told you, they were on their way to a medical convention when--"

"Shut your lying mouth, B. Look, I know I've

never been as smart as you. I still hear the same dumb blond jokes from the idiots and assholes who were saying that shit in high school, so I'm not delusional about how clever I am. But, of all people, you know I'm not as stupid as I look." Her eyes narrow and I see the lifetime of pain and disappointment hidden in them. A lifetime of living up to the very low expectations everyone had for her.

I want to argue, to tell her none of that is true, but I won't insult her intelligence. I was a musical prodigy in a tiny town with no competition. It set me up to be some kind of weird local mascot. I could do no wrong. I was pretty, sure, but I wasn't AJ's level of pretty. Instead, I was the smart one with all the talent. She was the blond bombshell who filled out early. Her nickname in middle school was jailbait. Her family life was shit, so she had no support. I became her family, with my grandparents doing what they could for her. But nothing we did could shake this town from their prejudices.

It's no wonder she never left John. She had nowhere else to go. I'm the only person in Rowley who's ever loved her back, and I was gone for half a decade.

So, I make a decision I hope I won't regret.

And I tell her everything.

She is completely silent through it all, the only sign that she's still listening is the occasional widening of her eyes.

When I'm done, we sit in silence for a long minute, both of us absorbing the absurdity of my tale. Saying it all out loud does nothing to make this situation sound saner. If anything, I feel like I'm in an alternate reality.

"So, Zev is the werewolf, Rune is the fae, and Darius is the vampire?" she asks, finally.

I blink. "Yes."

She nods. "Makes sense. I vibe with that."

I blink again. "You… *vibe with that*?"

"I mean, at first, I wasn't sure if Rune or Darius was the vampire. They both have a bit of that energy, but I for sure knew Zev was a werewolf the moment I met him."

"What the hell are you going on about?" I ask. "When you *met him*?"

AJ sighs, like she's trying to explain something basic to a child. "I don't know how you *didn't* know what they were the moment they walked into the bar, B. It was super obvious. You think I bought any part of that story about them going to a medical convention together?" She rolls her eyes. "I have read enough books and seen enough TV shows to know the real deal when I meet it. First of all, no normal men are that incredibly hot unless their last names are Hemsworth. Second, I could smell it on them."

Now my eyes are surely bugging out of my freaking skull. "You could *smell it on them*. AJ, what does that even mean?"

My best friend shrugs, all casual-like. "I dunno. They didn't smell human."

She glances at me sharply, her perfect little nose scrunching in disgust. "Speaking of, momma, when did *you* last bathe." It's not even a question, just a clear testament to my current hygiene. And she's not wrong, so I don't argue when she drags me to the bathroom and begins running the tub.

"Strip down. It ain't nothing I haven't already seen. We need to clean you up before we go deal with the mess my dead husband left."

She's so matter-of-fact about it all, I feel equally relieved and confused. Am I the only one surprised by the presence of the supernatural in our world? And what will the Sexies say when they find out AJ knows? I worry Darius will try his mind tricks with her, and no one is messing with my girl's brain if I can help it.

AJ hums as she works, adding bath salts and

bubbles, and when I finally sink into the hot water, I moan in pleasure. My body truly feels like it's been put through a military boot camp. Everything hurts, and I don't even care if baths are recommended after birth or not. It feels too good to be bad for me. Plus, my new bath came with jets, which work perfectly to massage out some of my aches and pains as I soak.

AJ washes my hair for me, bless her, and once I'm done and dressed in fresh clothes, I feel like a whole new person. Ready to face whatever awaits me on the other side of my bedroom door, more or less.

Also, I need my baby back. Being apart from her is strange, after carrying her in me for so long. My body doesn't feel complete without her. I glance at the clock and see it's already afternoon. The day is slipping away, soon we'll have to light candles because it doesn't seem like the power is coming back by tonight. Thank God for the gas water heater.

I can hear the three Sexies bickering as we walk into the living room together, though the scene that awaits us is not what I'm expecting.

"This has nothing to do with her," Rune says.

He's sitting in a rocking chair holding Rain so tenderly, my heart nearly melts.

Darius and Zev are playing chess in the corner, which is strange because I thought they hated each other and I'm very certain I don't own a chessboard. It's also strange that Zev can transform from wolf to human and immediately become lust worthy again.

"It certainly has something to do with her," Darius says, not bothering to look at the fae as he studies his next move on the chess board. "She died trying to sort out this prophecy, and now the three of us are here, just as she foresaw."

Darius looks over at Rune now. "You think that's a coincidence?"

Zev clears his throat. "I think we should discuss this later."

"Discuss what later?" I ask, when it's clear they won't keep talking like I'm not in the room.

"Nothing important," Zev says with a grimace. "Just digging up old bones that should stay buried."

"Speaking of bones and being buried, what did you do with…" I was about to say, the body, but I glance at AJ to see how she's doing first.

"The body," she finishes for me. "Where's that asshole's body?"

Turns out my girl is holding her shit together better than I could have imagined.

It also turns out John's body is gone. It's like it never happened. The floors are spotless, the ceiling is repaired, even the smell of burnt gunpowder is gone. The room now smells like cinnamon and apples, from something boiling in a cast iron pot over the fire.

Darius, who was just sitting across from Zev, is now standing before us in a blink.

"Stop doing that," I say. "Walk like a normal person unless it's absolutely necessary."

He narrows his dark eyes, but nods. "We have handled the situation." Then he glances at AJ. "All that remains is taking care of her."

I grip AJ's hand harder. "I've told her everything. There's nothing to take care of. She's in the know and it's gonna stay that way."

Zev growls under his throat and Rune looks up from the baby, but doesn't make a move to intervene.

Darius frowns. "That won't be possible. The more people who know, the more dangerous this situation becomes for the child and you."

Before I can argue with him, his eyes begin to glow a faint silver and he speaks to AJ in a hypnotic voice. "You saw nothing and heard nothing. Your last memory is being downstairs at the bar. There was no gun shot, and you don't know what happened to your husband."

AJ blinks, then begins to laugh. "Oh, this must be some vampire mind voodoo shit, right? I knew that was real. Yeah, sorry, buddy. Doesn't work on me."

Darius' face hardens and Rune chuckles under his breath.

Darius tries again. "You will forget everything that happened."

AJ shakes her head. "Sorry not sorry, dude. But A for effort."

"Looks like you've lost your touch," Rune says, amused.

Zev stalks over, his muscles flexing like he's on the prowl. He sniffs at AJ, who doesn't seem to find this weird at all. Zev's green eyes widen in surprise. "Hmmm. Seems like this one isn't human."

Chapter Seven

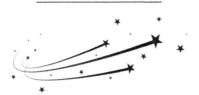

I'm shocked, confused, and conflicted. On the one hand, it's a relief to know AJ's mind isn't open for vampire business. On the other, my best friend for as long as I can remember, the godmother to my only child, the one person in this world I can trust--isn't human? What am I supposed to do with that information?

"What?" I ask Zev, ready to throw a massive fit if he doesn't elaborate.

"Yeah, what?" AJ echoes.

My head snaps to her, every sense I can control focused on studying her thoughts, expressions, and movements. I've always been able to read AJ's tells, knowing when she lied about where she spent the night, what was going on with her dad, which boy she was making out with. Throughout all of that, at no point did I think, *hang on, I wonder if she's lying about being the same species as me.*

Even as I look her over, getting close enough to take a discreet sniff and see if I can smell whatever Zev smelled--I definitely cannot--AJ keeps her eyes on the werewolf.

"What do you mean I'm not human? Bernie, what's he saying?"

AJ finally looks at me and sees how freaked out I am.

"Are you... Bernie, are you freaking serious? Do you not think I'm a person?" The look of disbelief on her face makes me wonder if I am being a little crazy about this. "We've been having sleepovers since we were like five. We've gone skinny dipping a thousand times."

She's not lying, but I'm not sure if anatomy is the defining human factor. After all, I've spent a fair amount of time thinking about the anatomy of my visiting Sexies, and I don't want those fantasies to be dashed right now.

"Why didn't you fall under the spell, A? I'll believe whatever you say, but I need you to help me understand."

She looks at me, then at Zev, then back and

Darius, who's still pretty steamed about having his mental advances rebuffed.

"I mean… I don't know. All he did was tell me to forget shit and it's like, why? So you're a gorgeous vampire, I don't have to hand you the damn keys to my mind."

The logic doesn't win me over, but analytics have never meant much in our relationship. Still, I need a second opinion.

"Zev?" I ask, still wanting an explanation from the doctor with K-9 smelling powers.

"Humans have a bitter smell," he explains, eyes wandering over AJ. "The toxins from your body, the harmful chemicals your brains produce, the scent is almost overwhelming."

He walks back to AJ, very much invading her personal space as he places his nose at the base of her neck and inhales deeply. She doesn't fight it at all, instead placing her hands on his hips to steady herself as she tilts her head to the side and gives Zev better access. From the way they're standing, you wouldn't know AJ's husband died twenty minutes ago and Zev's the one who killed him. As Zev takes in whatever otherworldly pheromone my friend's producing, he keeps his eyes locked with mine. For the briefest second I imagine standing where AJ is, Zev's face next to mine, his breath on my neck. A warm shiver runs through me and I shake my head to snap out of it.

Zev steps back, his gaze returning to the woman he just inhaled. "She has no such smell. You may have human blood, but there's more to you than that."

I need a break from this new reality, so I cross the room to take my baby back from Rune. She might be less than a day old, but she feels like the one constant I've got in life, now that I know AJ is an alien or a bird or a pile of crabs wearing a human suit.

Darius comes in hot, wanting answers like the rest of us, but also with a personal bone to pick since AJ beat him in a game of mentalist. "Where are you from?"

"I'm from Rowley, idiot."

Her immediate snark is so common for people in this area, it makes me think either Zev can't handle the smell of New Englanders or I've grown up amongst nonhumans. Frankly, both options sound plausible.

Rune's been quiet to this point, observing with a blank face. When he stands and strides over to AJ, Zev and Darius clear the way, almost deferentially.

"I sense nymph."

He speaks with a quiet authority. It's a side of Rune I hadn't seen until this point. He stares into AJ's eyes while describing her to us.

"She attracts, clearly. There's fluidity, grace... and fire. That must be the human side."

Zev and Darius join the fae, the three of them all standing inches from AJ, whose body is tense but unmoving. My mind drifts again to a quick body swap, placing myself in the middle of that Sexy circle, but I push the thought out for fear of fainting.

"It's on the father's side," Darius speaks barely above a whisper.

"How do you know?" asks Zev. It's the first time I've seen the werewolf seek knowledge from another, and it adds another layer to his intelligent charm.

"Because if the trait came from her mother," Darius says, turning away from AJ to show his inspection has concluded.

"...she'd know." Rune picks up the sentence where Darius left off. "She had no example of who she was. No role model."

"Hey, blondie, maybe stop talking shit about my

mom." AJ's heart is in the right place, even if she misses the point.

I've still got no fewer than a million questions, but the Sexies seem pretty content with this reasoning. AJ's a nymph, not on her mom's side, case closed, I guess?

"Hang on," I finally chime in, not ready for this conversation to move to the next point. "How many nymphs and wolf people and, friggin', I don't know, orcs are living around me? Or is AJ, and AJ's dad, are they the only ones?"

"Certainly not the only ones," Zev answers, reclaiming his role as the smartest man in the room. "But there are very few."

The werewolf walks into the attached kitchen, taking a glass and filling it with water from the sink.

"A small number of Earthlings aren't human," he continues, "many concentrated in this area."

"What, in Rowley?" AJ asks. I can hear from the tenor of her voice that she's not into the idea of other non-humans living in her town. She doesn't want anyone cheapening her Nymphness.

"Your world has a long history with paranormals," Rune explains. "Centuries ago, when witches sought refuge in this region--"

"Quiet, Rune," Darius says with a roll of his eyes. "You sound like a tired professor."

"Someone had to pay attention during seminars, Prince Darius," Rune fires back.

"Hang on," I say, not wanting the seminar detail to slip through the cracks. "You two went to school together?"

"All three of us," Zev says, walking over with his glass and joining the conversation. "We have a backstory that predates your country, Bernie."

"That's right," Darius says, a menacing look in his eyes. "Our friendship started lifetimes ago. Or at least *one* lifetime."

"We don't need to have this conversation now," Rune says, his anger starting to boil over.

"Then when?" Darius asks. "Generations have passed. When will you feel comfortable talking about Cara's death? Or are you happy to silently blame me until the kingdoms collapse?"

A hush takes over the room, each man staring daggers at the others. It would appear that the Sexies not only have history, but some heavy history.

"Later," Zev says. "You deserve the conversation, Darius, but not right now."

And with that, the werewolf turns to AJ and

shocks us all by throwing the water from his glass at her face.

"What the… you son of a bitch!" As mad as AJ looks, she's too startled to act on her anger, staying put while staring daggers at Zev.

Darius moves over to look at AJ. Rune also looks from her face to the floor around her, giving the scene of the crime a thorough inspection.

"Interesting," Darius says.

"Quite," Rune agrees.

"Water nymph," Zev announces.

"More like beat-your-ass-with-a-tire-iron nymph, you piece of--"

"A." I cut her off in part so she won't start a fight with three superpowered beings, but also because of the sight before me.

She might be livid, but AJ is completely dry. In front of her, there's a perfect ring of water. Like she had a forcefield that repelled it and, save a few drops on her clothes, kept her from getting wet.

I point to the floor and she follows my finger, noticing the water and then putting her hands to her face.

"Why… why'd you miss?" she asks Zev, who smiles in response.

"Because you're a water nymph," he responds

in an oddly reassuring tone. "You control the water around your body, just like you can control men."

At that, both AJ and I burst into laughter. Attract, seduce, allure, maybe. But control? If AJ could actually *control* men, her life would have been way different.

"I'll give you the water gag," she says, looking from Zev to me and then back to her assailant. "But I've got no power over men. If anything, it's the other way around."

"Do you live near the water?" Darius asks, a hint of annoyance in his voice at having to teach someone about why they could dodge his mind tricks.

"Yeah, dumbass, the ocean's like five miles from here."

"Can you see it from your home?" If Darius sounded annoyed earlier, he's now fully vexed.

AJ thinks, though she knows the answer. "No, not... no. But why does that matter? Also, plenty of people have thrown beer in my face and it hasn't, like, bounced off me."

"You don't have power over fluids, and just a minimal control over the water near your body," Zev clarifies. "I also imagine you relinquished your power over men."

"What? When? Why?" Her string of questions showcases how little either of us understand what's being said.

"If you don't believe in your own strength," Darius cuts in, "you turn what should be a power into a weakness."

It's a very backhanded compliment, and I think AJ takes it as such. She might've let guys walk all over her up to this point in her life, but if she actually starts to believe in herself, she could put a stop to it now.

"But," Darius continues, "a nymph in the house only complicates things further." He steps toward her, mouth open, teeth sharpening with each step. "I'd like to know what everyone proposes we do."

"How about this," I say, putting my foot down before this conversation gets further out of hand. "This is my house and you three are the entire complication. So why don't you go down to the bar, clean a little, talk things over, sit on the stools and try to look normal. With the power out and nothing to do at home, people will start showing up soon, and I'd love it if you refrained from killing anyone else today."

I look at AJ, still weirded out by her not being human, but nevertheless taking a lot of comfort in her presence. I need a shot of Jameson and a cry on a shoulder, and I know she'll help with both.

"AJ and I are going to have a quick talk and then we'll join you," I finish, trying not to leave room for any follow-up questions.

The Sexies seem content, or are at least eager to discuss the new situation. They move out of the apartment, with Darius being the last to go, his eyes lingering on AJ.

As soon as he closes the door, she turns to me with a twinkle in her eye I don't think I've ever seen before. "Can you believe this shit? I'm not human!"

I don't know why this makes her so ecstatic, but I guess it's better than her being devastated.

"Are you sure, though?" I'm not ready to buy into all this, especially because we don't know what any of it means. Can she breathe underwater? Talk to fish? Or just stay dry without an umbrella?

"I mean, not really," AJ says, and I take solace in her at least being a little apprehensive. "But that water trick was something, and I'm riding a wave of dead-husband endorphins."

Right. That's still a thing. At some point, when we know what's going on and, well, what she is, we'll need to address the issue of the murdered and now officially missing John.

"What I do know," AJ continues, "is that a sexy vampire tried to get in my head, and then a wicked hot werewolf sniffed my neck and told me I'm not human. Who am I to argue with those facts?"

I stroll into my bedroom while considering her words. It's time for Rain to have a proper sleep in her crib before I have to feed her again. My breasts are already starting to feel heavy again. AJ follows me in, her face going soft at the sight of my daughter.

"So," I say as I lay Rain down. "What now? What do we do?"

There's a quiver in my voice as I speak, and I know a monsoon of tears are on the way. I'm overwhelmed by everything and need to cry out some stress before I can use my brain or body again.

AJ recognizes all of this, of course, and brings me in for a hug just as the weeping begins. I bury my head into her shoulder to stifle my sobs and she leads me out of the bedroom away from Rain.

"First off, let's get downstairs and drink some whiskey." As expected, AJ's comfort game is unassailable.

"Second, let's remember who has the dead husband and yet is for some reason doing all the consoling."

It's a fair point, and one that forces me to break from crying long enough to let out a laugh.

"You're right," I say as I dry my eyes with my sleeves. "I've got a beautiful baby and run a halfway house for hotties from other realms. And that includes you, apparently."

"It's a pretty good setup," she says. "Even so, I'll kick your ass if you stay in Rowley longer than is absolutely necessary."

"AJ, I have to run--"

"Nope," she cuts me off before I can launch into my speech about being responsible for the family business. "No buts. You have a gift, it got you out of this place, and as soon as we deal with...whatever it is we're dealing with, you gotta go, girl."

We share a brief moment, speaking no words, just smiling gratefully at each other. Thank God for true friends.

"Okay," I say, feeling a bit of a second wind coming on. "I've got to figure out how to run this bar and… well, I've got to figure out everything."

"*You*," AJ starts, looking at me like I'm nuts, "don't have to do anything. I was going to step in for you after the baby came, and that doesn't change just because she's here early."

I knew AJ would help when Rain arrived, but I was always hesitant to put this on her plate. She's got--well, had--enough to deal with in her personal life, and I can't really afford to pay her beyond what the customers tip. Morgan's is a small bar in a small town, meaning we'll always have enough customers to stay open and never quite make enough money to pay all our bills. The fact that my family has kept this place going for multiple generations is nothing short of a miracle.

"I mean, I'm not going to turn down your help, but I completely understand if you need to go off and think or cry or just fire a gun into the sky for a while."

"Nope, I'm good," AJ says with a shrug. "I don't want to leave you, don't mind being around them, and I'll happily stuff some tips in my bra." She flashes a sexy smile. "I'm going to control the shit out of these human men."

She undoes a button on her shirt to show a little more cleavage. What a strange new version of the same old AJ.

"Great," I say as I turn back to my room. "I'm going to watch my baby sleep for a while, then we'll come meet you downstairs, Nympho."

AJ bounds off to the bar, not at all bothered by

the new moniker. I step into my room and catch a glimpse of myself in the mirror over my dresser; looks like the bath did me good. Face is still a little puffy and I'm not even going to think about my midsection, but I'm not the monster I felt like earlier this morning.

A cold breeze ripples over my skin, alerting me to an open window on the other side of my bed. What kind of horrible mother leaves a window open in the dead of winter next to a newborn? Even if she's only alone for like five minutes, she could still…

I stop dead in my tracks, standing between the window and the crib.

The empty crib.

My baby's gone.

Chapter Eight

I look out the window, my heart pounding so hard in my chest I fear my ribs will break. Panic crowds my mind, filling it, not so much with words, but horrifying images of all the things that could be happening to my baby.

Outside I see only sheets of snow blurring the town I know so well, covering it all in a blanket of white that earlier looked ethereal and beautiful, but now has a sinister undertone.

Rain is hungry. Cold. She needs me.

And someone has taken her.

Fear jolts me into action, turning to rage in a blink, and I raise my voice as I race downstairs as fast as my still-healing body can go.

"Which one of you assholes took my

goddamned child?" I scream, storming into the bar so hard the door hinge comes undone. The building seems to shake, startling me for a moment. The storm outside must be worse than I thought, which only makes me more angry and scared for Rain.

The three Sexies and AJ all turn to look at me, and none of them are holding my baby.

Darius is the first to blink over to me, and I don't even reprimand him for using his superspeed this time. "What has happened?" he asks, his eyes burning into my soul with their dark intensity.

"She's gone," I say, tears springing up as a wave of emotion threatens to drown me. "Rain is gone."

And then, Darius is gone. Presumably upstairs to investigate. I don't even know. My stupid human eyes can't track his movements.

I cover my face, sobs shaking me, and feel strong arms wrap around me. "We will find her. Trust us on this," Rune says, and his words hold power that seem to calm me despite myself.

With a howl, Zev, already back in wolf form, leaps across the bar and crashes out a window. Dude is really going to have to learn to use doors, but that's a lesson for less urgent times.

"Aren't you going to help search?" AJ asks Rune, who is still holding me close, like I might fall apart if he wasn't there to keep me together, and maybe that's not far from the truth.

"I must stay to protect Bernie. We do not know what we're dealing with yet, though I have my suspicions."

"If you're staying with B, then I'll go."

I push against Rune's chest just enough to create a bit of space between us. I need to clear my head, and whether it's his magic or natural magnetism, I can't do that when he's holding me. "I'm going too," I say.

"Not a chance, B," AJ says with a frown. "It's freezing out there. You just gave birth. You'll be no use to Rain if you get sick or dead."

AJ glances at Rune, who nods. But though her words make sense on some level, it feels wrong for me to stay behind doing nothing while my child is in danger.

As if reading my mind, AJ reaches for my hand. "I know this goes against everything inside you. You're a badass, no question, but you. Just. Had. A. Baby. Most women are still in the hospital recovering and getting fed sad, alcohol-free jello shots. You shouldn't be dealing with any of this. Let me help."

"Werewolves and vampires are the best trackers

you can find," Rune says. "And however else I might feel about Darius and Zev, they are powerful, even amongst their kind. They will find your child."

"And I've never been sick a day in my life," AJ says, and with a start I realize that's true. I never thought about it before, how odd that was. "Turns out, the cold never bothered me anyway." She shrugs with an impish smile. "Snow is just water in a different form, and apparently that's my jam. So, I'm gonna go out there and see what I can do."

She kisses my cheek. "I'll be back soon."

Then she glances at Rune. "Get her a shot, make her rest. And protect her with your life or I will carve out your liver and feed it to that wolf out there."

"Duly noted," Rune says with a glint in his silver-blue eyes.

I watch helplessly as my best friend heads outside, into the blizzard, and hiccup softly as a new wave of emotion overwhelms me.

My breasts feel about ready to burst, and when I look down I notice I'm leaking. Fantastic. As if I needed one more problem right now.

Rune takes my hand and guides me to the bar, indicating I should sit.

My legs are wobbly, my head is spinning, and now that the adrenaline is wearing off, the ache in my body from my recent birthing experience is returning, so I take the seat normally reserved for Joe and marvel at how odd it feels to be on this side of things.

Rune moves around like he belongs back there, pulling out two glasses and the finest whiskey we have. He pours a generous amount into each tumbler, then takes something from a hidden pocket and sprinkles it into mine. It makes the liquor sparkle, like liquid gold.

I take the glass, staring at the mesmerizing drink. "What did you do to it? And honestly, I shouldn't be drinking this while nursing. A tiny bit once a week is fine, according to Doctor Internet, but more than that could be harmful for... for Rain."

Saying her name brings up a surge of terror once again, and Rune comes around the bar to sit next to me. He takes my free hand, and at the touch of his skin that calmness I felt before flows over me. "That powder will change how your body perceives the alcohol. It will excrete it more slowly, breaking it down and keeping it from passing through your milk. I've also added something that will help you recover more quickly from the birth. It's quite safe, I assure you."

My eyes widen. "We could make a lot of money selling your magical drinks here," I say, sipping at the concoction. It dances on my tongue and burns going down in the kind of smooth, rich way only the best whiskey can offer.

Instantly I feel my body melt a bit. Every nerve is still on fire, worried for my child. Wondering what's happening. What the three of them are out there doing.

But the drink and Rune's presence take the edge off--which part of me resents. I have a right, a responsibility, even, to be hysterical and in full-on rage mode right now. At the same time, AJ is right. I'm no use to Rain if I'm sick, and I don't want to-- I don't know--feed her angry milk. Is that a thing? I don't even know anymore, but I don't want to risk it.

So I continue sipping the magic whiskey as my gaze locks with Rune's pale blue eyes. "You don't look like a fae," I say at last. "At least not how I imagined."

His lips twitch in a smile. "I appear how I must in this realm to not stand out too much. Would you like to see my true form?"

I suck in a breath and nod.

With a flick of his wrist, his appearance shifts. It's subtle, but I take in each detail. The irises of his eyes are larger, more luminescent. His face is more defined, his skin so perfect it doesn't look real. His hair glows silver, like moonlight. But the most striking difference is his ears. They are longer, with pointed tips.

"You're beautiful," I say with a shaky breath, temporarily overwhelmed by the vision of him.

He lifts a hand to caress my cheek, his gaze consuming me. "Would that you could see yourself through my eyes, to truly know real beauty."

His words send a shiver down my spine, but the temporary distraction is short-lived as my mind crashes back to why we're sitting here.

When a new tear slides down my cheek, Rune uses the pad of his finger to wipe it away. "They will be back soon. With Rain."

"How can you be so sure?"

"I just am," he says, as if that explains everything. "The cost of failure is too high."

"Tell me what's really going on here," I demand. Since these guys walked into my bar, it's been madness. The irony that this is the first pause we've had to actually talk is not lost on me.

"Your child is at the crux of a prophecy that will have a profound impact on all of us. Human, vampire, werewolf, fae, and all others. It is said she is the Last Witch that will be born, the last one of your kind who can save us all from extinction."

"My kind?" I ask, sure the magical alcohol is now playing with my hearing.

"Yes," Rune says softly. "You're more special than you know, Bernie. In time, this will all make sense, and you'll understand the true importance of your beautiful girl."

"Is that why she's been kidnapped? Because of this stupid prophecy?" I ask, my hand clutching the tumbler so hard it might crack as my anger returns more powerful than before.

Once again, the bar shakes, like a mini-earthquake, though we don't get earthquakes here. My baby is out in a storm so powerful it's shaking buildings. I'm beyond angry. I'm ready to tear into whoever did this the same way Darius and Zev tore into John.

"We are not the only ones who seek her," Rune says.

"Fantastic," I say, downing the last of my whiskey. "As if having three supernatural alphas showing up demanding my child wasn't bad enough."

Rune frowns. "I'm truly sorry our presence has been so disruptive to you. I will admit, I never quite thought about your role in the prophecy. For thousands of years, this edict has been passed down in my family, that we would be ready to retrieve the one who could save us. It has made us all a bit...myopic in our approach."

Ugh. I can't be like, sure it's totally fine you want to steal my kid, but also, I don't know what I would have done if they hadn't been around to help deliver so, shit. "Right now I just want her back in my arms. The rest can wait. But know this, none of you are taking her away from me. She's mine." I pause, fighting a sudden urge to overshare, then give in when I realize it would be nice to have someone to talk to about the things weighing on my heart. I hold up my glass, and Rune reaches for the whiskey, pouring me another and sprinkling in his magic glitter once again.

"I didn't want her at first," I confess finally, after taking another drink. "She wasn't planned... obviously. And I gave serious consideration to..." I pause, drinking again. It's so hard to think about. To talk about. To have her or not have her was the most difficult choice I've ever made. "I was in a master's program at Julliard--"

When Rune looks at me confused, I explain. "It's a music school in New York. Very prestigious, hard to get into it."

His eyes soften. "I'm not surprised you attained that level of acclaim. Your music is truly magical."

His words send a thrill through me, which I attempt to ignore. "I had opportunities coming out my ass," I say. "But I guess the prospect of success made me stupid. I had an affair with one of my teachers... and ended up pregnant. He wanted me to have an abortion, and I was ready to. Having a baby would derail my career, my life. Everything I'd worked so hard for. But on the day of the appointment, I couldn't go through with it. I stayed at school as long as I could while pregnant, but then my grandfather died and I knew it was all coming to an end. My life, my dreams. Everything."

I swallow my tears along with more whiskey. "And then she was born and I looked into her perfect elfin face and I knew I'd made the right choice. I would give up everything for her. Everything."

I glare at Rune fiercely. "She is mine to protect.

She is mine to raise. And that is non-negotiable. But I don't expect you to understand."

I turn away, overcome by my own emotions, hating myself for talking tough about my parenting moments after my baby was stolen from her room.

Rune reaches for my hand. "Bernie, I would like to show you something, with your permission."

"Show me what?" I ask, returning my gaze to his.

"Close your eyes," he says, as he places his hands on both sides of my face and leans in until our foreheads are touching. The gesture feels deeply intimate, and I inhale his scent of wildflowers and cinnamon. "I understand more than you know."

His fingers heat up against my skin and my inner mind glows silver, then everything changes.

I am standing in a forest at night, a gentle breeze tickling the hair on my neck and swaying the branches around me. Dozens of small glowing bugs buzz in the air, casting silver light against the iridescent flowers spread over a vast valley that starts at the edge of the trees.

The sound of insect life scurrying under layers of leaves and mulch fills my ears, and when I inhale, I smell a faint sweetness from the flowers and the musky scent of the rich green foliage surrounding me.

Everything feels so damn real, it's like being in the most advanced, futuristic virtual reality game.

"Come this way," Rune says, startling me with his presence. He reaches for my hand and a spark of energy dances on my skin when our palms touch.

He looks down at me, a look of surprise and something else… on his face before he schools his expression to neutral.

Our fingers link and I let him lead me through the trees towards the sound of running water. Of waterfalls and rushing rivers.

A man stands at the edge of the water, placing flowers into a narrow boat.

I gasp, tightening my grip on Rune's hand when I realize the man we are watching… is him.

He leans to whisper into my ear. "This is the night my wife and child died. I am saying good-bye." His voice is choked with emotion. "She was the last of our kind to get pregnant and give birth. We hoped it was a sign that the plague on our people was ending. That the prophecy we feared wasn't coming to pass. That perhaps our combined royal lineage could break this curse. But alas, the child came early, and was stillborn. The birth took her life in the process, and there was nothing I could do with any of my magic to save either of them."

We watch silently, our grip on each other's hands tightening, as the Rune of the past pushes the boat into the water. Once it's moving down the river, he raises an arrow and lights it with a blue fire, then draws his bow and releases. His aim is true, and the boat alights in glowing flames that fill the night sky. He falls to his knees as his wife and child sink, his cries of anguish raw and visceral.

The Rune by my side looks down at me again, his silver eyes glistening with emotion. "I know your fear. Your pain. Your worry. It is mine as well. It is what brought us all here."

He holds up a hand before I can say anything. "I'm not trying to justify taking your child from you. I just wanted you to understand why."

There's an argument to be had, but I see the point Rune's making. It's just… not a conversation I know how to have right now, after what I just bore witness to. So, I change the subject.

"I know so little about you three. Can you take me back further? To your time with Darius and Zev?"

A fleeting smile passes over the fae's face, quickly replaced by a look of longing.

"I'm sorry," he says, his eyes glistening with unshed tears as he stares into a past I cannot enter. "I'm afraid my heart cannot bear revisiting the memory of another loved one lost to me."

There are times to question and times to be silent, and I know this is the latter. As much as I want to know more, and even as much as I feel I have the right to know more, sometimes we must choose to be kind over being right. I give him what little solace a squeeze of my hand can provide.

I'm pulled out of the trance by the sound of the bar door slamming open, my heart heavy and my mind thick.

Rune is now sitting next to me, just as he was. But his eyes are still full of the pain I just witnessed. As powerful as our moment was, my mind switches gears immediately when I see AJ race in, a small bundle in her arms.

Darius follows, dragging a man with a hood over his head and his hands tied behind his back, a large white wolf nipping at his heels.

"Rain's okay," says AJ, handing my child to me. I grip Rain so tight, probably squeezing air out of her tiny lungs, but I can't help myself. Now that she's back, I finally let myself consider the thought I pushed back against so hard--I might have never seen her again.

"I'm so sorry, baby," I say to her. "Mama won't ever let you go again."

"And this," AJ says, reminding me there's more to this story, "is the bastard who took her."

I glare as she pulls off his hood... and then I gasp.

"Karl?"

The deadbeat who's always passed out in my bar? The man who's known my family for years? That's the person who kidnapped my baby?

What the hell alternate reality have I stumbled into?

Chapter Nine

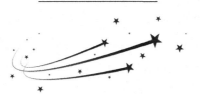

I stare into Karl's familiar face, snow sticking to his ever-present stubble. His large hazel eyes are full of fear and confusion. The fear I understand because he should know he's about to die; the confusion doesn't make sense, because there should be no question as to why he's about to die.

"Karl..." I let the word hang, carrying all the weight of a full sentence.

"Bernie..." Karl responds in kind, and I listen closely to his tone, hoping it will explain his inexplicable behavior.

It doesn't.

Darius, lacking the patience to read the man's facial expression, slams him against the bar, holding his face down on the copper surface.

"Who are you?" Darius snarls, his sharp teeth centimeters from Karl's pulsing jugular vein. "Who sent you for the child?"

Karl keeps his eyes trained on me, ignoring the vampire's questions.

"Bernie, you know me."

"I thought I did," I snap back. It seems like he's got some point to make, something to say in his defense, but he's not getting there fast enough.

"These guys, they aren't what they seem." If Karl thought that generic understatement was going to win any points, he's sorely mistaken.

"Neither are you!" My yell startles Rain and makes her cry, but AJ is at my side immediately with a blanket. In a surprisingly swift motion, I wrap the baby, pop out a boob, begin to feed and then return my fiery stare to Karl. I strut toward the bar, feeling incredibly emboldened with these three powerful men backing me up.

"Have you been plotting this? Pretending to be passed out in my bar so you'd know when the baby came?"

Of course, the answer will be no. Karl's too much of a deadbeat drunk to formulate a plan and then carry it--

"Yes."

The word doesn't come from Karl's mouth, but rather from Rune's. The two look at each other, reading one another's faces and movements, before Karl looks back at me. His silence confirms the fae's assessment.

"You don't understand, Bernie."

Another cliche one-liner, but he's not wrong. In a day where every single thing has been strange and stupefying, this is somehow the most unexpected event so far. A regular at the family bar for years, a guy who could never manage to drive himself home at the end of the night, a person everyone in town knows, stole my baby. From my window, on the second floor, in the dark, in a blizzard.

"I'm trying to help you," Karl says earnestly. "We're trying to save your baby."

"Who," Darius asks, stepping menacingly close to Karl's face, "is *we?*"

Zev circles around the captive man, sniffing. Rune grabs Karl by the wrist, inspecting his hand. I'm not sure what answers they're looking for, but they're looking intently.

Suddenly, Zev growls. At first I think something about Karl has angered him, but then I see his wolf eyes have moved to the front door. I follow his look and seconds later, the doorknob starts to turn. Jesus, who's here to steal my baby now?

The door opens about an inch, then slams shut and locks itself. As my frazzled brain tries to remember if the bar door has always made its own decisions, I see the vampire's hand extended in that direction and realize he did the closing and locking. It'll take a while for me to get used to all the magic.

AJ moves quietly to a window at the front of the bar and peeks out. "It's Joe and Frank," she says, then adds with a smile, "they brought flashlights so you can't make them leave when the candles burn out."

"Don't let them in," Darius says. "There are too many bodies in here as it is."

He makes a good point, but sending these guys home almost guarantees they'll come back fifteen minutes later with Frank's wife to check up on me. And if she shows up and starts talking, I doubt the most powerful magic in the universe could get her to stop.

"They won't go without a fight," I explain.

"Bernie?!" A voice comes from outside, right on cue. "You okay in there? It's Joe and Frank, we brought some baby toys, pacifiers and shit."

Sweet, stupid, drunk old men.

When I look back to Darius, he's gone. As is Karl. And yet I still hear his voice as if he's inches away.

"Where can I take this intruder?" the invisible Darius asks.

"Wait," I interrupt, too confused to let this go. "Where are you?"

"He's right where you last saw him."

Rune places his hand gently on my shoulder as he speaks, washing that wave of calm over me. God, I need him touching me always.

"I've created an illusion along the back of the bar. Darius, gag him now while we let these people in." Rune looks at me with a sweetness in his eyes, and I'm truly starting to feel he's on my side. "We'll run business as usual, if that's what you think is best. Though, may I suggest closing early so you can get some rest?"

"I'll be back in a moment," the invisible Darius says. "I'm going to stitch this cretin to the ceiling upstairs."

I don't really know what that means, but I'm also sure he isn't lying.

"Bern?!" Joe calls again from outside. It would never cross his mind that the bar might be closed, especially because my grandparents had the place open every day except Christmas.

Rune takes a seat at the bar, assuming the role of a customer, I guess. AJ comes over and takes the now-sleeping Rain, who fell asleep while feeding because she's just so goddamn cute. I walk over to the door, a little jealous I can't just unlock it from thirty feet away like Darius.

I open up and present Joe and Frank with a big, fake smile, even as a gust of cold nearly knocks me on my ass.

"Hey, guys! Sorry, the wind blew the door open earlier so I locked it. Come on in!"

I turn away to lead them inside, but don't hear footsteps behind me. When I look back, they're still frozen in place, staring at the far end of the bar. I follow their eye line and quickly realize the hesitation.

"Oh yeah, that. Ummm... I got a dog."

I wish I'd had a conversation with Zev about how to explain his presence, but it's too late for that. Now I'm a dog owner. When people come to my bar, I have a husky the size of a small horse. What a great way to drum up business.

"Where... where'd you get it?" asks Frank,

looking legitimately afraid to step foot in the bar. "Cuz that ain't no dog. That's a wolf."

"Maybe it has some mix in it, but he's totally tame," I say, as Zev looks up at me and growls under his breath. I want to kick him as a reminder to watch his manners, but that would definitely look bad. "As to where I got him, it's a long story, Frank. Now, get your ass inside so I can close the door, and I'll tell you once you've had a beer and loosened up."

They do as they're told, giving me a few seconds to start thinking of a husky-the-size-of-a-huge-wolf buying story that can't be verified. Fortunately, by the time they reach the bar, they see AJ and what she's holding. Joe spins back toward me.

"Whoa! Bern! Holy shit! Your baby!"

Holy shit indeed. It's like every time someone notices Rain, I remember that I'm a brand new mother who should be asleep constantly.

"Yeah, that's baby Rain," I say, walking back behind the bar to get her from AJ. "She arrived last night with the help of this guy. Rune."

Rune has been sitting at the bar, doing his best to be ignored, but I figure it's less suspicious to open up the introductions now than it is to wait for the guys to ask questions.

Joe and Frank size him up. Normally they'd make fun of a clean man with a handsome face, but Rune's obvious size and strength keep the jokes at bay. Plus, they take kindly to anyone who helped me out.

"Oh yeah, you were here last night," Joe says. "Are you a, uh, you know, you a…"

My tired brain is about to answer, "a fae," but fortunately AJ steps in to save me from myself.

"He's a doctor. He and another doctor friend are passing through town, thinking of opening up a practice somewhere in Mass. Couldn't have timed their visit to Morgan's any better."

Solid work, AJ. She's clearly better than me at lying on the spot, which makes it even more important to have her around.

"Where's the other doctor friend?" Frank asks. "And wait, weren't there three guys here last night?"

I look down at Zev the wolf, wondering how to answer this question. He returns my gaze, and I get a very strange feeling sharing a look with a wolf who I know is not just a wolf.

"No, just the two guys that I remember," I answer, unwittingly locking Zev into wolf form whenever the bar is open.

"The other guy, Darius, he is…" I launch into

this sentence before I have any idea of where it's headed, but the bar door swings open and finishes my story for me.

"He is here!"

Darius enters casually, giving me a slight nod and taking a seat by Rune. I watch the two lock eyes briefly and I'm positive they just linked brains, filling each other in on everything missed. When they finish their mind gossip, Darius turns to Joe and Frank, offering a forced smile.

"Do you gentlemen know Karl? I was speaking with him last night. He said he... had some lodging recommendations."

Joe and Frank start laughing immediately as I put my hand over my eyes. I've never seen someone so bad at lying to small town folk.

"Talking to Karl?" Joe says with a chuckle. "He must have been sleep talking, drunken fool."

"Of course we know Karl," Frank adds. "Grew up with his dad, our grandpas went to war together. Known his family for generations."

Joe nods, not going into his family history, even though I'm sure it's similar.

Rune and Darius share a knowing look and probably a little mental dialogue that I wish I could hear, despite my earlier insistence that they stay out of my head.

With Rain asleep in my arms and my own eyelids feeling like they're made of lead, I decide this is as good a chance as any to duck away for sleep. AJ's quick enough on her feet to answer questions, Rune can create an illusion if necessary, and as long as Darius doesn't lose his cool and rip someone's throat out, we should be fine.

I bid my goodnights and grab a candle as I head for the backdoor. Before I can leave, I sense the familiar feeling of another's words penetrating my mind.

I'm sorry to enter your thoughts and break my promise, Bernie, Darius says, *but I want you to know the intruder is bound to the kitchen ceiling with unbreakable ropes. You'll be safe upstairs, but perhaps avoid that room. Zev will join you.*

It's a fair warning, as I for sure would have shit myself if I walked into the kitchen and saw Karl magically roped to the ceiling.

I look back at Darius, who now has his eyes trained on the wolf. After a few seconds, Zev rises and clambers up the stairs. I turn back to Darius.

Thanks, I think, guessing at how telepathic communication works.

You're welcome, I hear in response.

I pat Joe on the shoulder, kiss AJ on the cheek, and head upstairs, baffled and amused at the state of my life.

MY DREAMS ARE full of Rune. We're standing in the snow, but everything feels warm. His hands touch every inch of my skin, starting at my shoulders, stroking down my arms, then moving to my torso, rubbing my back at first, then turning me away from him so he can caress my stomach and breasts. I feel him pressed against me, and it's clear we both enjoy the feel of each other's skin.

"You're beautiful," he whispers in my ear, over and over. I'm in the state of sleep where I know this is a dream, and yet it's as vivid as any I've ever had. His breath tickles my ear, sending shivers down my spine and raising goosebumps on my sensitive flesh.

When I turn back to face him, he's naked, his body chiseled and smooth. As I reach down for him, he puts a hand on my shoulder, stopping me.

"Bernie," he says.

"Yes?" I reply, moving my face to his, eager to taste his lips.

"Bernie," he repeats, this time a little more forcefully.

"Bernie," he says a third time, and now the snow drifts away, the white glow morphing into a dim flicker, and I'm suddenly in my bedroom.

I bolt up, an immediate sense of panic overtaking me. Where's Rain? Who's dead? What now?

Rune sits in front of me, his presence providing an immediate calm.

"Shhh, you're all right. Rain's all right." It's as though he can read my thoughts, which, duh, he probably can. Yikes. How much of that dream was he privy to?

"What time is it?" I ask. "How long did I sleep? Where's everyone else?"

"It's morning," Rune says. "You finally got some quality rest. Unfortunately--"

The rest of his sentence is cut off when we hear AJ bounding up the stairs, two at a time like she's done since junior high.

When she enters the room, I see worry etched on her face.

"I don't see him out front. No sign of a car, either. He must have gone out the back."

"What? Who?" I'm still groggy and there are too many "he's" that she could be referring to.

A lot of my grogginess dissolves when Darius

does his appearing act right next to AJ, nearly causing her to fall in surprise.

"Zev is trying to catch his scent in the woods," he says to Rune. "We saw no prints in the snow."

I'm still completely lost, but I think I've got a good guess.

"Karl?"

Darius says nothing, though the angry clench of his jaw speaks volumes. AJ just wrings her hands, confused and alarmed. Rune looks back to me, giving a slight nod.

"He disappeared."

"What do you mean, *disappeared*? He just escaped? I thought Darius had--"

"I had," the vampire cuts me off forcefully, a little defensive. "And he disappeared. The ropes are all in place, unmoved, unbroken. A human can't escape those bonds."

In an instant, Zev the wolf appears at the top of the stairs, and in just as little time Zev in human form stands beside Darius. It happens far too quickly, and by the time I notice he's completely naked, he's already started slipping into a pair of pants. But not before I see everything.

"No scent, no tracks, no sounds," the half-naked

werewolf says, his voice pulling my eyes up from his waistline to his mouth.

"Darius, what do you mean?" AJ asks. "He did escape those bonds, so what are you saying?"

"I can't be sure," Darius starts, choosing his words carefully. "But it appears that Karl spends his time in the company of witches."

Chapter Ten

"Awesome, let's bring some witches into the mix," I say sarcastically. My nerves are frayed and I'm definitely using snark to hide that. AJ sees right through me though, and reaches for my hand, offering what comfort she can.

"I anticipated push back from those who wish to thwart us," Darius says, "but I'm surprised the witches are getting involved."

"I'm not," Rune says calmly. "This directly affects all magical races, particularly the witches. If your kind hadn't hunted them out of our world, we might not be in this mess in the first place."

Darius bares his teeth, and fangs protrude, his eyes darkening even further. "Push me too far, fae, and I'll develop a taste for *your* blood."

Zev studies them both and shakes his head. "My kind has the reputation for being hotheads, but I think you're both stealing that title."

"Please," Darius says. "We've seen you at your angriest, Zev, and it's not something either of us can compete with."

The werewolf walks over and gets in the vampire's face, forcing me to take a few steps back just in case a fight breaks out.

"And if your cold, dead heart could make room for emotions, you would have been angry as well."

They're back at it again with whatever beef developed during their years at, I don't know, magic school. It's like siblings who can't let something go, and as an only child, I'm annoyed enough to put an end to it.

"Jesus Christ, what are you talking about? Get it out in the open so we don't have to pause every hour for this redundant shit fit."

Neither Darius nor Zev looks at me, still locked on each other and fuming. Rune steps forward to speak, putting a hand on Zev as he does so and hopefully delivering some calm to the furious wolf.

"We learned of this prophecy at the same time, centuries back," the fae says. "As it affected each kingdom, the three of us were part of an ancient council that aimed to work with some sense of a common goal."

"Four of us," Darius says, still not turning away from Zev.

"Yes, there was a fourth," Rune continues. "A witch named Cara. A dear friend to us all."

"Not dear enough," Zev says, leaving no question as to who he's addressing.

I look at Darius, a new level of rage on his face. It seems like he needs a chance to speak about this through a mediator, so I ask him the next question.

"Darius," I say in as gentle a voice as I can muster, "what happened?"

The vampire finally takes his attention off Zev and looks at me. The room immediately feels a shade less hostile.

"We all worked together to translate and understand the prophecy," Darius says, gazing at the wall like his memories are projected there. "Cara wanted to work on a spell that might illuminate the meaning of the language. We initially told her not to, that there was too much magic in play, but she insisted. And I was the first to take her side."

Zev opens his mouth to speak, but Rune tightens his grip on the wolf's shoulder and silences him.

"So… your friend died?" Their silence seems like a pretty solid affirmation. "And you were all there when she did whatever she did, and Darius maybe didn't push back as hard as you two would have liked. And instead of talking it out, you've been mad for, what, a millennium?"

More confirming silence.

"Okay," I say, coming to the end of my usefulness as a paranormal counselor when they continue staring in silence. "I'm glad that got explained. It's… a lot."

The tension breaks a little when Rain begins crying, and I feel bad at how happy I am to hear my child fussing. "We'll get back to that, because right now we need to find Karl," I say, my mind spinning with a plan. "Or whoever he's working with, since I'm pretty sure he's not a witch."

"He's not," Zev says. "Witches are exclusively women. Always have been."

Huh. That's interesting and slightly unexpected. "Okay, so as I said, we need to find him and figure out who he's working with and why they also want my baby. How many magical species will we be fighting to keep her safe?" I clutch her more closely, fear and a fierce maternal protectiveness clouding my thinking.

"If he has magic, he might not be easy to track," Zev says gruffly. "As for how many others might be after her, that's hard to say. There are many races, but the witches, werewolves, fae, and vampires are the primary. All others are derived from us over the course of thousands of years."

"So nymphs are, like, some kind of blend? A magical mutt?" AJ asks, disappointment clear in her voice. She definitely wanted to be higher on the pyramid.

"In a manner of speaking," Zev says. "But this all happened ages ago. Right now, we need to formulate a better plan for protecting Rain and Bernie."

"Agreed," Rune says.

Darius nods but says nothing.

"And who will protect us from you three?" I ask, my words thrown like daggers at each of them. Rain finishes feeding and I cover myself and burp her as I stare the three men down. "You came here to take her, just like Karl. How are you any different? The only reason you're still here is because you're all keeping each other in check."

The Sexies look at each other with some level of discomfort. "It is... complicated," Rune says.

I know it's complicated, especially after getting

insight from Rune, but that doesn't warm me to the idea of someone stealing my child. "You all have your reasons for what you're trying to do. So does Karl. And I appreciate that you're staying and helping. But at the end of the day, why should I trust any of you? You all want the same thing. My baby. And you all see her as a savior to your people without regard for me, or her as a person."

Tears sting my eyes and the whole situation crashes into me like a tsunami I can't contain. I turn away so they don't see me cry. "I'd like to be alone, please. Can you all leave my room?"

Before anyone argues it's not safe, I turn back to glare at them. "I'll protect Rain, and you can all wait in the other room, but I need a freaking minute with my child and myself, is that too much to ask after all this?"

I raise my voice for emphasis, and Rune especially flinches like I just slapped him, but I can't muster enough energy to care. I feel beaten and bruised after nearly losing my child, knowing it could happen again. AJ leads the men out, Rune leaving last and closing the door behind him with a sharp click.

I lock it, knowing damn well it won't make any difference to men with magical powers and super strength, but it gives me some small semblance of control over an entirely uncontrollable situation. I shuffle over to my bed and crawl into it, pulling the blankets over both myself and my child until it is just the two of us in my mini make-shift fort. She's already fallen back to sleep, content and safe in my arms, and I stare at her for some time, wondering what it is that makes her so special. I know what makes her special to *me*. But why is everyone else in all the worlds after her, and how can I possibly keep her safe against such threats?

Eventually, those guys will figure out how to best each other. One of them will take her from me, and I will have no recourse. No way of fighting back. I would die for her, of course I would, and it just might come to that, but I fear my blood is not powerful enough or valuable enough to matter in this battle. This is far beyond the skills of a barmaid turned pianist turned barmaid again.

The tears come hard and fast, and I'm solidly wallowing in my own pain when I hear the whir of the electricity coming back to life. Through the thick comforter, a flicker of light confirms our power has returned.

It looks like we'll be back to business as usual,

and I'll need to muster my own courage to get my business up and running before I lose that too.

I crawl out of bed and use a Baby Bjorn to strap Rain to my chest, then I freshen up in the bathroom before returning to the guys in the living room.

"We've got a lot of prep work to do now that the power's back on. Are you going to help?"

Everyone nods and follows me silently downstairs.

I spend the next several hours giving instructions and teaching everyone what to do. AJ insists she can handle everything, but I need something to keep my body and my mind occupied. The alternative is more wallowing, and I'm not a fan.

We clean, prep and have everything ready when our first customers arrive. Tonight it's all regulars. The power's back and the snow stopped, but tall snow banks and black ice keep people from venturing far from home, and we've never been good at pulling in tourists anyways.

That suits my mood just fine. I don't really want to deal with strangers right now.

Everyone who comes in oohs and ahhs over the baby, but I refuse any requests to hold her, and keep her strapped to my chest all night except when I sneak away to feed or change her.

AJ and my new sexy staff do their part. Rune and Darius wash glasses and buss tables while Zev just chills in his wolf body--and by just chills I mean he glues himself to my heels. I swear I nearly trip on him at least three times.

When we finally close up shop that night, I'm dead on my feet, though the guys look as refreshed as always. Damn them.

Rune approaches me with hesitancy as I straighten my back, cracking it in at least five painful places.

"Let me take her and put her to bed, Bernie. You need a break."

When I don't answer, and instead clutch Rain closer to my chest, Rune lays a hand on me, and a rush of warmth and calm flows over me.

I jerk away. "Stop. Don't manipulate my emotions right now. I get to be pissed and scared and… and pissed."

He nods. "You do. I apologize. I just hate to see you so unhappy. I come from a long line of healers. It is in my blood to want to soothe and help. Forgive me for overstepping."

Well now I feel like part ass, part justified mama bear and 100% exhausted. Rune has been nothing but kind to me and Rain. Tender even. And as I look up the staircase, I wonder if I can even make it with her on my chest. I worked too hard and didn't accept the help that was offered. It's classic Bernie and I usually push through, but my body isn't used to recovering from childbirth.

With a sigh and some nervousness, I unclasp the straps and hand the bundle--baby included--to Rune's outstretched arms. His silver-blue gaze drops to Rain, and his expression is so gentle, so loving, so full of awe and hurt for what he's lost, that the wall I built around my heart cracks just a little. "Go. Before I change my mind."

He nods and with fluid speed, hastens upstairs.

I pause a moment, trying to will my broken body forward, when I feel strong arms lift me up.

Zev flashes a cheeky smile. "You don't look capable of making it up those stairs, love. Let me help."

I'm about to argue, but he's probably right. Everything in my body hurts so much I feel tears coming, though I refuse to let them fall. I will not show weakness, but dear heaven I could use a bath.

Using that magically heightened intuition, Zev carries me to the bathroom and gently places me on the toilet as he runs the hot water. Rune appears with a vial of herbs and dumps it into the bath. "It will help with your pain," he says, softly.

I can see more words unspoken in the depths of his eyes, but he turns to leave before I can ask. Zev raises an eyebrow but leaves as well, allowing me to undress in private.

As I slink off my clothes and sink into the tub, I groan in pleasure. Worry for Rain still filters through the relaxation, but the scent of lavender and rose and the feel of my muscles unknotting does a lot to calm my mind.

My mind is drifting when a knock at my door pulls me back. "Uh, yeah?"

Zev walks in holding a small jar of oil as I try to strategically place bubbles to allow for some level of modesty. Though, the werewolf doesn't seem concerned about such things, and maybe it's just my prudish puritan culture getting in the way of things.

"Your back was bothering you. I thought I might offer my massage services to alleviate a bit of that discomfort," he says, his gaze taking in the parts of my body that are still exposed, and lingering on the parts that aren't.

His words send a promise directly to my body, which responds before my mind even gets a chance to talk me out of it. I pull my knees to my chest and lean forward, exposing as much of my back as I can.

Zev shrugs out of his shirt, revealing his perfectly sculpted abs of steel before taking a seat on the edge of the tub. I raise an eyebrow at that and he shrugs. "Wouldn't want to get it wet."

"Sure," I say, shaking my head. "I think you're just allergic to clothing."

He lays his large hands on my shoulders, the heat from his skin seeping into my perpetually chilled body, and I moan at the simple pleasure of it.

Zev leans in, his lips coming dangerously close to my ear, his chest pressing up against my naked back. "Not allergic," he whispers. "But clothes do get in the way of some of life's most delicious moments, don't you think?"

"They can be cumbersome at times," I agree, trying to keep my voice steady as he begins to massage the tension out of my muscles.

As he works his way down my spine, I'm lost to his touch. He knows every tender muscle and how to coax the pain out of my body. I try not to sound like I'm having an orgasm over this massage, but it's damn hard, and I can tell my attempt at silence isn't fooling the werewolf.

"I can smell your arousal," he says, once again bringing his mouth to my ear.

In a bold move that feels more like AJ than myself, I reach back with my hand and graze it over his pants. "And I can feel yours."

Even just the hint of my touch inspires a deep growl low in his chest. The timbre of it resonates through my body and ignites a fresh wave of desire that I do my best to fight.

So I ask a question that could definitely kill the mood, and most likely will.

"Do you have someone? Back home?"

I let my hair fall over my face as I turn from him. Whatever his answer, I don't want to wear my heart on my sleeve right now.

He clears his throat and pulls back, his hands lingering at my side, lightly grazing the sides of my breasts. "No, no mate at home."

"Never?" I ask.

His fingers dig into my flesh and he moves against me, his mouth hovering over my shoulder. "Wolves mate for life, love," he says, his voice cracking with emotion. "And you don't know how dangerous these questions are for you." His lips brush against my shoulder, then his teeth nip my flesh, followed by a soft kiss.

And then he stands and leaves, pulling the door closed behind him firmly.

My skin is on fire from his touch, from his bite and his kiss. I rub at the faint teeth marks left in my skin and lean back, closing my eyes as I try to process what just happened. I can't sort out of my emotions. All I know is my skin is buzzing and my heart is racing.

By the time I'm done with the bath and dried off, I feel like a whole new woman--and am mostly recovered from my time with Zev. Though I still feel a small bruising pain in my shoulder from his bite, and it brings to mind all manner of places I'd like to feel his mouth next. Shoving aside any sexy thoughts of the Sexies, I check on Rain, who's sleeping soundly in her crib. Ah, to be so sheltered from the reality of the world. I tuck a blanket around her and then head to the living room where the guys are all there.

"Where's AJ?" I ask.

"She said she had some errands to run and will be back in a 'hot second'," Darius says somewhat awkwardly.

"Okay... why do you all look so weird right now?" I ask, searching their faces. They're sitting around the kitchen table facing each other and seem to be in the middle of a very tense discussion.

"We have given thought to the situation," Rune says after a moment. "And we have all come to realize there is more going on than we initially...considered. Regarding the prophecy, your child, and... you."

Zev clears his throat, his gaze landing on my shoulder before moving to my face. "This is more complicated than my realm understood. I'm sure if my mother…"

"Your mother?" I ask, ignoring the way his forest green eyes make me weak in the knees. "Who's your mother and what's she got to do with any of this?"

Zev looks to the other two, who remain silent, so he continues, reluctantly. "My mother is the queen of our realm. All three of us are princes. It was--is--our duty to fulfill the prophecy in order to save our people. That's why we were schooled together, along with Cara, the princess sent by the witches."

Princes? Like actual freaking princes. Shit. No wonder they wanted to give my apartment a huge makeover. And here I've been putting them to work tending bar and cleaning floors. The thought makes me smirk just a smidgen.

"As I was saying," Zev continues, his eyes narrowing on my mouth, "we do not believe our families understood the whole picture. So we have decided to send messages back to our realms explaining plans have changed."

"Plans?" That snaps me out of any sexy thoughts. "The plans to kidnap my kid? So you're not going to try to take Rain?" I ask, hope rising in me despite my best attempt to quash it.

Darius grunts with a mixture of annoyance and impatience. "What *Prince* Zev is trying to say is that while the prophecy still holds, and the need is still dire, we want to try to find another way."

"So you're all leaving?" I ask, and my heart sinks at that thought despite being entirely pissed off at all of them five minutes ago. In a game of Kiss, Marry, Kill, all three Sexies would qualify for each column. These postpartum hormones are a bitch.

"No." Rune's voice is firm. More alpha than I've ever heard it. "You and Rain still need protection. We will not abandon you. But while we wait for word from our respective families, we have decided to take a pledge that will give you--and us--reassurance of each of our intentions."

Darius and Zev both shift uncomfortably as Rune speaks. Whatever he's talking about, it's meaningful. But… a pledge? Like… of allegiance? To the flag? That's the only pledge I can think of and it sounds pretty useless.

"So, what, this is like a glorified pinky swear? How is this supposed to reassure me?"

"This pledge will bind us to you--for the time being," he adds when Darius glares at him. "We will not be able to take your child without your consent."

"Pft. Then you might as well throw in the towel. I'll never consent."

Rune nods. "I know that is how you feel now. It is our hope you will reconsider, given the consequences."

Before I can interrupt to tell him where he can shove his pledge, and his hope, he holds up his hand. "Regardless, this pledge cannot be broken by any of us. It will run its course at the spring solstice, at which point we can all reassess. In the meantime, it will mean we no longer have to watch each other so closely. One of us can be with you while the others are tending to the bar or helping in whatever way you need."

Rune pauses, then locks his gaze with mine and says softly, "We will be here at your whim, to serve, care for, and assist you. And, most importantly, to ensure the safety of your child."

Oh my. Heat flushes my cheeks and my knees feel a bit wobbly suddenly. I want to fan my face but that seems a tad extra, so I hold myself in check. *Play it cool, Bernie. Play it cool.*

"Right. Okay. That sounds… fine. So when will you do this?" My emotions are tumbling around inside me. Relief, fear, gratitude, lust, all of it making me an emotional mess.

"We need the right ingredients," Rune says, still leading the conversation. "The proper herbs, a dusting of fresh snow…"

"Sure. That sounds… reasonable, I guess."

"And…" Rune hesitates, and Darius grunts again.

"Unicorn blood," Darius says, finally. "We need unicorn blood."

Chapter Eleven

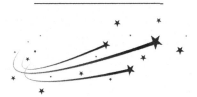

"Cool story, bro."

It's the answer I would have given, but it actually comes from AJ, standing in the doorway, having returned from whatever errand took her away in the dead of night.

"Unicorn blood?" She chuckles. "Yeah, sure, I'll just swing by my uncle's ranch and grab a vile."

Darius studies AJ seriously, as is his way. It's hard to tell if he's annoyed by her sarcasm or wondering--

"Who is your uncle? What's his family line?"

Yep. Wondering if her uncle really has a freaking unicorn.

AJ walks into the kitchen, laughing to herself, and pulls a beer from the fridge. Apparently grandpa didn't finish all his Budweiser before he passed. Jesus, have I not cleaned out the fridge since I moved home?

"My uncle doesn't have a unicorn, numbnuts," she responds, leaning against the counter and popping the bottle cap off with a lighter.

Darius bolts to his feet, fast enough to startle even his magical buddies.

"Watch yourself, nymph," he hisses, teeth bared. "Your powers are few and the stakes are higher than you can fathom. Cross me any further and you'll see--"

Rune grabs Darius by the elbow, and it looks like those fae calming powers have at least some effect on vampires. Darius takes a deep breath and then slowly moves back into his seat, like a predator biding his time.

AJ looks between the two for a second, then laughs. She smells a little boozy. I'm starting to think her errand was a stupid one.

"So, what's the plan?" I ask, trying to get the conversation back on track. "One of you goes to your world and comes back with some blood?"

"We can't return until the message has been received," Zev says, shaking his head. "For any of us to show up without the child and no prior notification would send the kingdom into a panic."

"Really?" I ask. "Even if you told people, er, your kind, that you were coming right back to protect the baby?"

Now all three of them shake their heads, solemn looks on their faces. I'll never be able to empathize with the severity of their situations, since I'm the mom of the baby they want to steal, but a small part of my brain recognizes the gravity of what they're dealing with.

"Okay, three things need to happen," I say as I turn toward the fridge, lost in thought and also immediately ravenous. I've been working too hard, sleeping too little, and acting as a full-time milk generator for a hungry newborn. I need to eat my bodyweight in carbs.

The minute I open the fridge door, AJ sprints past me, through the living room and out the door, yelling, "Don't eat!" on her way out. The guys watch her go suspiciously, then turn back to me.

"She moves, and thinks, erratically," Rune observes.

I nod. That's as good a way as any to describe AJ.

I hear her feet scampering back up the outdoor

steps, and she enters seconds later with a giant smile on her face and a massive pizza box in her hands.

"House of Pizza... " I trail off, hoping I'll still be able to chew while crying tears of joy. AJ and I spent half our high school years inhaling pizzas from this place. She opens the box, displaying a steaming, extra-large pie covered in sausage and mushrooms. It's the best gift I've ever received.

"I thought you might want something other than Rune's salad bar," AJ says. "Also, while I was there I had a couple beers and practiced nymphing, so the pizza was free."

"That's... not a thing," Darius says, perplexed.

AJ just grins. "It is now, bitches."

Oh Lord. Nymph AJ is going to be a lot to handle. But also a lot of fun.

I walk over to her and take the box, mouthing "I love you" as I do. Then I turn back to the guys. Not wanting the Sexies to see what I'm about to do to this pizza, I compose myself and finish my thought from earlier.

"All right, four things need to happen. First, I'm gonna eat every slice of this thing. Second, I want to know what's actually in this goddamn prophecy you keep talking about. Third, you figure out where you're going to get unicorn blood and then let me know if I can help. But, like, that better not involve killing a unicorn, okay? I've seen all the Harry Potter movies and read the books. I know how that shit ends. And fourth," I conclude, moving toward my bedroom, "I'm going to sleep, waking only to feed my baby, and I don't want to see anyone until morning."

I hear no protest as I walk off, excited beyond measure for the face stuffing I'm about to do. But then, an unexpected blast of nostalgia, one unrelated to AJ, punches me in the gut and stops me in my tracks. The smell of the pizza takes me back a couple decades, to a summer day when I was a child.

I spin around, facing my housemates.

"Sorry, there's a fifth thing. I need to go see my grandma."

RAIN ONLY WAKES me twice during the night to feed, otherwise sleeping like a little angel because that's what she is. When I get out of bed in the morning, I quickly eat one of the four remaining pizza slices and then sneak into the bathroom to brush my teeth before heading to the front room.

I'm not expecting to literally run into a naked werewolf.

I smack Zev with the bathroom door, and he gracefully dodges the brunt of the impact--though it would do little to harm him regardless.

He grins and steps in my direction, not bothering to hide his nudity or the evidence that he's happy to see me.

I pry my gaze away from his huge--

"Can I be of service?" he asks, and dear heaven help me I just want to throw myself at this man.

"Um. Sorry. I didn't know anyone was in here."

He takes another step closer, until our bodies are almost touching. "I don't mind sharing."

I don't even know what we're talking about anymore. All I can think is 1: why aren't we both naked? 2: how can I brush my teeth before this goes any further? And 3: who cares what my third thought is. Let's go back to one.

Why aren't we both naked?

I feel lost in the woods when I look into his eyes, and as his arm slides around my waist, pulling me against the hard length of his body, I go weightless.

He brushes his lips against my neck. "You feel it too."

I don't know what 'it' means, but yes, I certainly feel something.

He flicks his tongue against the spot he bit in the bath, and heat pools in my abdomen as my body aches in need of him.

"Careful, woman. You're playing with fire."

When he pulls away from me, I feel like a balloon that's been deflated. And as he walks out, closing the door behind him, I lean against the bathroom counter and take a deep breath.

Damn him.

Once I can stand without shaking, I groom and dress for the day, then head to the living room.

The Sexies are still gathered around the table, and I wonder if they just stayed up all night staring at each other like weirdos--with the exception of Zev, of course, who at least had a brief break to torture me in the bathroom.

They explain that they did not, with Rune and Zev sleeping in shifts, while Darius of course remained awake since he's a creature of the night.

While I slept, a few plans were hatched. I'm not allowed to travel without a guard, and I can't be alone with just one prince until the pledge takes effect. Therefore, Rune and Zev will accompany me on my journey to see my grandma. Journey is their word, not mine--we're driving like fifteen minutes down to Ipswich.

In the meantime, Darius will stay here to get his two hours of sleep and ask AJ questions about potential places to find a unicorn. AJ's still asleep and it makes me really, really sad to know I won't be in the house to see her face when Darius starts inquiring about the local mythical creature scene.

After feeding, changing, and bundling Rain, I get myself ready to step into the world for the first time since I became a mother. It's an odd sensation, thinking of who I might see and what they might say, and it's all made odder by the fact that I'll have to explain the gorgeous, mysterious company I'm keeping.

As I buckle Rain down in the carseat in the back of my 2004 Subaru Forester--affectionately named The Boobaru by AJ--I'm surprised by how excited I am. I'm outside! I get to go for a drive! I'm like a happy retriever.

I try to hide my giddiness as Rune gets into the passenger seat next to me. His presence is a strange mix of calming and electric, accelerating my heart rate while wrapping me in a warm sense of security. Two days postpartum and I'm developing a schoolgirl crush on at least two hunks from another realm. Hard to tell if I'm lucky or cursed.

The roads from Rowley to Ipswich are shit, which makes the drive longer but gives Zev and Rune more time to break down the prophecy that's upended my life and the lives of many others. From the way they talk, three realms are in the throes of chaos and on the verge of collapse because of this… situation.

"The issue for so many," Rune explains, "is that you have to look back to the beginning of time, the origin story of each race, to understand the problems underlying our societies today. Most of the brightest fae, werewolves and vampires are not capable of that scope of thought."

"Certainly not vampires," Zev growls from the back.

"Well, let's see how a human can handle it," I say. "Start from the beginning."

Rune nods, and it seems like both an affirmation to my request and like he's queuing up a really long story in his head. I ease off the gas a little; no need to hurry when I've got the history of an entire world coming my way.

"The story starts with the Fates, who originally spawned the--"

"What's a Fate?" I ask, crashing Rune's story before it even has a chance to begin.

"They were the original witches--sisters, who had great power," Zev offers from the back. He leans forward and grips my seat, his fingers brushing against my arm, not that I'm paying attention to that. "In addition to their own kind, they created all races of magical beings."

"The first witch created vampires from her blood," Rune says, continuing as if Zev hadn't interrupted. "The second turned a rib into the first of the wolves, and the third gave life to the fae with the air from her lungs."

"Okay," I say, skeptically. "So far it sounds like the parts of the Bible I find hardest to believe."

"I've read your Bible and I don't disagree," Zev says with a gruff chuckle that sends shivers up my spine. "But the fae have documented history from the second generation of existence."

"And vampires being what they are, many direct descendants of the Fate's creation still live today," Rune adds. "Darius is only three generations removed."

Well, shit. Looks like the paranormals brought receipts.

"Fine, you're all made from witch parts," I

concede as snarkily as possible. "What was the prophecy written on? One of the Fate's arm fat?"

"The different races dictated the Fate's words in their own way," Rune says, dismissing my attitude. "Werewolves maintained the story orally, speaking it to pups."

"Singing," Zev corrects. "We pass on our history through song."

I make a mental note to start a karaoke night at Morgan's and force Zev to sing this prophecy in wolf form.

"Very well," Rune says, "*sung* by the wolves. Fae, as Zev mentioned, wrote fastidious notes, and the vampires tasked a group of immortals to preserve the story. Aside from a slight discrepancy here or there, each of the three races maintains a similar version of the Fates' original decree."

"So, wait..." I'm now invested in the story and want to parse out some details. "What about witches? We've got three races invented by witches. Did the Fates forget to, you know, have babies or something?"

Rune shifts in his seat, brow furrowed as he thinks of the best way to answer me. Zev laughs again, and I swear he does this in the sexiest way possible, like he's rehearsed sexy laughs in the mirror so much that it now seems totally natural. But there's nothing natural about his level of sexiness. Nothing.

"The Fates did indeed spawn more witches," Zev says. "For many ages they were the most powerful race, then they stood on an equal plane for centuries as the other races grew and eventually began to outnumber the witches. Then…"

He drifts off, his gaze shifting toward the increasingly uncomfortable Rune.

"Until what?" I ask, my eyes spending way too much time on Zev in the rearview mirror and not enough time on the road.

Rune takes his cue from Zev and picks up the story, though it clearly pains him to do so.

"A feud began between the fae and the witches, over the rights to some of nature's gifts."

"The fae began killing witches for their land and the magical materials they cultivated," Zev says, clearly annoyed at Rune's milder retelling.

"Which led to the vampires taking advantage of a weakened race," Rune says, "and enjoying the powerful blood of witches fleeing the war. And, unless I'm mistaken, many a wolf helped the vampires with their tracking during that era."

Now it's Zev who's looking out the window,

unhappy with the truth that's just been leveled at him. I feel like they're both too close to the story and need a third party's summation.

"So... you shit-birds killed all the witches?"

"Not all," Rune quickly explains. "Once the vampires began to attack, a great many witches came to Earth, taking human form as we have done, and beginning new lives amongst your kind. They came to this very continent, around the same time as the Europeans, hoping to find a new world of their own."

When the story transitions from a magical realm I can't quite fathom to the land where pilgrims and puritans settled--where I grew up and studied the local history--a circuit breaker trips in my brain.

"Hang on... that witch shit from the 1600s was... that was real?"

Rune slowly shakes his head, giving Zev the opportunity to jump in.

"Yes and no," the werewolf says. "Witches were here, living alongside and even marrying humans. However, it was almost exclusively human women burned in your horrific trials."

"Easy there," I fire back, not wanting to be lumped in with the old white men who burned women at the stake because they were afraid of getting boners. "Those weren't *my* trials. But please, continue."

"Vampires tracked the witches to this world," Zev says, "now constantly thirsting for their blood. Once the rumor of witches spread, it was the vampires who took human form and pointed fingers at ordinary women, even controlling minds during the trials to create the needed spectacle."

I've known witches were real for a few hours, and I'm already ready to kick Darius square in the balls for what his kind did.

"Okay," I say, trying to put things back on track as I notice our exit is approaching. "That's super fascinating and I want to hear more, but how does this tie in to present day? Why are the races fighting, and what in God's name does it have to do with my baby?"

"If you'll remember back to the beginning of the story," Rune says with a professorial nod, happy to connect the dots for me, "the Fates created us all. They are inextricably tied to each race... and we to them. As they died out, hardships engulfed each kingdom, and the elders who had been crying about the prophecy for generations were finally heard."

"Each version of the prophecy," Zev explains slowly, giving my human brain a little breathing room as it processes the wildest shit I've ever heard, "acknowledges that if the witches die, so will all the beings they created."

I look from Zev to Rune, and they both return sullen stares, waiting for me to speak.

"I take it a lot of the witches have died?"

They both nod, then Zev speaks in a softer voice than I've heard him use previously.

"There are no more in our world, and very few here. Few enough… " he pauses, giving his words extra weight. "That we've come to the final part of the prophecy."

I can tell Zev is just going to stare at me until I guess again, so I turn to Rune in hopes he'll just spill the goddamn beans. The sweet and sexy fae doesn't disappoint.

"When the Last Witch is born," he says, as though reciting the thesis for his doctorate, "the kingdom that harnesses her life will survive while the others perish."

His words filter slowly through my ears and into my brain, with only one phrase having a lasting impact: *The Last Witch?*

I nearly miss my turn as I try to process the infor-mation, slamming on the brakes and skidding along the icy road, then fishtailing into a parking lot. Having driven in the snow since I was a teen, the move doesn't scare me that much. For once, the nerves of the fae and werewolf are more frazzled than mine. But that might be because I'm in a state of complete shock.

I autopilot into a spot right in front of Nanny's assisted living home in Ipswich and exit the car, still fighting with the words floating inside my brain. *The Last Witch?*

Zev and Rune get out and fall in line behind me as I walk toward the entrance. Thankfully Zev grabs Rain out of her car seat, as I'm in such a haze I walk away from the car without even getting my baby. I would have remembered within seconds, but it's still a moment I know I'll beat myself up for until I die.

We pass people as I walk through the door, only half noticing the looks given to my companions. My weary brain is pretty used to the way they look and dress, but ten seconds in public reminds me how much they stick out in these small New England towns.

The Last Witch? At this point I'm not just thinking the phrase, I'm mouthing it as well. We've arrived at the front desk and I'm about to sign in when Zev hands me my child and the obvious connection finally clicks.

"Holy SHIT. *She's* the last witch?!?"

Zev and Rune don't respond, probably because they're contemplating using magic to disappear. I look around the room, feeling no fewer than eighteen sets of eyes on me. The harshest glare comes from the young nurse working the reception desk.

"Hi," I say, trying to compose and cover for my outburst. "They're catching me up on a TV show and just gave away a huge spoiler." I playfully punch Zev in the arm for effect, forgetting again that his body is made of muscle armor.

I give a half-hearted smile, sign in at the front desk, and lead the way toward Nanny Tilly's room. There are more questions I want to scream, but this clearly isn't the place for it.

When we get to Nanny's door, I stop, the trailing Sexies halting behind me. I face them, giving as serious a look as I can muster, even while Rune's eyes melt me and Zev's eyes consume me.

"I need you two to wait out here," I say. "There's a window in the door so you can keep an eye on me, but my grandma's been in a… let's say, disturbed mental state since my mom died when I was 11. She's been worse since she started living here a few years ago, and I never know what kind of mood she'll be in. I don't want any extra bodies in the room that might stress her out. Also, be prepared for no fewer than a billion questions when I get back."

Neither of them likes the idea of me going in alone, but they both give a subtle nod of agreement. I put my hand on the cold brass handle, overwhelmed by this revelation but still excited about introducing Rain to her only living relative.

I have such fond memories of life with my grandparents, Matilda and Edwin, or Tilly and Ed. They'd always take me to get pizza, even when my mom told them I couldn't eat more junk food. We'd spend long days on the beach, take camping trips into the mountains, sail to the Cape and drive to Boston to go see movies my mom said I was too young to watch.

Everything changed in an instant when my mom died. Nanny was reclusive for weeks, and then I became very sick and she just went insane. Couldn't speak in full sentences, would wail and point at things that weren't there. I recovered from my mysterious illness, but she never did. Gramps could keep her calm most times, though she was in and out of institutions until I went away to school.

Once I was out on my own I became focused on my life and didn't check in with my grandparents as much as I should have, and suddenly Nanny was moving into a home. I came back for a week to help Gramps make the transition, getting her room set up and personal items in order. She and I took a walk in the woods before I helped her settle into her new apartment that day, and it was the most peaceful I'd seen her in years.

I've visited with her a handful of times since moving back, but I can't tell if she recognizes me. I don't know if she's aware her husband died. I struggle to come see her because it makes me sad; I regret not spending more time with her, and I miss the moments we had before everything changed.

I take a breath to steady myself and then walk into her room.

She's lying in her bed, staring out the window. She's still beautiful in her old age, long silver hair hanging just below her shoulders, deep lines on a face that was once so youthful. When she's still, it's easy to see the old Tilly, and it warms my heart.

"Hi, Nanny."

She slowly turns away from the window until her eyes meet mine. We hold each other's gaze for a second, and she gives me a soft smile.

But then her eyes drift down to Rain, locked into her harness, blissfully unaware of the world around her.

Tilly stares at the baby, her smile fades.

And then she screams.

Chapter Twelve

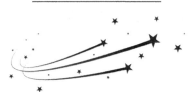

Nanny's screams wake the sleeping child in my arms, whose own wails join the cacophony of crazy. Within seconds, Zev and Rune burst into the room, Zev already partially shifting into a wolf, both of their gazes trained on my grandmother like they're going to attack.

"Stop!" I shout, startling everyone except Rain, whose lungs seem to have grown exponentially since we got here, if her volume is any indication. "Do not hurt her," I tell the guys. "And get back into full human before someone sees you," I hiss at Zev, whose arms are already paws. Looks like I stopped him in time before he ripped through yet another outfit.

He's barely shifted back when a nurse hurries

into the room. "What happened?" she asks, breath-less from running down the hall. She immediately checks on Nanny, who stopped screaming but is moaning and clearly agitated as she shifts around in the bed like she's fighting her blankets.

I hand Rain to Rune, whose gifts of calm wash over the child until she's back asleep in his excep-tionally chiseled arms. Prying my gaze from his guns, I move quickly to Nanny's side and try to calm her. "You're okay, Nanny. It's me, Bernie. Shh..."

The nurse checks her blood pressure and temperature and tsks at me like she's scolding a child. "Tilly doesn't need this kind of stimulation. It isn't good for her health."

"I'm aware of that," I say, trying to hold back my irritation. "We didn't do anything. She just started screaming the moment I walked in. What's wrong with her? Has she had more episodes? I normally get notified if it seems like she's taking a turn for the worse."

"She's been just fine until today, just now," the nurse says with more than a little accusation in her tone. "I think it's best if you go. Her blood pressure is much higher than I'd like it to be."

"I just need a few minutes with her," I say. "And

my cousin, he always knows how to calm her down, don't you, Rune?"

Zev smirks. "That's right, *cousin*."

Rune frowns at the werewolf but hands him the baby as he joins my side. "Of course. He smiles at Tilly. "Hello, great-aunt." He places a hand on hers, and her thrashing slows as she responds to Rune's calming powers.

The nurse narrows her eyes at us, then shrugs. "Fine. Five minutes. Then you must let her rest."

Once the nurse is gone, I focus my attention back on Nanny. Rune stays by her side, holding her hand. "If I leave, she will become agitated again," he says sadly.

I nod, blinking away unwanted tears.

Zev joins us, and kneels next to me while holding Rain so Tilly can see her.

"This is your great-granddaughter," I say, fighting the emotion making my words crack. "And Rain, this is your great-grandmother. She raised me through my terrible tweens and teens. She made sure I always had a tutor for my piano, even when they could barely afford to keep the bar open. She made me a dress for prom so I wouldn't feel left out when we couldn't afford to buy one." I can no longer fight the tears that stream down my face. "She's the best. You're a lucky little girl," I tell my child, then I turn to the woman who's been everything to me for so long. "Oh Nanny, I wish you were here. Really here. I don't know how to do this without you. You always had the answers, and now I feel so lost."

It's more than I wanted to say in front of the Sexies, but the words pour out of me before I can sensor them.

"Come back to me, okay? To us."

Zev slides his free arm around my waist and helps me stand, my legs already cramping.

Rune nods and pulls his hand away. He and Zev take Rain out while I say a final goodbye. I feel a sickening sadness as I smooth her brow one more time before leaving. "I'll come visit you as soon as I can, Nanny," I whisper.

When I pull my hand away, she reaches for me, grabbing my wrist with an iron grip that surprises me. Her voice is monotone and her eyes glazed over as she speaks. "Beware the stars, beware the moon, beware the language that ends with doom." Her nails dig into me and she hisses. "I am you. She is here. You are she."

I pry my wrist out of her grip, a bruise already forming. "Nanny, what do you mean?" Tears stream down my face and I watch helplessly as Nanny's face scrunches up and her body starts to seize.

The nurse returns with a needle. Without preamble, she injects Nanny with it, and my grandmother instantly calms, her eyelids fluttering shut.

I don't want to go, but the nurse stands by the bed watching me, her expression clearly annoyed.

I leave with a heavy heart, pulling the door closed behind me. Rune and Zev are waiting for me in the hall, and when Zev sees the tears in my eyes, he pulls me into a hug.

I want to resist, to push him away as I think about my Nanny instead of this witch business. Instead I melt into his arms, grateful for his strength, for his comfort, even for his presence. If I can set aside why he's here, the fact that I'm not alone is a relief.

Zev rubs my back as I cry into his shoulder. He smells like the woods and feels so solid, so grounded, that my heart slows and my mind calms just by being this close to him. "You okay, love?" he asks softly, his lips brushing against the top of my head, creating a whole other sensation in my body.

I nod against his chest. Then, when I feel strong

enough, I step back to look into his forest green eyes. "I've never seen her like that before. She's had breakdowns in the past, but nothing like that."

"I heard what she said," Zev says, which seems impossible considering he was on the other side of a closed door, but then I remember he has dog abilities and is probably listening to everyone in Rowley all the time. "Did her words mean anything to you?"

I think for a second then shake my head. "Not really. Something about the language of doom? But she's always spouted strange things, ever since her mind started to go. I just don't understand why seeing Rain freaked her out so much."

We head back to the car, and I feel distant and drained as Rune locks the baby into the carseat and stays in the back with her while Zev sits up front with me. "I guess it's time to find some unicorn blood?" I say with all the enthusiasm of someone about to go to the dentist.

"That can wait," Zev says gruffly. "You're shaking."

I look down at my hands and realize he's right. And I can't stop. I feel panic rising in me, unlike anything I've ever felt before.

Zev takes one of my hands in both of his and

the warmth from them infuses my skin, spreading over my body.

"Crazy shit has been happening to me, ever since the three of you walked into my bar," I say, turning to glare at each of them. "And then you spring on me that you think my daughter is a witch. Oh, and by the way, she's not just a witch, she's the last witch. What does that even mean?"

Zev turns my hand over and brushes the pad of his thumb over my palm in rhythmic strokes, like he's trying to calm a wild animal--which maybe isn't far from the truth. "That night we followed the signs of the prophecy. At this point I don't know much more than you, I'm afraid. We followed the fallen star and it led us to you both."

"The rock." I haven't thought about it since that night, but the rock I pulled out of the wall; it didn't look like a regular stone because it most definitely is not.

"So Rain's a witch? How? This isn't like AJ's situation. Rain's dad isn't magical. I'm sure of it."

"This wouldn't be passed down through her father's lineage," Rune says softly.

The implication of his words takes a moment to settle into my frazzled mind. "So you're saying she got it from me?" I choke out a laugh. "I'm definitely not a witch."

Zev frowns. "Stranger things have happened... but you almost certainly are."

My eyes widen. "So, you're saying my mother was a witch? And--"

"--And your grandmother," Rune, finishes my thought. "I could feel her power. It was confused. Untamed. But very strong. Overwhelming, perhaps. I've never felt more clarity regarding the prophecy."

"Tilly is a witch?" I feel like I'm in an episode of The Twilight Zone.

"Undeniably," Rune says.

I look to Zev who's nodding, clearly no question in his mind either.

The next ten minutes pass in silence, as Zev and Rune respect my need to process. I can't just accept this witch business the way I did with AJ being a nymph (especially since with everything they've said about nymphs that one makes *perfect* sense).

They're saying I'm a witch. My daughter, who can't yet see an inch in front of her face, is a witch. Before my mother died, I was apparently being raised by a witch. And after she went, when I spent my days and nights with Nanny and Gramps, I was still under a witch's guidance.

What is a witch? I don't know what this means on the most basic level. And yet, the more I reflect, the more I have to consider the possibility. Tilly was always a little off, but in that quiet, grandmother kind of way. She fully departed reality when my mother died, but even then she went mad in her own, interesting way. A lot of nights spent at the cliffside where my mom killed herself, and a lot of lucid conversations with Gramps about why they needed to go look for Lauren (my mom). I remember overhearing those talks from my room, knowing Nanny was losing it but still wishing she was right.

As we get closer to Morgan's, I decide to break the silence with a question. "If my mom was a witch with powers and shit, why'd she kill herself?"

Zev looks over his shoulder at Rune, the two sharing a thoughtful stare before replying. Is Zev trying to figure out what the answer is, or are the two conspiring about how much I'm allowed to know. Rune finally speaks up.

"As you know from my story, magical abilities don't keep one safe from anguish."

It's a good answer. Doesn't help me at all, but I can't blame Rune for that.

· · ·

WE PARK the car and I get Rain out of her carseat. She's going to wake up screaming for food any minute, but I'm hoping she'll put that off just a bit longer to give my mind time to settle.

It's only a little after 1 pm, a much earlier return time than I expected thanks to Nanny's episode and the nurse with no manners. I figure Darius is still sleeping or hanging out in one of his darkened rooms and AJ is either on a unicorn scavenger hunt or taking a nap in preparation for another long night of bartending.

As I walk into the living room, those expectations get dashed in a hurry. AJ's sitting on the kitchen counter, drinking a beer and looking very proud of herself. Darius sits in the corner, furthest from the blacked out windows and safe from errant rays of sunlight.

And in the middle of the room, tied to a chair and looking woefully confused, is Michael Lawrence. My high school boyfriend.

"Mike?"

"Bernie?"

We speak at the same time, matching exasperated tones.

"What are you doing here?" I ask before my

brain can catch up to my mouth. *He's tied to a chair, Bernie. He's not the one you should be asking.*

I whip my head toward AJ, who's stifling a laugh. "AJ, with God and three creatures from other realms as my witness, I will beat you to death with a ham hock if you don't tell me what's so funny right now."

My burst of anger only makes her laugh harder, and she coughs up some of her beer in the process.

"Bernie," Darius starts, "There's no need to worry. We've brought this man--"

"No, no," AJ cuts him off, "I need to tell her. You don't understand comedy, Darius, your timing will suck and the joke won't land."

"I don't believe there's anything to joke about in this situation, Anna."

There's a real sibling vibe developing between Darius and AJ, one that I'm sure she likes and he can't stand. I think for a second about what AJ would have been like in high school if she had an older brother who was a vampire. That's not a thought I want to revisit.

"Okay, Jesus, just tell me!"

"Yeah, and tell me!" Michael looks terrified, and it's clear he's been told nothing.

"Okay!" AJ snaps back. "God, it's not like

anyone's late for anything. All right, hold on, I have to set this up right."

She takes another sip of beer, but neither Michael nor I say anything this time because we know another interruption will just set her off and she'll take longer. Silence from Darius shows he's learned the same lesson.

"Bernie, this is Michael, you may remember him from high school when you two dated and he took your V card... "

I did not expect this part of my past to come up, and my face immediately turns fire engine red. When I turn away so Michael doesn't see me blush, I point my face at Zev and Rune, who look entirely confused.

"Anyway," AJ wisely gets back to her story before they can derail this ludicrous conversation with more questions, which is the first good thing that's happened to me all day. "Turns out that while you and Michael were getting your hump on, Michael was also busy making little girls' dreams come true."

I couldn't possibly be more confused, and I'm about to say as much when AJ finally spits out what she's been dying to say this whole time.

"Because your high school beau was a freaking unicorn."

Chapter Thirteen

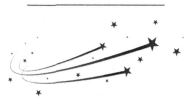

" **AJ**, what the damn hell is wrong with you?" I shout, waking Rain who begins to howl at the top of her lungs. I sigh, pull her from her car seat and pop out a breast to stick into her greedy mouth.

Michael's eyebrows raise, and he clears his throat. "Um, can someone let me out of these restraints and explain to me what's going on?" He speaks in a very formal and polite tone for a kidnapee.

AJ hops down from the counter and saunters over to him. "You know what's going on, Mikey Mike. Why don't you tell Bernie here what you really are?"

He glances at me, then back at AJ, then his shoulders sag. "How did you find out?" he asks.

I nearly choke on my own tongue. "Wait, it's true? You're a... you're a unicorn?"

He nods, not able to maintain eye contact with me.

I switch Rain to my other breast and begin pacing the room while she feeds. "What the hell is going on? Does Rowley have any humans here? Is Joe an ogre and Frank, what is he? A leprechaun?"

No one answers as I vent. I think back to high school, to the giddy days of new lust that felt like love. Michael was unquestionably the best looking guy in the school, with his golden hair and matching eyes, his perfectly tanned skin and sleek muscles. He was on the track team, and won more medals than I can remember. We used to make out under the bleachers when he snuck away from practice. He seemed magical at the time, but a unicorn? That's beyond the scope of what I can handle right now. Though maybe it helps to explain him being such a fast runner.

"Let him go," I command everyone--anyone--in the room.

AJ sighs and goes to release his bonds, but not

before glaring at him. "One wrong move and my vamp boy will eat you, got it?"

Michael's eyes widen and he nods his head nervously. I throw a look at AJ, a little annoyed that she's talking tough to the majestic creature she brought here against his will.

I haven't seen Michael since graduation. Last I heard he moved out of town and didn't keep in touch with anyone here. It's the goal for most people growing up in Rowley, and he's one of the few who accomplished it. I bet he's really loving this homecoming party.

"So now we're kidnapping people?" I ask. Rain finishes feeding and I hand her to the closest person--Darius. The vampire looks at Rain in confusion, then walks over to the changing table while I try to figure out what to do next.

"It wasn't kidnapping," AJ says, barely containing her laughter. "More like... horsenapping." Now she's literally doubled over in laughter, and as much as I want to be mad, I start to laugh too, because this is just too absurd.

"I'm so... sorry, Michael," I say, as my hysterical laughter escalates. Now I can't control the fits and AJ and I are both doubled over as the guys all watch us warily.

Well, everyone but Darius, who seems to be having some trouble at the changing station. "Is this normal? I think the young human is ill."

I dash over there, worry replacing all other emotions, then my laughter returns when I realize what he's going on about. "Nope, that's just normal newborn poop. Fun, right?

He wrinkles his nose. "It's smelly. And oddly colored and formed."

AJ hoots and slaps her leg. "I can't with these guys. It's too much."

"Listen," Michael says, sidestepping us. "I'm just gonna get going if that's all right."

Darius stands and in a blink has handed the baby off to Rune and is blocking Michael's path to the door. "You may not leave."

Michael looks around nervously as Zev growls under his throat and Rune, who's skillfully getting Rain diapered up and ready for a snooze, watches casually--in the way a cat is casual until it strikes.

"What do you want with me?" Michael asks, giving up and sinking into my new, luxurious couch. "No one knows what I am. I live a quiet life. I don't want to cause trouble."

"We need your blood," Darius says with his whole 'I'm gonna eat you and you'll like it' vibe.

"How much of it?" Michael asks, in an exasperated tone that makes it clear someone--or something--has asked for his blood before.

But Darius, who clearly doesn't like being questioned, hisses, flashing extra pointy teeth. "Who are you to question us? Do you know who we are?"

Oh Lord. "Chill your tits, vamp boy." I step forward and grab Darius by the arm. "You need some serious schooling in how to win friends and influence people."

His ink-dark gaze locks with mine. "I am fully capable of influencing people," he says.

"I mean without voodoo powers," I say. "You catch more flies with honey than vinegar."

His brows crease in confusion.

"Nevermind. Look, just let me handle this. You and AJ have done quite enough." I focus my attention on Michael, and as I look closely at him for the first time, I realize how ageless he is. Like a model stepping off the cover of a magazine, sculpted from clay and photoshopped to perfection. He's obviously matured since his teenage years, but he hasn't been ravaged by time in the way one would expect. Now I can see it. The supernatural beauty at work in him. "We just need a vial or so," I say. "I'm sorry they brought you in like this. I had no idea they were going to do that. And, to state the obvious, I had no idea you were a unicorn."

He stares at me for some time, the room quiet. "It's good to see you again, Bernie," he says, surprising me. "It's been too long."

"It has," I say, cocking my head.

"I meant to come by... when I heard." He pauses. "I'm sorry. For your loss. But. I didn't know if you'd want to see me after--"

"After you dumped her like the piece of shit you are," AJ says, getting in his face. "You broke her heart, you bastard. She was a wreck for weeks over your pathetic ass."

"For crying out loud, AJ, shut the hell up! That was like ten years ago."

She glances at me, nonplussed, but steps back a fraction. She still looks ready to cut a bitch though.

Michael shrugs sheepishly. "Yeah, I'm sorry about that. I was worried. We were getting so close and if you found out what I was... I was scared."

"It was a long time ago," I say, and I know I'll be sitting with this later, worrying over every memory of Michael, reframing the end of my first serious relationship in light of all I've learned. But I'm a big girl now and have too much on my plate to stress about my high school broken heart. "I would be grateful if you could spare some blood though. I know it sounds weird and all but--"

"It's fine," he says as he pulls up his sleeve and holds out his arm. "Take what you need."

"We can't take it from your human form," Rune says, inserting himself into the awkward conversation.

"Right," Michael says. "Um. You'll need to stand back. I don't want to hurt anyone."

I move towards the kitchen to give him room, the realization washing over me that I'm about to watch the first guy I ever slept with turn into a horse.

A unicorn, not a horse.

I glance at Darius, who smirks.

Out of my head, vampire. And excuse me, a unicorn.

But I soon see that the distinction is an important one. Before my very eyes, Michael begins to glow an ethereal white. He doesn't contort and bend out of shape like Zev. Instead, I'm blinded by the light he emanates, and in a flash, he's transitioned from man to a gleaming white unicorn standing in my freaking living room.

"Michael?" I step forward tentatively and hold out my hand to him. He leans his head down and I touch the softness of his mane and let my hand slide over his golden horn. A tingling pulses up my arm, like magic infusing me, and a euphoric kind of happiness overwhelms me. I smile, soaking up the feeling like it's water and I'm dying of thirst.

Darius clears his throat, rudely interrupting the exchange. "I will extract his blood now."

Rune shakes his head. "I don't think so. You'll contaminate it with centuries-old bacteria. Allow me." Rune produces from some pocket or another a small silver blade and a crystal vial covered in etchings.

I cringe as he slices into Michael's back leg and golden blood drips into the vial.

Once it's full, Rune waves his hand over the wound and mutters a few words in, I don't know, Elvin or some shit, and when he removes his hand, Michael's unicorn flesh is once again unblemished.

"This should be enough," Rune says, studying the glowing golden contents.

Michael nods and, in another blast of light, turns from unicorn to man once more. Unlike Zev, he still has his clothes on, and I try to convince myself I'm not the least bit disappointed by that. But I am curious. "You keep your clothes when you shift?" I ask, totally nonchalantly.

AJ blows my cover by snorting.

Michael grins like he knows what I'm thinking. "Sorry to disappoint. But yes, unlike shifters, my powers are pure magic. My body isn't changing form, my essence is returning to its true nature."

"Right. Sure. Makes perfect sense."

Michael looks around and frowns. "If there's nothing else, I assume I'm free to go?"

The Sexies don't object, and I sigh, assuming that means it's fine. "Let me buy you a drink first. It's the least I can do." I glance at Rune. "Keep an eye on Rain?"

He nods, and the other two narrow their eyes like they're jealous, though that can't possibly be true.

Michael and I walk downstairs to the bar, and I pour us both a shot of whiskey. "Cheers," I say.

He downs his drink and I refill, then move to the other side to sit with him.

"I see your apartment's gotten an upgrade," he says.

"Uh, yeah. Those guys, they're kind of a big deal and decided they wanted to live in style while here."

Michael frowns. "They're dangerous, Bernie. I don't really know what's going on, but I've got a bad sense. Be careful with them."

"I know," I say. "It's... complicated."

He chuckles. "It always is with you."

"What does that mean?" I ask.

"Just that life was never easy for you." He pauses. "I hated ending things the way we did, but after your grandmother talked to me, I--"

"Nanny talked to you?" I ask, shocked. "About what? Why?"

"She didn't tell you?"

"Tell me what?"

He sighs and sets his tumbler down. "After prom, she came to my house. Said she knew what I was and that I needed to leave you alone. That being with you would ruin your life. She was-- convincing. I didn't want to hurt you, but really didn't feel like I had a choice. It was the hardest thing I've ever done."

I lean back against my barstool, a wave of conflicting emotion flooding me. "She didn't say anything to me, for obvious reasons, I suppose. All of this magic shit was kept secret from me up until Rain was born."

"Congratulations, by the way. On your baby. She's beautiful, just like her mother."

His compliment makes me flush. "What about

you? I heard you left town. Just north of Boston, right? What do you do? Do you have kids? A wife?"

"Yeah, we're in Saugus." He pauses. "And I write fantasy novels for a living."

I can't help but smile at that. "They say write what you know. I guess that works out for you."

He laughs. "Yeah, something like that. And, I have a daughter. Ellie. He reaches for his phone and pulls up a picture of a blond girl with big blue eyes who looks about kindergarten age.

"She's lovely," I say. "I'm glad you found happiness. Is her mother still in the picture?"

"Actually, my husband and I are her parents. We used a surrogate."

"Husband?" I'm not sure if I'm more shocked my old flame is a unicorn or gay. Both are unexpected.

"Yeah. I didn't know, or didn't want to acknowledge it fully when we were together. It wasn't until college that I finally came out. That's when I met Robert. We've been together ever since." He looks at me cautiously, waiting for my response.

I smile and take his hand. "I'm so happy for you, Michael. How, um, did your parents take it?" I ask with a sheepish look, already knowing the answer. Michael came from the type of family that wouldn't be too keen on a gay son.

He returns my look and shakes his head, but then relief fills his eyes as he swipes the picture on his phone to one of him and his husband. "This is Robert."

"You two make a gorgeous couple," I say honestly. "Does he know about... "

"That I'm a unicorn?" he asks with a chuckle. "Yes, it was kinda hard to hide. We used his DNA for our daughter to avoid any... complications with her down the road. And he'd never betray my secret. Just like I won't betray yours."

I raise an eyebrow. "Yeah, about all this. I can't apologize enough. I've been thrown into the deep end of this supernatural shit, and it's been a hard ride. You shouldn't have been pulled into this."

"It's okay. I'm glad I could help." He takes one last swig from his glass. "But next time, just ask?"

I laugh as we both stand. "I will."

We hug and he pulls away to look at me. "It was good seeing you again, Bernie. Even under the circumstances."

"You too, Michael. Don't be a stranger. And bring your family by sometime."

I let him out the front door and lock it behind

him, then walk back up to my apartment, my mind lost in the past to what was and what could have been. What did my grandmother know about this new world I now find myself thrust into? And why didn't she tell me the truth back then?

Rune is in the kitchen cooking something in a pot when I return. Darius and Zev are playing chess, and AJ is sitting at the piano picking at keys. She looks up when I walk in. "Wild, isn't it?" she says with a cheeky grin.

"That's one word for it," I say grimly. "How on earth did you know he was a unicorn?"

"Well, Darius pieced it all together," she explains. "He asked about the families that have been in Rowley the longest, and I said the Lawrences since I've never heard of a Lawrence leaving town, until Michael, and even he didn't get too far. Then he asked some weird questions about who was whose son and suddenly I'm off to kidnap Michael while Darius waits in his bat cave." She gives me a ho-hum shrug and glances at the clock on the wall. "Time to open the bar. Ready boys?"

"I cannot leave the potion until it is complete," Rune says.

"How long will that be?" AJ asks.

"You cannot rush magic."

"Are you cooking Michael's blood in my kitchen?" I ask, marching over to look into the pot. It has a golden hue and sparkles, just like something that would come out of a unicorn.

"Once it is done, we can complete our pledge and you will feel safe," Rune says softly, and I realize in that moment he's not just doing this to keep the three of them honest, but so that I will trust them. It softens me just a little.

"Thank you," I say. "For trying to make me feel better about all this."

Rune stops stirring for a moment to turn to me, his eyes looking a deeper blue than before, like the ocean pulling me into its depths. He takes my hands in his, stepping forward so our bodies are mere inches apart. "I cannot say that I know how hard this has been for you, but I can feel your pain, your worry, your fear. I know it's hard to trust us, but I hope you can at least believe that I want to make this easier for you while we work out what must be done."

He drops one of my hands and brushes his knuckles lightly against my cheek. "I did not expect to feel the way I do about you and the child. It has complicated things. But I would not change that for anything."

I suck a breath in, my body humming with pent up desires I can't act on. His eyes drop to my lips, and I want more than anything for him to come closer, but then AJ tugs at my sweater, breaking the spell between us. "Let's go, before our regulars show up."

"Right," I say, reluctantly pulling my hand--and my gaze--from his. I turn away as Rune resumes stirring his pot. "AJ and I will go open up while you finish brewing up your potion," I say, trying to clear my head. "Bring Rain down when you're done. I don't want her left alone while those nutcases are out there."

The three of them nod and AJ and I head to the bar. Even before they finish their pledge, I'm already comfortable with them being around Rain. A lot has changed in a couple days. Everything, really.

We wipe down counters and prep the bar for whoever might wander in tonight. AJ peppers me with questions about Michael, from what we talked about to whether he was 'hung like a horse' in high school.

"You're terrible, you know that?" I say, spraying her with the water hose at the sink.

She shrieks, but before it hits her, she holds up

her hands and the water turns to steam and dissipates into the air.

I shake my head. "I need some powers of my own." I wipe up the mess I made and walk to the door to unlock it. "Speaking of, I found out some news about me and Rain today. Apparently we come from a long line of witches."

She stares at me for a second, mouth agape, then rushes over and pulls me into a hug. "I always knew you were special. More special than me for sure."

I lean back to lock eyes with her. "AJ, that's not true. I don't even have powers, not that I know of. You're special. You've always been more special than you know."

"Pft," she says, walking back to the bar. "You're just saying that because you're a very friendly, accommodating witch."

"No, it's because you're my best friend and it's true," I counter, grabbing a rag left on one of the tables. "You just turned water into steam with your mind and you can make dudes do whatever you want. You're, like, the most special. And maybe Rain has some hidden powers, but I'm just as ordinary as I was yesterday."

She flicks me with the rag in her hand. "Stop it.

I see how those three sexy men upstairs look at you. Rune is ready to lay down his damn life for you. Zev looks like he's about to hump your leg. And Darius wants to eat you, in the best possible way." She wags her eyebrows, and I can't help but laugh. "They didn't hunt a unicorn and make a vow for nothing. They want in your pants, bad. So don't give me any bullshit about being ordinary. There's never been anything ordinary about you."

Our conversation is cut short when the bell at the door rings. I expect to see Joe and Frank, but am surprised when it's Chief Roland.

I stand and smile. "Hey! Can I get you a drink?" I ask. "Scotch on the rocks, right?"

He smiles grimly. "Good memory, but no, I'm not here to drink. Unfortunately, I'm on official business."

"About what?" I ask, my heart suddenly pounding nervously in my chest. "Did something happen to Tilly?"

He shakes his head. "No nothing like that. It's about John Marsden." He looks over at AJ. "A few neighbors said he was driving this way the morning he disappeared."

AJ freezes and I hold my breath, waiting to see how she responds. "And? You can drive this way without coming to this bar," she says, and I can almost feel the blast of her powers being thrown at the chief.

His eyes widen and his mouth drops open as he struggles to find his words. "We found... we found some blood, and the lab results finally came back."

"What do you mean?" I ask, repeating AJs words like an idiot.

"It was John's blood. And we found it in front of Morgan's. I'm going to need to talk to both of you, and definitely to those strange men that have been hanging around. This has officially become a murder investigation."

Chapter Fourteen

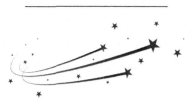

"**H**ow can I help you, Officer?"

AJ and I both turn to see Darius walking into the bar from the back entrance. He's inexplicably wearing a designer suit and tie, rather than his usual cos-play dress up, and his dark eyes are locked onto the Chief, who startles at the unexpected arrival.

"Uh, yes, I have a few questions for all of you about the night of John Marsden's disappearance. But I'll need to speak with your... the other men as well?"

Darius crosses the room quickly--normal human quickly not vampire quickly--and stands in front of the chief, towering over the stout man by at least two feet. "There were only two of us, and my colleague is in the middle of an important meeting. I can answer any questions you may have."

What kind of brain damage is the good chief going to suffer after being blasted by both AJ's nymphness and the vampire's mind melts, I wonder. Poor guy. I feel bad for him, but not bad enough to intervene, cuz I sure as shit do not want to get caught up in John's well-deserved murder.

"Right, well, this is... as I said, a murder investigation," Chief Roland mutters, looking around like he needs that drink after all.

I reach for his arm to guide him to a table. "Why don't you have a seat, and I'll get you something to wet your whistle while you talk to Darius and AJ, hm?"

He nods vaguely and sits as I direct him. I give AJ and Darius pointed looks that I hope communicate something along the lines of 'do not mess him up too badly but also get us out of this stat' and start pouring a scotch on the rocks, which I serve with a napkin and a smile as Nanny always taught me.

I take the fourth seat at the table and wait for the chief to begin.

Relying on familiar habits, he pulls a small notebook out of his breast pocket and puts his reading glasses on, then takes a swig of the drink before clearing his throat. "Where were you the day of Mr. Marsden's disappearance?"

"We were all here," I say. "I had just had my baby, which Darius and Rune helped deliver by a miracle from heaven. AJ came over as planned to help take care of me, the baby, and the bar while I recovered, and we were dealing with the power outage and the storm."

The chief nods, pushing his glasses up onto his nose before it slides off. "Right. Right. Can anyone else corroborate this?"

"Other than all four of us?" AJ asks with way too much snark. I kick her under the table and she flips me off when the chief isn't looking.

Darius rolls his eyes like an exacerbated teacher and leans in. "We know nothing of this man's disappearance. We were here throughout the power outage with no visitors. You will stop looking into this and determine John left town of his own volition. He was abusive, angry, and erratic. He walked around town looking for his wife, cut himself on a broken bottle of beer, grew frustrated, and left."

I sit silently, waiting to see if his Jedi mind tricks work.

The chief takes notes, then nods. "Right. Right.

Yes, just had to dot all my i's and cross all my t's. You know how it is."

"Sure," AJ says, sitting forward in her chair, her face a mask. She doesn't have the same benevolent relationship with the chief that I do. To her, he's the dickhead who never stood up for her when she called in John's abuse. The jackass who always berated her for her youthful indiscretions. It's taken me too long, but I'm finally seeing the truth. AJ and I did not have the same childhood, despite growing up the exact same way.

My heart hurting, I reach for her hand and squeeze it, as the chief and Darius stand.

"How do you know Bernie, again?" The chief asks as they walk to the door.

Darius glances back at me. "Oh, I'm an old friend of her grandmother, Tilly's. We go way back."

His cheeky answer grates my nerves, but I hold in my ire until the chief is in his car and driving away. Then I walk up to Darius and punch him in the arm.

The act of defiance predictably hurts my fist more than it hurts his steel arm, but I don't care. "Don't you dare bring my grandmother into this again, you hear me?"

He stares at me long and hard, making me think the punch was a bad idea.

"First of all," he says, "it was a good cover. Second, it was a warning shot."

I raise an eyebrow, now more confused than angry. "A warning... what, to warn the police chief not to do his job?"

"You think we would have left any trace of the man we murdered?" Darius says, his voice utterly patronizing. "He's here on behalf of the same people who sent Karl. The nymph's dead husband is just his excuse to get us all talking."

AJ and I share a look, both a little miffed by the vampire's assessment. Does this mean the whole police department's in on this? That seems excessive.

In any event, I can't think about that right now. I've got to save my baby from literally everyone and try to run a bar while I'm at it.

"Let's just get this pledge over and done with," I say, preparing to follow him upstairs, but he stops me.

"You cannot be present. It must be done with only those taking the pledge in attendance for it to work."

Sounds like a lot of bullshit to me, but honestly, I don't even care anymore. "Fine. Whatever. Go."

I wave dismissively, sending Darius off to join the others for their little pledge, then turn to AJ. She's chewing her nails and staring at the wall. With as much as I've been through, it's easy to forget the tumultuous times that befell my friend these last couple days: getting shot, losing her dickhead husband, finding out she's not human, becoming a full-time bartender.

"Hey," I whisper as I put a hand on her back. "How are you?"

She turns to me quickly, the distant look gone from her face and replaced by a sweet smile.

"I… I think I'm fine."

She sounds earnest, but it's still a little hard to believe. How could either of us be fine right now? She sees my doubt and works to convince me.

"I'm almost ashamed about it, but I've only felt relief since John… you know. And I might go home and look at a picture or find an old birthday card and get hit with some grief, but right now I'm only worried about you. It sounds a little messed up, but the last two days are the best I've had in a long, long time."

"That does sound messed up, A," I agree. "I

wish we could have turned this page a long time ago."

She smiles again and puts a reassuring hand on my shoulder, turning the tables on who's doing the comforting.

"No use thinking about what could have been. I'm a godmother to an angel and a freaking nymph now. Let's open this damn bar!"

A FEW HOURS LATER, Morgan's is in full swing. And by full swing, I mean nine people are quietly drinking beers. We get a little rowdy on St. Patrick's Day, but otherwise we're just a place for locals to escape into a pint and bide their time before they have to go back to lives they've mostly grown tired of.

AJ's pouring drinks and I'm letting Joe tickle Rain's toes while she's wrapped in her little holster. As much as I'd love to let him hold her, I'm still too afraid. Joe's as trustworthy as they come, but no one in my life is what they seem anymore. I remind myself of that everytime I look at Karl's normal spot in the back.

Finally, the three Sexies arrive. Each looks a little off. Darius lacks his normal aggressive intensity, Rune has slight bags under his eyes, and Zev, in wolf form, is panting a bit. I guess the hangover from a pledge potion is legit.

The fae and the vampire sit at the bar next to a younger guy named Max who's been coming to Morgan's since his 21st birthday. He's a couple years older than me and pops in a few times a week then goes home and lies to his wife about how much he drank. Max looks at Darius questioningly.

"You're not from around here, are you?"

"No," Darius mutters back.

"Where you from?" Max says, unaware of how poorly this small talk will go.

"Elsewhere."

Max looks at me, eyebrows raised. "Got a real chatterbox over here, Bern."

"I know, Max. He's an old… *family* friend," I say, my inflection dripping with distaste. "Can't get rid of him, despite how much we want to."

"I hear that," Max says with a smile. "My wife's two sisters are staying with us. It's like the three of them can't talk without screaming. Don't matter if they're happy or mad, just constantly yelling."

Jennifer's sisters are in town, huh? The beginnings of a plan start to percolate.

I look from Darius to Rune, then down to Zev.

All three are here for the long haul, whatever that haul may be. They also just chased down a unicorn and chugged some serious moonshine in order to earn my trust. I'm not shutting down the bar because I need money and a home for my daughter, so I think I ought to make the best of this hand I've been dealt.

"Max, call Jen and tell her to bring her sisters here."

"What?" Max says, terror in his eyes. "Not on your goddamn life-"

"Max, call your wife and tell her to come to Morgan's," I say, "and I'll tell her you've had two beers instead of six. And your kids can play out back with my husky."

There's a moment of silence, then Max reaches for his phone. I knew this would be an easy win.

I look down at Zev, his head cocked to the side, undoubtedly thinking angry thoughts. I scratch him behind the ears and coo at him like a dog. Darius almost laughs at that, his permanent frown twitching into a near-smile.

While Max begrudgingly texts, I move over to the stool where Rune is sitting. He's sipping what looks like a rum and coke, but I'm pretty sure it's just water with some rum-colored magic.

"How are you doing?" I ask softly, feeling an almost uncontrollable urge to care for the man who's done so much for me recently.

"Rather ill," he answers. He doesn't look up from his drink, but he does place his hand gently on my waist. It's intimate and exhilarating. In response, I put my hand on his leg, my fingers falling over the inside of his thigh.

"Well, if you're feeling up to it," I say, fighting the urge to let my hand creep higher, "I have a favor to ask."

"Anything."

His response comes immediately, his eyes penetrating mine, and suddenly I want to ask an entirely different favor that would require a trip to the bedroom.

"They'll be here in ten, Bern."

Max's voice reminds me of what I really wanted to ask, and possibly keeps me from passing Rain to the nearest person with hands and leading Rune upstairs.

"Thanks, Max," I say quickly before turning back to my Elvin crush. "There are some ladies on their way. Think you can make a cool looking drink that's the most delicious thing they've ever tasted and it gets them good and drunk but with no hangover in the morning?"

My request is utter BS and I'm about to laugh, but Rune answers with a curt nod.

"Of course. Should it be fizzy? Perhaps an alluring shade of pink? I'll provide a few options."

With that, he's up and behind the bar, looking through my liquor selection and pulling small vials from the inside of his coat. AJ, now a little territorial as my head bartender, gives Rune an angry look.

"A, you're on break," I say. "Come hold the baby while I play piano."

She smiles widely, jumping at the chance to hold Rain. It feels like weeks since I had my baby, but it's only been days, and the opportunities for AJ to snuggle her goddaughter have been few and far between.

I may not trust many people right now, but I trust AJ with my life. Always will.

As she gently embraces my sleeping angel, I glide toward the piano, wondering what I'll play. I'm instantly overcome with emotion, thinking back to my youth when I'd play for bar patrons all the time. Gramps used to tell me the bar would go out of business if people didn't come to hear me.

I sit on the bench and uncover the keys. So many memories are tied to this instrument and this bar. My mom bought the piano when I was five, then a couple years later Tilly moved it into this bar, right where it still sits today. This is where I grew up, and now I feel like I'm trying to grow up all over again.

"Play, Bernie."

Joe's voice is soft and sweet, tied in with all those memories. It's the perfect motivation to get my fingers moving.

I decide on Chopin's Nocturne Op. 9, No. 2 in E-Flat Major, which was always Tilly's favorite. Even after her mind went, this song would make her smile and give her a moment of respite from whatever was ailing her. It's not the most complicated piece, which made it one I mastered early, and as my fingers glide over the keys, pulling from strings and ivory a hypnotic melody that carries its own kind of magic, that same relief washes over me. The music takes me out of myself and away from all the fear and uncertainty that have plagued me since Rain arrived.

I can't wait to teach my baby to play piano.

I don't realize how quiet the bar has grown until I finish, the pads of my fingers resting on the last notes. After a breath of silence, there's a smattering of applause that seems much louder than our few patrons should justify. I turn towards the bar and notice AJ has tears in her eyes, the kind of crying you do when you're incredibly proud of your friend. Rune has stopped mixing drinks, his enchanting face looking extra enchanted by my music. Darius looks calm and content, which is a big mood change for him. Even Zev seems affected and is now curled up by my barstool watching me.

"Girl's night!! WOOOOOOO!!!"

No voice shatters a mood quite like Jennifer's.

She and her sisters waltz through the door, looking like three women who refuse to let spring break end. They're all attractive enough, even if each of them is wearing a dress that's one size too small.

"Bernie, I'd kiss your baby but Miles has been wiping snot all over the house for three days and I don't want you to have to deal with that shit. Holy Christ, who the hell are you?"

God, I love Jennifer. She's finally spotted Rune behind the bar, where he's got his sleeves rolled up as he firmly muddles some mint leaves.

"Good evening," he says before throwing a quick wink at me. Rune is totally in on my plan.

"We've got a special drink tonight if you ladies would like to try it."

Jennifer and her sisters, who I think are named Rebecca and Amy, belly up to the bar, none of them even taking the time to acknowledge Max. He almost has to raise his hand to get his wife's attention.

"Babe, where are the kids?" Good question, Max.

"At your parents' place, playing video games with headphones on," Jennifer answers, eyes still on Rune. "I told your mom to call you if they get too annoying."

Max studies his wife and her sisters for a moment, then polishes off his beer and waves to me. It's a clear signal that he wants another, and I'm to remember not to tell Jennifer how many he's already had.

"A," I half-whisper, loud enough to get her attention. "Time to get back behind the bar and do some beer pouring and nymphing. I'm going to make Jennifer's night and really piss off a vampire."

AJ nods her understanding and hands me Rain, who somehow slept through Jennifer's booming entrance. I walk over to the girls, all three of them so entranced by Rune that they don't even notice my approach.

"Thanks for coming in, ladies," I say with a semi-forced smile. Older men have always been the lifeblood of this bar, and I'm not entirely sure how to feel about three women here for "ladies night." Still, I've got bills to pay and sexy men to exploit.

"This is Rune, he's visiting from Europe and he'll be making some fancy, foreign drinks. And this... " I say, putting a hand on Darius' shoulder and feeling him tense as I do so, "is Darius."

The vampire stares at me, looking unamused as he waits to see what kind of description he gets. I can read in his eyes that he fears what I'll say next.

"He's an exotic dancer."

Time practically stands still. The girls turn their heads in slow motion, pulling away from Rune and focusing on a new object of desire. Darius stares into my eyes and I feel the familiar, uncomfortable sensation of a voice entering my mind.

You'll pay for this, Bernie.

It's not an empty threat, but he doesn't scare me like he used to. I send a thought back his way.

Maybe I just want to see you naked, Darius. And this is the best way I can think of to make my dreams come true.

A little of the anger leaves his face, replaced by

a slight trace of intrigue. I turn away, proud of myself for the sly reply, and also wondering how much truth there is to it.

I join AJ behind the bar, surveying the scene I've created: a few girls swarmed around Darius, all of them sipping magical cocktails whipped up by Rune, Joe scratching a man-turned-wolf behind the ears. Also, we've got five guys lined up at the bar staring at AJ, ready to order a tenth beer if it means she'll give even the slightest smile. Not a bad night at Morgan's, I'd say.

"I'm sneaking upstairs to feed and change Rain," I tell AJ. "You keep everyone happy and drinking."

"Try this before you go." AJ hands me a cocktail that fizzes with magic. "It's called a Sexy Runedezvous," she says, unable to hold in her giggling. "Get it? *Rune*dezvous, like rendezvous but--"

"I get it," I say with a laugh, 100% sure Rune did not name or approve of the name for his concoction. That's all AJ. I sip on the drink and the flavors burst on my tongue, then the magic and alcohol mix in my body to create a nice mellow buzz. "Damn. No wonder this is such a hit."

I hand the drink back to AJ and duck over to

the back exit, hoping to make a discreet getaway since I know the Sexies get nervous if I'm out of sight. Once I get up the stairs and into my bedroom, I quickly change Rain and then start to feed her. When she's got a good latch and a steady gulp going, I head into the living room--

--And run smack into Darius.

"Jesus!" I yell, causing Rain's eyes to flare open before going back to a contented half-mast. "What the hell are you doing up here?"

He stands very close to me, closer than he's ever been, aside from the times he was showing his teeth and hissing some kind of threat.

"We don't want you and the child alone, Bernie. Under no circumstances, no matter how quickly you think you'll be back."

He's serious but sweet, a tone I've never heard in his voice. Then he does something even more unexpected.

"I was very upset I had to follow you. I was about to start dancing."

Oh my God. Darius made a joke. I'm too surprised to laugh. His lips twitch into something close to a smile, and that's about as much of a reaction to humor as I can expect from him.

"Right, sorry," I say. "I thought maybe the pledge would have mellowed that protectiveness."

Darius shakes his head. "We aren't worried about each other. We worry about whoever else might be out there."

Again he smiles, this time it even reaches the edges of his lips, and I'm getting exposed to a whole new Darius. He steps even closer, our faces now inches apart. With all the antagonizing, I'd forgotten how perfect his features are, how easy it is to get lost in his dramatic gaze. As he starts to speak into my mind, it nearly causes my knees to buckle.

I must say, Bernie, the thought of you dreaming about me in the nude was… stirring.

Oh shit. I awoke a lusting vampire.

Minutes ago I was ready to take a fae right there on the bar, not long ago I was sharing bathroom space with a naked werewolf, and now my body's begging to be wrapped in a vampire's arms. This kind of sexual energy can't be normal for a new mother. The werewolf hair stitching must be having an effect. That feels like a safe thing to blame all this on.

Before I can think of how to respond to this advance, Darius stiffens. My gaze had been locked on his lips but now I glance up and realize his eyes have gone completely white. His body trembles and he stares blindly into the empty space above my head.

"Darius? Darius, what's wrong?"

I don't want to raise my voice, but I'm seconds away from running down the stairs and screaming for help. Just as my nerves are about to break, he comes to, his body relaxing and his eyes returning to their normal piecing darkness.

He stays still, thoughts clearly whirring around in his mind.

"What? What happened?" I ask, afraid of the answer.

"I've communed with my father, the King. He received word of our predicament... and passed on some news."

All news is bad news at this stage of my life, so I don't have any question that I'm about to hear something terrifying.

"Apparently... " Darius continues, "The Order of the Star has returned."

And, once again, the bad news makes zero sense to me.

"Okay. And I care because...?"

"Because that's the group after your child," he says. "It's a collection of witches with bad intentions, but the members disbanded over a decade ago. It appears they've reconvened."

Of course. More magical enemies to deal with. "If they're witches, do I know any of them?"

Darius thinks for a moment. "I don't know." He looks at the floor, then back into my eyes to deliver the real bombshell.

"But it was amongst the Order that I first met your grandmother."

Chapter Fifteen

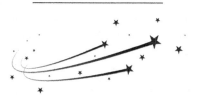

"What the--" I lean away from Darius, so far that he has to reach out and catch me before both Rain and I fall ass over tea kettle. I have so many questions, I don't even know where to begin. "What does Nanny have to do with this Order of the Star? And what do you mean that's when you met her?"

He looks deep into my eyes. There's a pain in his gaze, and I can't tell if it stems from a past hurt of his own, or if he fears hurting me with his words. Either way, he's showing a vulnerability I never expected to see.

Just as he opens his mouth to speak, I hear footsteps pounding up the stairs. They're coming up two at a time, so I know it's AJ.

"Hey, what are you dorks doing up here?" She seems a little out of breath, and I can tell it's not just from her trip up to the apartment.

"The bar is, like, packed. Jennifer called a hoard of horny moms when you said there was an exotic dancer."

I peek back at Darius who's already staring my way. I no longer notice that sweet vulnerability from two seconds earlier.

AJ is oblivious to the non-verbal conversation happening as she talks. "They brought cash and they're like, I dunno, tigers at feeding time. If someone doesn't start dancing soon, I think they're gonna burn the place down."

Stubborn as he is, I've got no idea if Darius will actually help us out. As much as I want to see him dancing while the ladies of Rowley stuff dollar bills into his thong, it's a little hard to imagine. On top of all that, we still have to deal with the bombshell he just dropped on me.

To my surprise, Darius simply nods at AJ. "Mustn't disappoint the ladies," he says. He winks at me and then follows her quickly down the stairs.

Not one to let someone else have the last word, I mentally shout at him. *This conversation isn't over, vamp boy.*

He doesn't reply, but I do hear him laughing in my mind.

He's such a damn pain in the ass.

I strap Rain into her carrier and follow them down. The moment I open the door to the bar I stop short, staring in wonder at a sight I've never seen in my life.

Like AJ said, the place is packed. Mostly with women, which is definitely a first for Morgan's. The few men I see are regulars, all looking fairly uncomfortable. I'll have to remember to comp their drinks tonight as an apology. Or maybe AJ can nymph them all into high spirits. That might be a better plan. I also spot Michael and his husband in the corner drinking a few of Rune's magical elixirs. When Michael sees me, he grins and raises a glass.

I smile and nod, then follow his gaze to a makeshift stage one of the guys must have rigged while I was upstairs. Rune, no longer behind the bar, is playing a harp--where the hell did we get a harp?--in a way I've never heard one played before. It's majestic, both the song he's playing and the way that he plays. I could watch him all night, but it appears the crowd is getting antsy for something else.

"Where's the strippah?!" A female voice yells

from the middle of the room, inspiring a cheer of assent from the ladies around her. I scan the room for Darius but don't see him. Did he bail? Is dancing the one thing in life that scares him, and he's fled back to his realm?

I get my answer almost immediately, as a shadowy figure drops from the ceiling and lands in a crouch on the stage. I don't know if he climbed to the ceiling earlier or just tricked the crowd with some vampire shit, but either way they all lose their freaking minds.

Darius is still fully dressed and he doesn't move anything except his eyes as he surveys the audience before him. The crowd falls into a hush, waiting for what will come next. I see Darius give a quick look at Zev, then he turns to Rune who begins to play something different.

This new harp song is nothing like the first. It's fast and intense, and it has me imagining a bunch of serious-faced fae at a rave.

As the music ramps up, the Dance of Darius begins. It's rhythmic and fast, almost violent, but controlled and intoxicating. It's like he's break-dancing and gyrating and booty shaking all at the same time, and he hasn't even taken his clothes off.

That's going to have to change if he wants to keep all the ladies interested.

As if on cue, Zev lunges at Darius, his teeth sinking into the vampire's black silk shirt, pulling it off dramatically. The crowd screams with fear and excitement. A wolf just attacked the dancer, but now the dancer is shirtless with his six… no wait, eight-pack on full display. Good grief vamp boy is ripped.

If there was any question as to whether or not Darius would enjoy dancing for a crowd, that doubt has disappeared. I dare say he's in his element. As he moves into a handstand and does an aerial split, I wonder if he worked as a dancer to pay his way through vampire college. Then, when Zev approaches again to bite off Darius' pants, I wonder if the two of them had a traveling stripshow act.

I move behind the bar to try and get a better view, since the place is packed with patrons. Before I can find the perfect vantage point, AJ taps me on the shoulder.

When I turn to her, I'm met with an enormous smile. Her eyes are wide as saucers as she opens the register to show me piles of cash within. "Rune's drinks are a hit. And the guys are tipping me like money's going out of style. Plus, two kegs are tapped and we're running out of all the well liquors. As long as these guys are around, you might have to start running this place like it's a successful bar."

The thought is equal parts exciting and sobering. What happens to the bar, to us--to me--when the Sexies leave? Surely this can't be the status quo forever.

My sad musings are put on hold when Zev growls and pounces from across the floor, pinning Darius to the wall, who's now only wearing a pair of red silk boxers that do little to hide his significant... size.

AJ snorts as my gaze locks on the sexy vampire. His muscles glisten like he's been rubbed in oil, and as he continues his dance-fight with the wolf, I'm mesmerized by his fluid grace and his flexing muscles.

"Looks like someone's falling for vamp boy," AJ whispers with a mischievous smile.

I tear my eyes off of the stage to glare at her. "I can admire the view without wanting to pay the price to live there," I say.

"Suuuure," she says as she saunters off to fill a drink order.

To avoid falling into a lust-filled daydream

about Darius, I focus instead on Rune, whose long, graceful fingers strum the strings of the harp with such mastery, I can't help but feel a kindred connection to him. To his music. To his craft and skill.

As if he knows I'm thinking of him, he glances over to me, his silver eyes gleaming in the dim light of the bar, and he winks. My cheeks heat with the attention and I turn away, flustered by all of them.

"Bernie, where did you find these guys?" Jennifer asks, her eyes glazed from too much drink. Or too much man meat. It's hard to tell.

"It's a long story," I say, shrugging. I'm super tired of the doctor lie, and I don't think this particular crowd will buy that one anyways. It makes me a little nervous; we may be digging ourselves into too many lies and sooner or later the walls will cave in. But that's a problem for future Bernie. Today's Bernie has enough to deal with.

When Darius and Zev finish up their weird-- and perhaps rehearsed?--routine, the crowd screams and shouts, begging for more, but it seems the boys are done.

Darius locks his dark gaze with mine and smirks. *Was that sufficient?*

I swallow, still a little weak-kneed as he stands there mostly naked. *It'll do.*

He raises an eyebrow, then disappears with his clothes to the bathroom, where he emerges a few moments later completely dressed, to the utter disappointment of everyone.

For the rest of the night, Rune's drinks flow, Darius and AJ charm everyone with their powers, and Zev sticks close to me and Rain, nearly tripping me several times.

When Rain demands to be fed again, I sneak upstairs to take a break and rest. AJ, Rune and Darius are handling things well enough, and I'm exhausted. When I think of how little time has passed since I gave birth, I'm amazed. I should still be in the hospital. Or at the very least resting a lot while kind neighbors bring me casseroles.

I read *What to Expect When You're Expecting* at least three times. There for sure wasn't a single chapter on what to expect when a werewolf, a vampire and a fae walk into your bar and try to steal your baby, then proceed to protect you, then you find out your best friend is a nymph and your ex-boyfriend is a gay unicorn, and your grandmother is a witch who might have been part of a secret society. Someone should publish a new addition that takes all these issues into account, if you ask me.

Once in my apartment, I sink into the couch,

my feet aching, my back about to break, and my head pounding.

I close my eyes as I pull my breast out to nurse Rain and am startled when my front door opens and a large white wolf walks in. "Jesus, Zev, you scared the living daylights out of--" I lose track of my thoughts when he transforms from beast to man and stands before me naked. I've already seen the goods, but I'm sitting and he's standing and he's on full display at eye level. Forgive me, but it's really hard to not stare. Holy hell, do all paranormals come packing, or just my three?

"Not all of us, no," Zev says in a deep voice, his green eyes twinkling flirtatiously. I blush three shades of red when I realize I spoke out loud. I must be more exhausted than I thought. "But if it bothers you, I'll clothe myself."

"It's not that..." I start to say, but then I stop. Of course he needs to put clothes on. I can't just hang out with him naked. Pull yourself together, Bernie.

"What's that?" Zev asks, turning toward me as he walks to the guest bedroom, his ass cheeks like perfectly sculpted boulders that I have to resist the urge to stand up and touch.

"Get dressed," I finally say when my brain starts to work again.

He chuckles as he disappears into the room, as if he knows what I'm thinking. Undoubtedly I'm not hard to read at the moment.

When he returns, he's only wearing jeans. Which I guess helps a bit. But those chiseled abs are just as distracting as everything else. "Did you lose all your shirts?" I ask, bundling Rain into a burrito and walking over to the living room crib to let her sleep.

Zev grins. "I'm not a big fan of excess clothing."

"Right." My throat feels suddenly dry, so I head to the kitchen for a glass of water, then go back to the couch to sit down.

Zev joins me and without asking permission, pulls my legs over his lap, forcing me to recline against the sofa. "What are you doing?"

"Giving you what you need," he says, which brings to mind all manner of tempting ideas, none of which involve my feet.

"Is that part of the pledge potion?" I ask. I have no idea how this thing works, so while my question is a bit cheeky it might also be spot on.

"In a way," he answers. "We're committed to respecting your wishes, as a mother and a woman. But, pledge or no pledge, I understand what you've been through and the care you need. And deserve."

He begins massaging my legs. As he works his way up my calf and toward my thigh I give in completely, moaning as his strong hands relieve the tension in my body.

"You've pushed yourself too hard too soon," he reprimands, his voice as much of a caress as his hands. "Rune's potions will help, but you still need your rest."

"I didn't exactly schedule this craziness to come into my life right now." I lose my words for a moment when his fingers dig into a particularly painful spot on my foot.

"By the way," I say, switching gears to a much more pressing topic. "Do you know anything about the Order of the Star?"

I haven't had a chance to ask Darius about his involvement, and since the Sexies have a mysterious shared past, I figure Zev might be able to answer some of my questions.

He frowns, his lips tightening. "Why do you want to know?"

"Okay, sounds like you do know something. Explain.""

"Others will have more information than I do. The Order has a torrid history amongst my race. It was an organization of witches who used their magic to attack my kind, targeting our pups and killing our mates in order to weaken our packs."

"Tell her the whole story," a new voice demands. Darius has appeared out of practically nowhere, and now stands before us, glowering. "The witches organized in order to protect themselves from persecution. From being hunted."

Zev stops rubbing my feet, much to my great sadness, and stands to face Darius, bristling at the interruption. "We weren't the only ones, nor the first, to hunt the witches," he growls.

Rain--disturbed by the men raising their voices--wakes up from her nap screaming, and I scowl at the two of them. "You've already had this fight, and now you've woken the baby. Shame on you both."

I sound like an old school marm, but I don't care. A sleeping infant is not to be messed with.

Zev's demeanor changes in an instant, turning from combative to repentant. He shuffles over, tail between his legs, to change Rain's diaper and try to get her back to sleep. I use the moment to confront Darius.

"Now's the time you explain how, when, and why you met my grandmother," I say, patting the cushion next to me and inviting Darius to sit.

The vampire casts a glance at Zev, who

pretends like he's not paying attention, but I know he totally is. Darius takes a seat beside me, close enough for our legs to touch and the recent memories of his gleaming body to flood my brain. His words snap me back to the reality at hand.

"I had business with the Order, before you or your mother were born. That is when I met Tilly. She was a powerful witch--their leader, and we were at war."

"So you were some kind of emissary?" I ask.

He gives a shrug that could mean anything.

"And what did you learn?"

"That they were waiting for the Last Witch to be born as well. The one who would spell the end to all other kinds and return power to the witches."

"Oh good, another power grab," I say dryly. "So their motives are about as pure as all of yours."

Zev grunts, proving he has in fact been listening, and Darius just scowls. "At least we now know who Karl is working with and what they want."

"But we don't know who's leading the Order now," I say. "It's clearly not Tilly."

Darius looks out the window and Zev tilts his head back, staring up in thought. They don't know.

"No, we don't," the vampire says as he lays a hand on my leg.

The touch makes me shiver, and not just from his unnaturally cold skin. Why are all three of these men so good at gentle touches that make me want to be ravaged when there are so many other things I need to be thinking about?

"But if the leader is not from your bloodline," Darius continues, "that's something of concern."

"Why's that?" I ask just as Rune and AJ enter the apartment, finally done closing the bar just after one in the morning. On our best night pre-Sexies, the place would be empty by 10:15.

"Not all witches have the best intentions," the vampire says, a knowing look in his eye. "Outside of your lineage, we can't really know what the Order intends to do with the child."

FOR THE NEXT FEW WEEKS, things fall into a bit of a routine--certainly more routine than the first few chaotic days of Rain's life. AJ moves back to her own house to escape the cramped quarters at my apartment but continues to bartend and incorporate more of Rune's drinks into our regular menu. Darius--much to his eternal consternation-- becomes a favorite amongst the locals, and even folks from out of town. He and Zev perform their act nightly now, bringing in tourists from Salem, Boston, and all over to witness their ever-changing show. Rune plays the harp and has talked me into playing piano with him, and I have to admit, the effect is pretty damn magical. Several patrons record us and put us up on instagram, which delights Rune beyond measure for some reason.

And I can't deny, having these hunky paranormals around has made my bar a whole new type of intoxicating.

I thought Rain's arrival would kill Morgan's financially, and the antics that ensued made me sure the business would collapse, but things have turned around drastically. In addition to all of our new female patrons, now that AJ has a grasp of her seductive powers, men who would stop in for a beer after work are now staying for three or four drinks.

Meanwhile, I get to be a mother. I tend to my baby without constantly looking over my shoulder, and I wrap her in a Bjorn and stroll through the bar when I feel like it. I've set up a swing next to the piano and Rune and I play her to sleep while the patrons watch and listen. For fleeting moments, I feel a happiness I haven't experienced in years.

But it's a momentary sensation, clouded by the uncertainty of what isn't happening. Despite our best attempts, we've learned nothing new about the Order of the Star or what Karl was involved in. We don't know who else might be part of this. I'm half expecting sweet old Joe will turn out to be the Devil himself, maybe with plans to burn me alive? At this point, nothing will surprise me.

So when we have yet another week of no new leads, I make a decision. One that won't be popular with anyone.

"I need to see my grandmother again," I announce one afternoon, looking at Darius specifically. "And I want you to come with me."

"Why me?" the vampire asks, setting down the leather bound book he was reading.

"Because you knew Tilly back in the day, and you've got those voodoo mind powers. Maybe you can get through to her. We'll leave Rain at home with Rune and Zev so she'll be safe. And hopefully we can avoid triggering my grandmother into another panic attack."

Darius frowns. "I cannot go out during the day, and there are no visiting hours at night," he reminds me. Like what, did he study the damn brochure?

I smile. "I know. That's why we're going to break in."

Chapter Sixteen

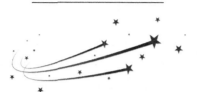

I'd love to leave right after sunset, but AJ tells me I should wait until after the bar closes so Zev doesn't have to be in wolf form and she's not too busy creating a "lust tornado of nymphiness." Her words, not mine.

So Darius and I plot behind the bar between his dances, deciding how exactly we'll get inside.

"I should go in first," I say, trying to take charge of our strategy. "If anyone's inside, at least I'm a family member and I can make up some story about being worried."

Darius smiles condescendingly, and I realize immediately that my plan is unrealistic. "You understand that we're breaking in, yes? Trying to enter unnoticed."

He makes a very good point. Planning for an encounter with a nurse or a custodian sort of handicaps the whole operation.

"Fine," I say, reluctantly relinquishing my authority. "How do we get in undetected? Without tripping the alarms?"

"Well," Darius says with a casual shrug, "the alarms sense either motion or heat, and since my blood runs cold and I move too quickly, I'll just go inside and disable the system."

Right. The fact that I thought I should take the lead on a heist with a vampire shows my mom brain still isn't firing on all cylinders.

We agree on the strategy and that we'll leave as soon as the bar doors lock, and I decide I'll catch a quick nap before we go. As I start for the stairs, Darius stops me.

"Remember, we've pledged not to take your child without your permission."

"Right. That's why I can leave her while we go." I feel like I've got this, but Darius gives me a look that suggests I'm missing something.

"That's correct," he says, "as long as you don't give permission."

"So, what, I need to just leave her on the floor and walk away?" Either I don't understand what the word permission means, or these paranormal pledge rules are a little vague.

"No," Darius responds, doing a better job than normal at staying patient. "You can hand the child to any of us, as you've been doing. You can say 'play with Rain,' or 'hold my baby.' The only phrase you cannot say, without breaking the pledge, is '*take the child.*'"

Take the child. This is good to know, and the type of thing someone might have told me earlier, but maybe each of them was hoping for a slip. So strange to think that these men, now my companions, maybe even friends, definitely objects of many affections, could still turn on me. But it's nice to know they can't do it unless I give them the go-ahead.

"Can I say, 'take the *baby,*'?" My question's half in jest, and yet these semantics seem to have cosmic importance.

Darius nods. "Only the phrase *take the child* will break the bond."

With that, he struts toward the dance floor and I head upstairs, happy to know I have powers--and terrified I might slip up.

. . .

AT FIVE PAST MIDNIGHT, Rune carries the last drunk out the door and AJ locks up. I pass her the baby, ensuring I won't misspeak and destroy my life, and head to the car with Darius.

As we buckle in, I realize I'm alone with him for the first time. Yes, we've had moments in one room while everyone else was in another, but now we're in a car, driving away. A few weeks ago I would have accepted this as a death sentence, now I can't help but feel a thrill run through my body. Ever since our shared moment in my room, the chemistry between me and Darius has changed. Less antagonism, lots of sexual tension. It certainly doesn't help that he strips down to almost nothing in the bar night after night.

Darius stares out the window as we drive to Ipswich, taking in the scenery, which I'm sure he can see just fine even though it's dark.

"Does anything look familiar?" I ask, wondering how much time he's actually spent in this area. He's been alive forever, so maybe he's summered in Eastern Mass for eons. Who the hell knows? I realize with a sudden sobriety no matter how much we talk, or how long I end up living with the Sexies, they will always remain mysteries. They have lived longer than I can even imagine. This is nuts.

"Only vaguely," Darius answers, pulling me out of my thoughts. There's a hint of sorrow in his voice that he covers quickly. "A lot has changed since I last visited. Both here and in my world."

He seems a little melancholic, so I leave it at that. Plus, I've got to start stealing my nerves for the crimes I'm about to commit.

There are three other cars in the lot when we arrive, which doesn't seem like a lot. Maybe two nurses and a security guard? Thin staff to care for a building full of invalids. I'm worried for Nanny, but also relieved that our scheme might be easier to pull off than expected.

We pull around to the back and Darius does a quick survey of the building.

"Are you sure about this?" I ask. "They might have a more complex system than you're used to."

He looks at me, the condescension roaring back into his striking eyes. "I've broken into kingdoms protected by magic spells and guarded by dragons."

"Dragons? You're just going to throw that out there willy nilly? Dragons?" But he doesn't respond. He's already out of the car and moving swiftly toward a ladder that leads to a ventilation duct near the roof, leaving me to stew about dragons and unicorns and whatever else might exist that I always thought was fairytale. It's probably safest to assume everything is real, but that might make my brain explode.

I shove my existential crisis to the side as I get out of the car and glance around, not really sure what to do next. Darius has taken full control of the plan, and I'm just along for the ride, which isn't a position I enjoy being in.

It only takes a few seconds before the back emergency exit pops open and he waves me toward him. I jog over, noticing how good my legs feel. I've recovered very quickly from this birth, and if anyone asks me how I did it I'll just say some bull-shit like kale smoothies and yoga. Namaste, bitches. Who would believe the truth anyways? I can barely wrap my mind around my current situation, and I'm living it.

As soon as I get inside, I see Darius hasn't gone totally unnoticed--a security guard lies unconscious on the ground by the door.

"I assume this was necessary?" I say in an aggressive whisper.

Darius looks down at the guard and shrugs. "Sometimes an elbow to the temple works more effectively than mind control. Let's go to Tilly."

Before I can show him the way, Darius starts striding down the hall toward her room.

"How do you know where you're going?"

"Magic," is all he responds. At first it seems like he's brushing me off, but then I think about it a little more.

"Your magic? Or hers?"

Darius throws a quick glance over his shoulder, "the latter."

When we get to her door, I'm about to ask how we'll get it unlocked, but my brain catches up fast enough for me to keep my mouth shut. With a flick of his wrist, I hear a soft click and the door pops open. I'm excited to someday learn the extent of his powers, because right now the man feels like a walking cheat code.

With a final look behind us, we tiptoe into Nanny's room. Well, I tiptoe. He just walks in his normal stealth mode.

Enough moonlight spills through the window that we're able to see her bed. Nanny's asleep, but tossing a bit like she's having a bad dream. As I move toward her, Darius stands back by the door.

"Stop," he quietly commands. I do as I'm told, though I can't imagine what his concern is with me getting closer to my grandmother. "She's not well."

I roll my eyes at the obvious statement; *that's why she's in a home, bro.* I realize immediately that my thoughts have been heard, because Darius takes slow steps toward Nanny while explaining the dilemma.

"She's powerfully afflicted. The episodes you've talked about have nothing to do with you or her surroundings, and everything to do with what's going on in her mind."

He arrives at her bedside and kneels, every step taken in silence. Ever so slowly, he reaches up and grasps her hand. The move is done gently, but Darius seems to tense as the two connect, like a shock has gone up his arm.

Seconds later, Nanny's eyes start to flutter open. She looks at the ceiling, then slowly turns to me. After my last visit, I'm terrified at how she might react. Screaming would be bad for our cover, of course, but I assume the vampire could fix those problems. I'm more worried about the emotional damage another episode might cause her and me both.

However, instead of becoming agitated or distressed, my sweet Nanny smiles. It's a smile I haven't seen in years, not since I was a little girl and my mother was alive.

Then she lets her head fall to the other side, facing Darius, and something even more unexpected happens.

"It's you," she says softly, the smile still on her face.

"Hello, Matilda," Darius responds, his voice so full of kindness that unexpected tears spring to my eyes.

It's beyond beautiful, seeing Tilly recognize a face and speak coherent words. At the same time, I just want to scream until everything makes sense. After all these years and so much mental unrest, she recognizes the effing vampire?

"Where am I?" she asks Darius, who's still holding her hand. His jaw is clenched tightly and his muscles are tense, like he's the one in distress.

"In a room that keeps you safe from the outside," Darius answers, "but not safe from yourself."

"Can you take me away?"

The vampire shakes his head, a look of pity etched on his brow. "I can't take you anywhere you'd be better off. Matilda, do you recognize your granddaughter?"

She turns toward me, the warm smile still there, and nods her head.

"Bernie. I'm so sorry."

"What for, Nanny?" I can't imagine what she feels the need to apologize for. The tears I've been holding back begin to spill as I rush to her side, kneeling next to Darius, and only slightly resenting that it's his hand she's holding instead of mine.

"I couldn't save you," Nanny says. "I couldn't save my Lauren, and after I tried, I couldn't save you."

"Save me from what?" When she doesn't respond immediately, I turn to Darius. "Save me from what? What's she talking about?"

He throws me a quick look, and with it a mental warning. *If you want me to learn anything, you'll stay calm.*

I nod, his point well taken, and he gives his attention back to Tilly.

"You've more power than I remember," Darius says, a slight quiver in his voice. "Do you know what changed? What happened to your mind?"

Nanny keeps her eyes on the ceiling, and I see a tear fall down her weathered cheek.

"I thought I could end the line," she says matter-of-factly, her voice clear and strong. "I thought, perhaps, I could be the last one."

I don't understand what's going on, and I can't

quite tell if Darius does either. His face looks pained, like he's having this conversation while squatting a thousand pounds.

"Why didn't you know better?" the vampire asks. The question isn't so much scornful, as one filled with regret. A sadness born from whatever my grandmother did.

She turns to him again, the smile coming back, though this time with a mischievous curl in her lip. "Why don't any of us know better, my sweet?"

My *sweet?* That better be some endearing grandmother shit, because I'm not prepared to hear that Nanny and my vamp boy had a thing before I was born.

"Matilda," Darius says, the strain in his voice more pronounced. "The Order is back. Or perhaps never left. We know they want the baby, but we don't know their intention. Without your guidance, I fear they're being misled."

Tilly's smile fades, replaced by a look of concern.

"I know nothing. Leadership came through my bloodline, protection spells from our family books. It... it must be a new--"

Before she can finish her sentence, the door to

her room crashes open, shattering the fragile silence.

"Get away from the bed!" screams a male voice.

I look over to see a man dressed in black, his face covered by a hood just like Karl's, only it's not Karl's voice. It's obviously not medical staff, unless they've really changed their methods since last I was here.

"You! Get up. Let go of the woman's hand!" he shouts, holding up a gun and pointing it at Darius.

The vampire raises his left hand, the one not locked with Tilly's, to show he's defenseless. Then he leans in and whispers to my grandma, just loud enough for me to hear.

"This will hurt, and I'm sorry. But you're strong."

With that, he releases her hand and she immediately starts to convulse violently. It's worse than I've ever seen before, and I'm sure her neck is going to snap.

"What did you do?" the man at the door shouts, stealing my question. He makes a move toward Tilly's bed, but as soon as he lifts his leg, Darius waves an arm and sends the man flying through the doorway, crashing against the wall on the opposite side of the hall.

"More will be here soon," Darius says, his voice raspy and his eyes bloodshot. "Follow me through the window."

"I can't leave Nanny. What if they hurt her?"

"They won't," he says as he unlocks and opens the window frame. "If the Order of the Star wanted her dead, she'd be dead."

"That's not as comforting as you might think," I hiss, but I know he's right. We have to get out of here, and we can't take Tilly. I glance once more at my Nanny, my heart breaking that I have to leave her like this. "I'm sorry, Nanny," I whisper, but before I do as Darius says, I dart into the hall, needing whatever answers I can find.

The man he threw against the wall is barely conscious, definitely concussed. As he moans, I lift the ski mask that was covering his face.

It's Alex.

Joe's son.

What the hell?

The sound of footsteps running down the hall forces my hand, and I sprint back through Nanny's room and Darius hoists me through the window. We run around the building, the sound of sirens in the distance and getting closer by the second, and finally reach the car.

There's only one driveway leading away from the facility, and that road's about to be filled with cop cars or Order members. The other option is to drive through the fence in front of me and down a hill. So that's what I do.

I start the engine, leave the lights off, and slam on the gas. We crash through the chainlink and roll into the darkness, just as the lights from the squad cars blink in my rearview mirror.

As my Subaru rolls downhill, I realize I just drove us off a snow-covered slope in the dark. I pump the breaks to no avail, the car still rolling and picking up steam.

"Um, Darius? Think you could...?"

I don't bother finishing the question, assuming his best solution will be better than whatever I could think up.

When he doesn't answer I give a quick sideways glance, and don't love what I see. He's breathing hard and still looking haggard. The one time I decide to rely on his magic, and he's got the flu or something.

"Darius! I know you can't die, but I've still got bones and organs and shit that will not survive when we hit a tree. So WAKE. UP!"

As I yell the last part, I dig my nails into his leg

and feel a jolt of electricity shoot through me. It's strong enough to knock me against the car door, my head bumping hard against the window.

I try to shake it off, but my vision is blurred and it's pitch black anyway. Instead of last-minute ideas for how to save us, I've just got pictures of Rain dancing in my head. Her tiny toes, her sweet little nose. Who's going to take care of my baby?

And then my body lurches forward, my sternum slamming painfully against the steering wheel. My eyes are shut and I'm positive we just collided with a huge maple tree. The only reason I'm not feeling intense pain is because I'm already dead.

For a moment, there's nothing but silence. Finally I pry open my eyes, for no other reason than to see what heaven looks like. Or hell, I guess. No point in being presumptuous.

Instead, I see the inside of my car. I look to the side and see Darius, his hands pressed against the dashboard in front of him. He looks at me, his face less pained than before, the beginning of a smile at the corners of his mouth.

When I turn my head again, I can see faintly out the windshield. No more than ten feet in front of us is a crumbling stone wall, one of those old property lines people made with huge boulders in the 1700s. If we had stopped a second later, I'd be dead.

I look back at Darius. "Why'd you wait?!" I yell, the emotion from the near-death experience boiling over. "We... *I*, almost died!"

He puts his hand on my knee, trying to calm me as he speaks.

"When I clasped hands with your grandmother, I took on the burden of her powers. She has a tremendous amount of magic inside her, that's the reason she's been... the way she's been."

He takes a moment, clearly still recovering from whatever he's trying to describe.

"The longer I held her hand, the stronger it became. Had we stayed in contact a moment longer I might have been knocked unconscious. It took everything I had to disable that man. I barely made it to the car."

"And then...?"

"And then you grabbed me. I'm not sure what you felt, but I felt whatever power that had been constricting me release."

I raise my hand to my head, feeling the knot forming where I bounced off the window.

"I felt something, all right. Guess Nanny's powers almost took us both out."

I smile at Darius, glad he's okay, even more glad I'm alive.

"So I timed it out perfectly, then," I say with a slightly unhinged chuckle. "I screamed and pinched your leg just in time for you to stop the car."

Darius returns the smile, though he also shakes his head--there's still something I'm missing.

"No, Bernie. I didn't stop the car." He looks out at the line of rocks that would have instantly killed me, then returns his focus to my eyes, a new and exciting energy brewing there.

"You did."

Chapter Seventeen

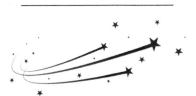

"**I** 'm sorry, I must have hit my head harder than I thought, because it sounded like you said *I* magically stopped our car from killing me and--I don't know--wrinkling your outfit?" My voice carries in it all the disbelief I feel, mixed with an unhealthy dose of adrenaline and raw nerves.

"That is correct," he says, tugging on his jacket. "My clothing is not wrinkled."

I raise an eyebrow. "*That's* your takeaway from this?"

"My takeaway is that a small thread of your grandmother's powers traveled through me and into you, though I do not know how such a thing would be possible." He tightens his lips in annoyance.

"Oh, is that hard for you?" I say, laying the

sarcasm on real thick. "Something's out of the ordinary and confusing? Poor little vampire."

He ignores my comment, so I ignore him, and instead I look down at my hands like I just grew them from scratch and they might start spitting out lightning or magic balls any moment. When nothing extraordinary happens, I sigh, a little disappointed. I've never understood in books and movies why the heroine or hero resists when they find out they're special or have magic. Music was what made me special, and I was--and am--grateful for it. Otherwise, I would have been just another small-town girl who ended up married to her high school sweetheart and popping out kids while stealing away every week for a night at the pub.

I close my eyes, letting the painful truth wash over me. If it weren't for the Sexies showing up, that's exactly where my life was headed even with this musical gift I've been cultivating for years. Well, maybe except the part about being married to my high school sweetheart.

How did I end up here? I was on the right path, the path that led out of Rowley and into the great wide world where all my dreams lived, when I self-sabotaged and ended up right back where I started.

I wouldn't trade Rain for anything, but I wish I

could have had her under...smarter circumstances. But then again, aren't these the circumstances that brought these men into my life? Things might be difficult and complicated, but I'm not particularly eager to see them leave, if I'm being honest with myself. Even though that's what will ultimately happen, with or without my baby.

Okay, enough self-loathing. Jesus, a fleeting moment of thinking I was magical and now I want to throw a huge pity party. *Buck up, Bernie.*

I look back at Darius, who's watching me carefully.

"What? Did I grow horns or something?"

He shakes his head. "But you are exhibiting signs of a serious concussion."

"Pft. I'm fine." But even as I say it, I realize I've been slurring my words this whole time, and everything is a bit fuzzy around the edges. The fact that I didn't even notice scares me more than the actual symptoms. "Let's just get back to the bar."

But as I try to start the car, it sputters and dies. "Shit."

"You are in no position to drive. Nor is your vehicle, it would appear."

"Ha, very funny mister. What do you recommend?"

"First, we must heal you. Then, I will carry you home."

My head begins to pound, like the pain was on a temporary leave of absence and is back in full form. I slump against my seat and close my eyes. Just for a moment.

I start awake at the sound of Darius calling my name.

"Shhh... " I hiss, not opening my eyes. "You're making it worse."

"Bernie, you need to look at me."

I really want vamp boy to back the hell off and let me sleep, but then I remember where we are and what just happened and my heart starts thumping aggressively against my rib cage, jolting me back to reality. "Shit. Okay, I'm here. You mentioned healing? Yes, let's do that before I lose it again. Do you have something like Rune's magic elixirs?"

Darius smirks. "Something like that. But it's more... direct from the source."

"Right, well, lay it on me. I'm ready to go home."

I expect the vampire to pull a vial of some glowing shit out of his pocket, like a normal magical dude. Instead, his eye teeth elongate and he brings his wrist up to his mouth and... bites!

"What are you doing?"

He offers me his blood, pulsing out of his vein, like it's a delicacy.

"What am I supposed to do with that?" I ask, my stomach roiling in displeasure.

"Drink. It will heal you."

"Um, no thanks, I'm good. Plan B."

"There is no Plan B, Bernie. This is the plan. The only plan. We need to get you home, but not in your current condition." He stares at me, his dark eyes wide and pleading. "Now, drink."

I feel the compulsion and I smack him without thinking. "Don't you dare mind control me," I hiss. "That is against the rules."

"What rules?" he asks with all the arrogance of an eternal being of beauty and power who's used to getting whatever he wants.

"The rules I put in place. I'm the queen of this castle, and what I say goes."

He narrows his eyes at me. "Fine, then drink before you pass out, you foolish, stubborn woman. Or do you want to leave Rain without her milk source and mother?"

"That's a low blow," I say, but I can't argue with him. Not about that. I would do anything for that little girl. Including, it would seem, sucking on some vampire blood.

Just as I lean in, I pause. "Wait, this won't make me a vampire will it?"

"No. Our transformation ceremony is much more complicated."

"Good," I say. "I'm rather fond of the sun."

Bracing myself for the grossest shit ever, I move my mouth apprehensively toward his bleeding arm, nervous about how his blood will taste, what it will make me feel... and how I'll react to having my lips on his skin.

My mouth reaches the wound and I feel a drop of blood on my tongue. There's not a strong taste to it, maybe a little bitter, but it's thin like water and doesn't have me gagging.

As soon as I swallow, I feel a surge ripple through my body. It's like the feeling of getting goosebumps, but the bumps are in my veins. The rush flows to every part of my body, and as it reaches my head I feel the ache start to fade. Add this to the list of things to sell at the bar: Tylenol capsules filled with vampire blood.

"Do you feel better?" Darius asks, but the tone of his voice shows that he already knows the answer. I realize I must be sucking pretty hard on his wrist, but I can't make myself stop. Every drop makes me feel better and gives me more energy.

Finally, the sexy vampire takes his arm away from my hungry mouth. "Enough," he says with a playful smile. "I need to keep at least a little in my veins."

He starts to pull his sleeve back down, but I notice a drop of blood trickling down his wrist. Before I can stop myself, I lunge at his arm, my tongue flicking out for that last drop of powerful blood.

Our faces are now inches apart. I hold his gaze as I lick my lips, savoring every molecule of his life-force. What started as an unappealing proposal has turned into an arousing endeavor, and I'm quite sure Darius feels the same way. Perhaps this was his plan from the beginning.

I'm already so close. I already tasted him.

What's the harm in a little kiss?

No harm at all, he whispers into my mind, and before I can think another thought, our lips are touching, our tongues swirling around each other's. It seems Darius has regained all of his strength since being overwhelmed by witch power, as he reaches around me and pulls our bodies tighter together.

His kisses are forceful but soft, firm but sweet. I run my hands through his pitch-black hair and over his neck, his smooth skin so intoxicating that I just want to touch him everywhere. I bite his earlobe as he moves a hand slowly down my side and then slips it under the waist of the back of my jeans. The feeling of his touch on my bare skin makes me nibble his ear almost too hard, so I move my mouth back to his.

He continues to rub and caress in all the right ways, and I find my hands undoing his pants and dancing my fingers along the top of his silk boxers. I break the kiss so I can look into his eyes as my hand starts to move under the waistband. He returns my stare with a fiery passion, and I know exactly where this "little kiss" is headed. If we weren't in a car, our clothes would be scattered about the room and we'd already be under the sheets.

But we are in my car. My car that won't start. Miles and miles from my home... and my baby.

As much as my body is screaming for this, it's not right. My mind is elsewhere, and that's where my body should be, too. Even if it means I have to stop touching the beautiful man in my arms.

Darius senses my hesitation, and it seems he

understands the timing is all wrong. He also probably snuck in and listened to my thoughts.

"You're right," he says, his lips still brushing against mine, my fingertips still inches from their prize. "When we finish this--and make no mistake, we *will* finish this," he says, his voice deep and hypnotic against my ear, "it will not be under such limiting circumstances. I will take my time memorizing every inch of you, playing your body like you play that piano, making you sing for my touch until you are begging uncontrollably."

His words, the thrill of them, the feel of him still pressed against me, does nothing to deescalate the growing need in my body.

And then, as if he knows just how aroused he's made me, he pulls away with a smirk. "In the meantime, I will carry you back."

He starts to retreat, but no way am I letting him get the last word. I pull him back for one last kiss, and as I claim his mouth with mine, I grab his hand and slide it up to my breast until he is arching against me, as full of desire as I am. Then I force myself away and try to put myself back together.

"*Now* your clothes are wrinkled," I say with a wink.

When I emerge from my car, everything feels

different. Not only are all my injuries healed, but it's like I've gained extra senses. I can hear a night owl in the distance, its wings ruffling as it hunts its dinner. The sound of snow falling. The breathing of a small critter hiding in a log fifty feet away. It's all overwhelming and I don't know where to focus.

I look to Darius, wide-eyed. "Is this your blood or more of my grandmother's power?"

"My blood," he says, his gaze taking in my disheveled clothing.

Despite the cold, my cheeks heat as I think about how close we got to... everything. How close we will get again if either of us have our way.

Traditionally, it would be a bit too soon to explore these urges after giving birth. But I'm pretty sure the fae magic, vampire blood and... I cringe at the thought, but werewolf hair... have all done their part in getting my body to a better place than it was even before I got pregnant.

"You might notice... other side effects as well," he says, and before I can reply or ask what he means, he literally sweeps me off my feet and into his arms.

There is no chance to talk as Darius begins to run. I would have expected it to be uncomfortable, bouncing around in his arms, but he's so fluid, so graceful, it's like we're flying. The wind blows through my hair, snow collecting in it, but I don't even notice the cold. My body is still hot from within, and with my face tucked in his shoulders and his arms gripping me firmly, it's so very easy to get lost in the fantasies of what we almost did.

By the time we arrive home--which should have taken hours or days, I'm almost disappointed the trip happened so fast. It's just after 2 AM when we walk into the apartment, where Rune, Zev and AJ are waiting in the front room.

One look from AJ and it's clear she knows I had some sexy times with vamp boy. She arches her eyebrow and looks between us in a not-so-subtle way.

Since that wasn't the point of the trip, I ignore her and head straight to Rain, who's happily snuggled in the arms of a werewolf. As I quietly approach my sweet, sleeping girl, Darius fills everyone in on what we discovered.

"Tilly possesses more power than I've ever seen in one witch, and tonight we were confronted by another member of the Order of the Star."

Rain is sleeping, and she looks so peaceful with Zev that I don't want to disturb her; instead I slide onto the couch next to him. He glances at me with a warm smile as Rune brings me a cup of coffee sprinkled with magic--like coffee needs anything extra to make it wonderful. It is the drink of the gods, after all.

"Did they hurt Tilly?" AJ asks, hopping from her chair like she's ready to cut a bitch.

I shrug, my eyes stinging again at the memory of leaving her so vulnerable. "Darius doesn't think they will. But, A, you should have seen her, when Darius held her hand, I got her back. Just for a few moments, but I got Nanny back."

Zev uses his free arm to wrap around my shoulder and pull me into a warm hug, dispelling any remnants of chill from the trip through the snow, and offering me unspoken comfort as I grapple with my emotion.

"And that's not all," I say, before Darius can continue. "You're never going to believe who it was this time." This is obviously directed at AJ, since no one else in the room would specifically care.

"Who?" AJ asks, her eyes widening.

"Joe's son!"

My best friend's jaw drops. "Alex? That's... that's impossible," she sputters.

"I know!" I say, as flabbergasted as she is.

The guys just stare at us, waiting for one of us to make sense.

AJ explains. "Alex was in an accident on prom night years ago. He was in a car crash and flew through the windshield. His brain… it never worked right after that. He's been in a home ever since."

I shake my head. "I don't get it. He seemed… normal, given the circumstances. But it was definitely him. I checked myself."

AJ begins to pace the room while I snuggle more into the nook of Zev's arms. He looks down at me, concern in his eyes. "You've had vampire blood. What happened?"

"Oh yeah, that's the other thing. I wrecked the car. Hit my head. Darius healed me."

A growl forms deep in Zev's chest. "I'm sure he did."

Darius scowls at the werewolf. "It was that or let her pass out and suffer worse injury. What would you have me do?"

"Not bind her to you," he says gruffly.

Rune comes over and lays a finger on my wrist, while staring into my eyes, then nods. "Darius did the right thing. It could have been much worse if he hadn't acted quickly."

This shuts Zev up, but I can feel the tension in his body. The werewolf is definitely pissed, and now I have a lot of questions about this binding shit.

But Rain has clearly not enjoyed the change in Zev, and she wakes up screaming and ready for her midnight snack. The werewolf's demeanor changes instantly, cooing and loving on her as he passes her to me. It's really incredible to see how each of the Sexies are with my baby. All their bad boy bravado shuts down when my little one is around. She's got them wrapped around her tiny, adorable, little finger.

I take her into my bedroom and close the door, wanting some privacy for myself and knowing Rain could use less stimulation right now. You could cut the tension in the living room with a knife.

I ease into my bed and cuddle my child as she feeds, my mind worrying over all the different threads in my life that seem to be unraveling. I want to get Darius back in to see Nanny, but that seems risky after the ruckus we've made. Even if Darius doesn't come with, I need to check in on Nanny to make sure she's okay. I also need to get my car back. And...I'm going to need to talk to Joe and find out what the hell is going on with his son.

Determined to do just that, I fall asleep with

Rain in my arms and am ready the next day to confront a man I've known literally my entire life.

Only catch is, he doesn't show up to Morgan's that night.

Or the next.

Or the next.

I ask Frank about it, but Frank is as perplexed as me, saying he hasn't heard from Joe in days.

By the end of the week, I've called to make sure Nanny is safe: she is. Though the staff gives me very few details about 'an incident' that disrupted her. I also know something is definitely off with Joe. At the close of the night, I pull the Sexies aside and voice my concern. "I think something happened to Joe. We need to go check on him and find out what's going on."

Leaving the baby with AJ and Rune, Zev, Darius and I head to Joe's. One of the Sexies managed to bring back my car, but Darius determined it was a waste of metal and somehow acquired me a brand new Jaguar.

"You realize you've painted a big red target on me with this, right?"

Darius sniffs. "You can just tell people it is mine, if you must."

Zev snorts in the back. "Darius has always been a bit pompous. He can't help it."

"You know, when AJ and I were little and would get into fights, Nanny would lock us in the bathroom together until we resolved our differences," I say, turning onto Joe's street. I park in front of his house and twist to face both of them. "We would 'pretend' to make up, and we thought we were so clever, but of course in the process of negotiating our fake peace, we actually made up in the end. I'm thinking you three need some quality time in the bathroom together. Seems like you were close once upon a time, and I think you could be again. You have a lot in common." I wink and get out of the car, with the boys following.

We approach the house cautiously, but we don't get far before both Darius and Zev stop and look at each other, their faces unreadable.

"What?" I ask, walking to stand between them.

Zev glances at me. "I'm so sorry, Bernie."

The werewolf just stops there, leaving Darius to finish his thought.

"Joe's dead."

Chapter Eighteen

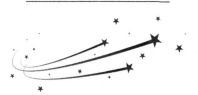

I stand in stunned silence staring at the house AJ and I had visited many times as teenagers, back when AJ and Alex dated. Before John came along and before Alex's accident. It wasn't something I ever talked about with Joe or my grandparents, what happened that night. Michael and I went to the prom with AJ and Alex, but Alex got too drunk and none of us were willing to drive with him, so he left alone. And then he crashed.

It's a night that weighed heavy on all of us. I always thought it was part of the reason Michael broke up with me. Now I know better, but still.

Emotion clogs my throat and my eyes pool with unshed tears as Darius and Zev each take one of my hands. They don't speak, and they don't demand anything from me. They just stand by my side, holding my pain in the silence.

After several minutes, a tear finally escapes and falls down my cheek. Darius turns to face me, using his free hand to catch the tear with the pad of his thumb.

It takes me a moment before I can speak. "H--how?"

"We'll find out," Darius swears.

I nod and release their hands, missing the contact instantly--the cold touch of the vampire and the heat of the werewolf, but I know they can't get me answers if they're tied to my side.

Crossing my arms over my chest to ward off a chill, I watch as Zev sheds his clothes and shifts into wolf form, then sniffs around the perimeter of the house. Darius dashes toward the side door with his impossible speed and is inside before I can blink.

Nothing makes sense in my world anymore, so logically I know Joe could've been evil or mixed up in some dark magic, but my gut says otherwise. Maybe Alex did recover from permanent brain damage, and maybe my ex is a unicorn and my best friend's a nymph and I'm from a line of witches. But it'll take a lot more than that to convince me Joe is anything but good. He was always so sweet, looking out for Tilly while she still lived at home, then taking care of Ed once he was alone. And then he took care of me.

Even if Darius and Zev come back and tell me he was part of this ridiculous Order and he got killed for not stealing my baby when he was supposed to, I'm not ready to believe them. Some people are still good. Not everyone is tricking me with magic and lying about their past. Joe's on the right side of this, I'm certain.

Zev returns first, shifting back into human form and standing naked on Joe's front lawn. Darius arrives a moment later as Zev is getting back into his pants and shirt. I'm just hoping none of Joe's neighbors are watching us. If so, they just got an eyeful.

Now clothed, Zev steps over to me. "I'm so sorry, Bernie," he says as he pulls me into a hug.

"What happened?" I ask, hoping they'll say it was natural causes, but knowing they won't. Nothing is natural in my world anymore.

Darius answers first. "I can't say. He's seated at the dining room table, a glass of water by his hand. No blood, no sign of struggle."

Zev nods, stepping away from me but keeping his hands on my shoulders. "The smell works with our timeline. He's been dead for four days, five at the most. I will say…" He pauses mid-sentence, taking a long, full breath, then slowly breathing out. "Bernie, do you know Joe's wife?"

I shake my head. "I *knew* her, past tense. She died a couple years back."

Darius and Zev share a look.

"What do you smell?" the vampire asks.

"I don't know," Zev answers. "But it's not a scent that should be here. Not if Joe's wife really died two years ago. Not if he's been living alone."

"How… how the hell do you smell that?" I probably sound angrier than I am, but I take so many impossible outcomes as fact these days that I just need a little piece of logic to hold onto.

The werewolf frowns, bringing me in for another hug and whispering the answer in my ear. "The same way I smell your fear and your sorrow. And the many other things you feel."

His answer doesn't really have a science behind it, but it'll have to do for now. It also makes me a little bashful, knowing that not only can the vampire hear my thoughts but the wolf can smell my feelings. Not a lot of privacy around a group of men who make me think and feel the types of things I'd rather keep secret.

I pull out of Zev's arms and take a deep breath, trying to steady myself and think clearly. "What do we do? About Joe?"

The question brings a steady flow of tears, as the reality of his death starts to sink in. Darius steps forward, putting a hand on my shoulder and softly running it down to my elbow.

"Anything we do will only bring attention to us, and there's already too many watching."

"But we can't just leave him there. I'll call the police, or an ambulance…"

I start to pull my phone from my pocket, but Darius stops me. "Make that call, but not while we're here. We need to be back with Rain. I'm more convinced of that now than ever."

My phone is in my hand, and I have half a mind to ignore Darius even though he's probably right. Joe just deserves so much better. He's a stone's throw away, lying dead at his table, and I'm just going to leave?

I nod, acquiescing to the vampire's point. As I look down, I notice I have a new text message.

It's from AJ. Two minutes ago.

And it just says, *Help*.

. . .

THE INSTANT I show the message to Darius, I'm in his arms and we're bounding through the woods of Rowley. Joe lives just a few blocks from Morgan's, and clearly this vampire thinks it will be quicker to leap over fences and barrel through snow banks than take my fancy new ride. Zev follows close behind, once again in wolf form, sprinting on all fours.

Darius comes to a stop when we get close to Morgan's, waiting two seconds for Zev to catch up. I watch the two of them make eye contact, surely discussing an unspoken plan, and then Zev darts off into the shadows. Before I can ask where he's going, which, like an idiot, I was about to do, Darius whispers into my mind.

We mustn't speak. Zev's going to check the perimeter to make sure we're not being lured into a trap. Then we'll follow him inside.

I think some sort of affirmation, probably just the phrase "uh-huh," and then hold my breath while I wait for Zev to lead us in. My baby's in there, and while I take the slightest bit of comfort in knowing Rune's nearby, I'm starting to think that there's a limit to the powers my Sexies possess.

There, Darius mind-speaks, and I follow his gaze

to the roof where the wolf now stands. *Hold tightly to my neck.*

I wrap my arms around him as firmly as I can and a rush of wind hits my face as Darius takes three huge steps and then leaps into the sky. I guess he's jumping, but I feel like springing from the ground to the top of a two-story building is more like flying. And just as impressive as him going airborne is the silence with which he lands. Dude is high level stealth mode.

Zev gestures us forward, leading us toward the roof above the bathroom. As he nears the edge, he shifts back from a wolf to a naked human. The cold doesn't seem to bother him. It also doesn't affect him in the ways it might affect other men, I can't help but notice.

"The baby is in the bedroom," Zev says in a whisper, not nearly as aware as I am of his nudity. "I'm guessing she's being concealed by Rune. There are at least four bodies in the front room, though I can't hear all their movements because... well, because AJ won't stop talking. She seems very angry."

I bet she is. But whatever rage she's dishing out now, it's going to look like a soft rap on the knuckles compared to the fury I'll unleash.

"Darius, go in first," Zev continues. "Careful of any energies you feel--I'm not sure what's Rune's magic and what's not."

"I'll know," Darius says in a deathly serious tone, then he quickly vanishes over the edge of the roof.

I shiver, glad I'm not on the receiving end of him when he's angry.

Zev turns to me. "We need to get inside, but I want you to stay in the bathroom."

"Not a chance," I hiss with as much quiet rage as I can. "I need to find my baby."

"You won't be able to see her," Zev says. "I'm sure Rune took every precaution, and now you need to do the same. You're too important, Bernie. Please do as I ask." His forest green eyes, practically aglow in the moonlight, plead with me.

I give the slightest nod, knowing he's right, but not trusting myself to heed his advice. I've said before that I'll die for my child, and I don't think anyone can talk me out of that.

Zev takes me under an arm, then uses his free hand to lower us down to the window that Darius left open. I can't imagine the strength it would take to hold two adult bodies with one arm, but I suppose his strength is as magical as all the other magical shit that's taken over my life.

Once in the bathroom, he returns to wolf form and creeps to the door, listening to whatever sounds are coming from the bedroom. He's probably trying to hear movements and smell feelings or some shit, because the dialogue is plenty audible from where I'm standing even with my bullshit human hearing. Mostly because of AJ.

"I don't care, Alex!" my friend yells. "There's nothing you could say that would make me give two shits about our past, because what you're doing is wrong. Now get this goddamn blindfold off of me!"

"How can you trust these guys and not me, AJ?" Alex sounds serious.

"How can I... you pretended to have brain damage for ten years!" AJ makes a really good point.

"I wasn't pretending, I was... look, you don't understand, and you're not--"

"Alex, stop." Another voice enters the conversation, this one a woman's. She sounds familiar, but I can't place her.

"We don't have time to debate these issues," the woman continues. "I've come for the child, and I'm not going to waste time trying to convince you."

"You sound familiar," AJ says, mirroring my own thoughts. The voice has a nostalgic quality. Like a high school teacher or someone I once knew long ago. Chances are pretty strong that's who it is. AJ and I definitely called Ms. Day a witch all the time; maybe the reason she got so mad is because we were right.

The voice ignores AJ entirely and speaks directly to Rune. "Fae, you're running out of options. I've got plenty of spells left to try, and sooner or later you'll lose consciousness and any mystique you've created will vanish."

Jesus. I can't tell what's going on, but it appears Rune doesn't have the upper hand. Whatever he did to help hide Rain seems to have put him in a bind. Zev's hackles are up, and his left paw is raised, like a hunting dog ready to strike. But where the hell is Darius?

I hear Rune clear his throat before speaking. "Like you said, Witch, we're not debating anything. Please, continue with your spells." His voice is extremely strained, even if he's still putting up a verbal fight. I can only imagine what's been done to make such a strong man suffer so much. I wish I could do something to help him, but I know I'm way out of my depth.

"Very well," the voice says with a trace of disappointment. God, she sounds more familiar with every word. *Who is she?*

I hear the clinking of some glass, maybe a spoon hitting the edges of a cup as it stirs. "Would you like to drink this one on your own, Fae? Or shall I pour it in your eye like the last?"

Before Rune can respond--or not respond, depending on how he prefers his torturing--Alex speaks up.

"Hey, we might have a problem."

"What?" the mystery woman asks sharply.

"I, um… I just looked at AJ's phone." Alex fumbles his words, sounding pretty nervous, just like the guy I remember from high school. "She… she sent a text to Bernie before I took it away, I guess."

After a second of silence, I hear a loud slap.

"Ow! Goddammit, that hurt!" Alex screams, obviously on the receiving end of a smack across the face.

"Did it?" the woman asks. "Because if that hurts, you're not going to enjoy being ripped apart by a werewolf at all."

"You certainly won't."

Darius has joined the mix, probably appearing out of nowhere in his annoying way, which I swear

I will never reprimand him for again if he can get us out of this mess.

His arrival seems to put a temporary halt on conversation as fighting ensues.

I hear crash after crash and loud growls from Zev, who sped out of the bathroom without me even noticing.

"Hold on, Rune!" Darius says. I don't know what he's asking the fae to hold on to, but the fear in the vampire's voice is tangible and makes my own fear that much stronger.

Snapping myself out of panic mode, I scan the bathroom, searching for any sign of Rain or a weapon I can use, anything to make myself useful. Maybe this is my chance to sneak into the bedroom and try to find my baby.

I feel the urge to help, to do something more proactive than just sit on my ass like a damsel in distress. I want to help Rune, or distract the attackers so Zev can maul them or Darius snap their spines. But more than that, I want to find my baby.

I creep toward the door, trying to be wary of the fight that's going on while staying under the radar. Peering down the hallway, I see a whirlwind of activity. Chairs crash against the wall, flashes of light scorch my plants, and AJ lies slumped against the floor, a blindfold tied around her eyes. I'm about to throw caution to the wind and rush to help when I see her push herself up.

"Rune!" Darius sounds more anxious this time, causing my anxiety levels to spike as well. How dire is the situation out there? Is Rune going to die? Where the hell is he?

But before I can worry about the guys, I need to find Rain. I take a deep breath and slink down the hallway toward the bedroom, hoping I can turn the corner into my room before someone grabs me.

I make it through and close the door quietly behind me, leaning against it while I reach behind my back to turn the lock. I search the room, starting with the crib and moving over to my bed, hoping a mother's intuition will help me find a baby that's shrouded in a magical illusion.

As I fumble around checking the most obvious and oddball places for a baby, I hear a soft cry. It doesn't sound like she's in distress, but it still makes me that much more panicked about finding her. I move more slowly, listening as hard as I can, inching closer to the source of the whimpers...

And then the world goes dark.

I can't see anything, and sounds are muffled.

My first guess is that the lights went out. My second is that I've been knocked out. My third is that a bag's been put over my head.

When I try to lift my hands up to my face, someone with an iron grip grabs my wrists and thrusts them behind my back, binding them with something warm. It ties too fast for a normal rope but doesn't hurt like a zip tie. Before I can guess what's holding me in place, I'm hoisted over someone's shoulder and carried toward the back wall. I'm helpless with no hands or vision, and I can only scream as I feel myself falling out the window and through the cold night air.

I DON'T HAVE a clue where I am when I come to. It's still dark, my hands are still tied behind my back, and I'm shivering from cold.

At first I panic, trying to fight out of my tethers and shake off whatever's covering my head. All that does is fill my hood with noise and make me less aware of my surroundings, so I stop. I take a few deep breaths, then try my best to be still and listen.

There's the sound of a fire crackling nearby. Not close enough for me to feel its warmth, but not too far away. There are also voices--soft and distant, but loud enough to make it through whatever fabric covers my ears.

Another sound cuts through it all. The same sound that rose above the chaos in my apartment. Rain is crying.

As I listen, her tiny voice gets closer, as do the voices of others, along with the sound of footsteps crunching in the snow. My heart races as I prepare for the people, witches, or monsters that are coming my way. To kill me? Maybe. To kill my baby? That's the only thing that worries me.

I feel a body come close, stopping right beside me. Suddenly, the hood over my head gets ripped off, and cold air hits my face. The distant fire provides the only light, and I blink my blindness away, allowing my eyes to focus. The first thing I see is trees everywhere, branches heavy with the recent snowfall, the ground covered by a fresh layer. I can't hear or see any signs of city life. We must be deep in the woods.

Whoever lifted my hood steps behind me and unties my wrists. Moments later another captor passes me Rain. I cry through a painfully dry throat and pull her close, trying to give her every ounce of warmth in my body, doing whatever I can to protect her and make her feel safe. My touch seems to settle her a little, which in turn calms my nerves the slightest bit.

"Beautiful."

I hear that same voice, the familiar woman from my apartment, though now she sounds soft and nurturing. I look up to find the source of the sound, and see a cloaked figure a few paces away. She's outlined by the fire in the background, so I can't see anything except her profile.

"She's absolutely beautiful," the woman says again.

Who the hell is this? Who kidnaps a mother and child, only to tell the bound-up mom how pretty her baby is?

The figure steps closer until she's right next to me, and as the moonlight illuminates her face, I finally get to see her.

"I'm so proud of you," she says as she kneels down and touches my cheek.

It takes another moment before I can place her, because it's been almost twenty years... but that smile. Those eyes. That voice. The small scar on her forehead that I used to run my finger over.

I'm staring into the face of my dead mother.

Chapter Nineteen

"...**M**om?"

My voice catches on the word. Is this a trick? Some kind of magical illusion making me see things that couldn't possibly be here? My mom is dead, and therefore this can't be real.

An icy numbness burrows into my heart, steeling me against unwanted emotions. My entire adult life has been defined by the day I lost my mother. A part of me died with her, as I shut myself off from feeling the type of love that could lead to that type of loss. More than one therapist tied her death to me seeking companionship with unavailable or inappropriate men, like my music professor. Her death crushed me in a way nothing else ever would or could.

But now she's here. And I don't know what to feel.

"Hi, Sunshine," she whispers, tears rolling down her cheeks and coming to rest on her smiling lips.

Sunshine. She always called me Sunshine, and I haven't heard that nickname since. I wonder how much that word, stuck deep in the recesses of my psyche, led me to name my daughter Rain. Like somehow the opposite word would lead to the opposite outcome. I squeeze my baby a little tighter, needing her for emotional support right now far more than she needs me.

My mom looks from me to the baby, a grandmother's love radiating off her face. She doesn't move to touch Rain, probably because she knows my guard is still way up. If she was hoping for a joyful mother-daughter reunion, she picked the wrong way to go about it.

"How?" I ask, choosing the only question I can give voice to right now. A deep hurt in my chest is threatening to crash over me, and I have to keep it at bay if I want to get through this.

"Come, join me by the fire," she says, extending a hand to help me up. "I'll tell you everything, but I also need to prepare you for what's to come. You're still in danger."

Yeah, no shit. I'm surrounded by the people who have been trying to steal my baby.

Seeing no other choice if I want answers, I stand and follow, my gaze taking in everything I can as I try to figure out where I am and who I'm with. About a dozen figures cloaked in dark robes form a circle around us, pretty much exactly what you'd expect a creepy cult to do. Their faces are cast in shadows from their hoods, and none of them move. They could be statues for how still they are, but I wouldn't bet on it. My guess is they are armed, with magic and weapons. Whatever they're packing, they're no doubt ready to intervene if I go off-script. I clutch Rain harder to my chest, then ease off when I realize I'm about to wake her. My skin thrums with the power in this place, and I suddenly feel desperately alone.

I try to quiet the sound of my heart pounding in my head and reach for that small strand that still connects me to Darius. Will he feel where I am? Will he know I'm in danger? Try as I might, I can no longer sense him tethered to me, and this breaks me almost more than anything else has. That sense of loneliness is now completely consuming.

With hesitant steps, I join my mother by the fire. My uneasiness is at war with another, deeper part of myself--the child in me who recognizes with longing the way my mother walks as if her feet barely touch the ground; the way she flicks her wrists like a ballerina, so graceful and lithe. She had been a dancer once upon a time, and though she mostly abandoned her studio sessions when I came along, my fondest memories are of us dancing together in the kitchen while baking banana bread.

I study the woman before me now, and I see that same grace, that same easy fluidity, and I know that part of my mother couldn't possibly be faked. Which makes all of this so much harder. While I'm desperately clinging to my fear to keep me alive, I'm also trying hard not to fall into that safety net she always provided. It's a dichotomy I don't know how to justify within myself, and I'm torn apart by it. Once I'm close enough to the flames to feel their warmth penetrating the cold that has sunk into my bones, I look for a place to sit. My legs feel unstable, whether from exhaustion or from the recent revelations I'm not sure. As I search for a stump or a log, I hear my mother speak in a slightly affected tone.

"*Lángol.*"

I look her way just as she finishes waving a wand--like, an actual witch's wand, and suddenly two flames leap from the fire, turning a radiant blue as they split from their source, one landing behind each of us. I jump a little, afraid of getting burned--since that's what fire does. Meanwhile, my mother sits back into the blue flames beneath her, and the fire expands around her body like a really bizarre bean bag chair.

"Go ahead, Bernie," she says in her soothing tone. "It's safe."

Safe is debatable, but I'm curious despite myself. I inch closer to the blaze, noticing that it's warm but not painfully hot. I ease my body down and feel a resistance come up to meet me. It molds around my body like a cushion, and just like that, I'm relaxing in a fire chair. Well, relaxing may be too strong a word, but tensely sitting for sure.

I have plenty of questions about the seat she just conjured, and my mom must notice because she starts to explain.

"Fire is one of the greatest tools for a witch," she says. "It's part of the reason we've been able to survive despite--"

"Why are you after my baby?" I ask, cutting her off.

As much as I want--and need--to know what she is and where she's been all these years if not dead, my most immediate concern is keeping Rain safe.

My mom just shakes her head, a pained look in her eyes and a quiver in her lip. "To save you, sweetheart. We've been trying to save you."

She seems entirely earnest, but things haven't been as they seem for quite some time. Recent events have primed me to stay skeptical of everyone, and that definitely includes my dead mother.

"I don't understand." I really don't. I don't know what to ask, because I'm too overwhelmed. Too many questions are crowding my thoughts to pick just one.

"I know, Sunshine. There's no way you could. Even after I explain, there will still be parts that don't make sense, but I'll do my best to ease your mind." My mom takes a moment to compose herself, wiping away some tears and dabbing a handkerchief under her nose. In the most extreme, unnatural circumstances, she's still kind of normal. Like a regular mom, sitting in a chair made of fire after pulling off a supernatural kidnapping. Someone sign us up for our reality TV show, stat.

"You might never trust me," she says. "I accept that, and part of me expects it. But I won't stop trying to save you, and hopefully, you'll come to understand…" she pauses again, her voice cracking with emotion. "You'll come to understand that everything I've done is because I love you. More than anything."

I want to believe her, almost as much as she wants to be believed. She sounds so sincere. Her tears, the emotion straining her voice, the look of love she gives me that's so reminiscent of my memories of her. It's almost too perfect. Too much like a movie scene. Either I've become jaded, or I'm missing something here. Still, the child in me wants more than anything to trust what she says, because the alternative might just break me.

She leans forward, her gaze locked on mine, her words earnest as she continues. "I found out I was a witch on my twelfth birthday, which is the year most girls' powers manifest. I fought it for a long time, not wanting to believe I was different. You know how it is at that age. You just want to fit in. Then I went through a rebellious phase, discovering all the worst uses for my powers and--"

"And what does this have to do with me?" I ask sharply, leaning forward with Rain held firmly in my arms. "With what's happening now? Kidnapping me and my child?" I really do want to hear my mother's life's story, but there's a time and a place. This is neither.

"Everything changed when you were born,

Bernie," she says quickly. "I'm not trying to ramble on about my past, but I think you understand how becoming a mother upends your world. And you're starting to understand how much crazier it is when you know magic exists, for better and for worse."

Her words give me pause as I realize my estranged mother and I have something very much in common. *Well-played, mom.*

"Nanny filled me in on the prophecy after you were born, and I briefly lost my shit on her for waiting until I'd had a child to drop that bombshell." It's nice to hear mom sounding a little like me. "But once I cooled down, I knew what I had to do. I went all in. I wanted to master my powers, to harness my capabilities, all so I could protect you. And then…"

My breath catches, knowing she's about to talk about the day she died. Or, rather, didn't die.

"I still didn't really understand my magic, but I knew that I was part of this prophecy, and so were you, and it was too much to bear. I didn't want you to suffer the way I and your nanny had."

"So to ease my suffering you faked your own death?" I ask bitterly, on the verge of losing the battle to control my sorrow and anger.

She shakes her head. "I tried to cast a spell, just

before you turned twelve. I wanted to protect you. I just… I wanted you to be safe forever."

"What happened?"

"I almost killed you," she says, wiping away more tears wetting her cheeks. "I put my baby girl in a coma. Nanny had to pull out some deep, dark magic to bring you back."

"Wait, when I was eleven? I don't remember any of this." Even if I didn't remember the coma, wouldn't I have at least remembered all the magic spell stuff leading up to it? Wouldn't I have any memory of missing school? Wouldn't AJ remember something this big?

"Tilly took care of your memories," she says.

"What about school? Friends? AJ?" I ask, shaken to the core that my kind old Nanny messed with my brain.

"It was summertime, and Nanny handled the rest."

The rest being AJ. Jesus, what kind of family do I belong to?

My mom continues, seemingly oblivious to my own horror at learning all this. "She tried to tell me it was okay, that you would be okay and I should forgive myself, but I couldn't. I couldn't look at you after what I'd done. So…" she forms a fist with her hand like she's trying to hold in all the pain as she speaks. "I decided you would be safer without me. I chose to end my life."

I exhale, letting out a breath I didn't know I was holding. "Except you didn't," I point out.

"I tried," my mom says, sounding even more remorseful than before. "I threw myself off a cliff into the ocean."

I shiver as the memories I keep carefully suppressed come rushing back. Finding her suicide note. Searching the shoreline for her body. Friends with fishing boats patrolling the coastline day and night. Her body was never found. She was presumed dead. After all, how could anyone live through that fall?

"How did you survive?" I ask. "And where have you been all these years?"

She sighs and looks away, her gaze lost in the darkness of the surrounding trees. "I woke up here, in this very forest, staring into my mother's face."

That's actually something I can imagine quite readily, though her circumstances were a bit different. "So what, this is like some weird recreation reunion for you?"

"No. But I wanted you to understand why I did what I did. Why Nanny did what she did."

My heart skips a beat. "What did Nanny do?"

My mother stands and approaches me, then kneels down and takes one of my hands into hers. "She stole your magic to bring me back from the dead."

My throat goes dry and a cold sweat covers my skin as I yank my hand from hers. "What do you mean, stole my magic?"

"I didn't want her to. I never meant for any of this to happen. I didn't consider what it would do to a mother to lose her child. She snapped, even before she absorbed too much power. The grief turned her into someone else." My mother rocks back on her heels, her eyes, the same deep blue as my own, locked on mine. "She used dark magic, blood magic, to pull your power from you and then harnessed it to find my body and bring me back. When I woke up in this forest, I was yanked from the afterlife. The use of that much power made her crazy."

"That's why she lost her mind? Why she's in the hospital now?"

My mother nods. "It is. Magic. Power. It isn't natural. It's always been a curse, causing more problems than it solves. And those monsters who are living with you, they are born of the oldest magic, and they are using you, and your daughter, to empower their own races."

"I already know what they want," I say, impatiently. "I know why they came. But it's more complicated than that."

I think back to all the shared moments, the private conversations, the memories I've already made with each of them. Complicated definitely describes my current relationship status.

My mother smiles sadly, then stands and waves her wand over the fire. The golden-red flames turn blue, like our magic chairs, and begin to dance against the night sky, forming shapes that tell a story.

"They told you what they wanted you to know. They used their powers of mental manipulation and seduction on you."

As I watch, I see scenes played out from my life with Darius, Rune and Zev. Private moments none other were privy to.

"Did they tell you what they will do with the child, once they have her?" she asks, the form of a baby appearing in the flames.

"They need her to save their people," I say softly, feeling sick to my stomach.

"That much is true," my mom says. "But there's

much more to it than that." With another flick of her wand, the flames change shapes once more. "Each race believes they understand the prophecy of the Last Witch. And each believes they know what must be done to save the magic flowing in their veins, giving life to their race."

A wolf appears in the flames, several wolves, in fact, surrounding the baby laying on the ground. The wolves then descend upon the child, ripping it apart. I turn my head from the gruesome scene, but cannot erase it from my mind.

"The wolves would eat her, consuming her flesh and bones in order to take in her magic and save themselves."

I glance back at the flames as they shift again, this time to the fae, who lay the baby in a hole dug in the ground. "The fae would put her to earth, burying her alive so that her blood, bones, and final breath can become part of the nature they worship, so that she will become one with the Great Tree and give them their lives and magic back."

I clutch Rain tighter to my chest. "Stop this," I whisper, anger and fear and disgust boiling in me.

"You must see the truth, my daughter. You must know, otherwise, I cannot save you."

The flames dance again, this time bringing forth

the vampires. The baby in the fire is strapped to an altar, her blood drained as the vampires feed on her. My mother doesn't need to explain this one. It's all too clear.

She circles her wand a final time and the flames die down, turning back to their normal color. "You see? They've been using you. They don't care about you or the child, only their own immortal selves. They were never meant to exist. Not in the world of humans. Not anywhere. They are aberrations and they must never get their hands on the Last Witch. We must keep Rain safe, for her sake and for the sake of all of humanity."

"So you've been trying to kidnap her to keep her safe?" I ask.

My mom smiles, relief in her eyes. "Yes. Exactly!"

"And what about Joe? Why did you kill him?"

She flinches. "That was out of my control. Joe found out about Alex, and he…"

She drifts off but I press on, needing info faster than she seems prepared to give it.

"And Nanny? Why send Order members to her room?"

"To keep her safe," she says. "The Order has been watching over Nanny since her mind went, trying to keep other creatures away from the powers stored in that frail body. Like that vampire who nearly killed her before Alex arrived."

Except… that's not what happened. Nanny had been relieved to see him. Happy. Or was that just what Darius wanted me to see?

I rub my temples, a massive headache forming. I don't know what's real and what's not. Who to trust and who to fight.

"Then why not come to me yourself earlier? Why all the theatrics? You put me and Rain at risk."

My mother sinks back into her fire chair, looking slightly defeated. "I wanted to. Sunshine, I've wanted to come see you every day since I disappeared. Being so close and yet so far has made life almost unbearable. But how could I explain myself? How could I tell you anything and still keep you safe? I wish I got to you before those monsters did, and now I'm trying to fix this, I swear it."

I close my eyes, squeezing through tears as I try to find the truth in my heart, when a voice invades my mind.

Bernie, do not trust her. It's not what it seems. I'm coming to save you both.

My breath hitches. *Darius.*

Chapter Twenty

Don't move.

  Darius' final command makes me hold my breath and my eyes go wide. The reaction is not lost on my mother.

  "What is it, Bernie?" She leans in, inspecting me, clearly on high alert. I don't know if she senses something, or if she's just constantly on edge because she lives in a secret society in the woods.

  "I'm... I'm afraid, mom." I decide not to mention the voice in my head, because I still don't know who to trust. The only thing I can think to do is keep this conversation going and hope the truth appears in big, flashing, neon lights.

  "I'm afraid of everyone. Including you."

Probably not what a mom wants to hear from her daughter, but she takes it in stride.

"Of course you are. I lied to you and broke your trust, and I don't expect to fix that just by showing my face. I only hope you take it better than Joe did when he saw Betty."

And the hits just keep on coming.

"Betty? His wife who died from cancer, whose funeral I went to?" I mean, has anyone ever actually died? And like… stayed dead?

Mom nods. "She's here. She's a witch."

As shocking as that is, I'm more heartbroken for Joe.

"And Joe found out?"

"About her, and about Alex," my mom says. "Betty worked for years on a spell that would bring her son's mind back, and it was finally a success. But the deception and the loss--and the knowledge that his wife was a witch, it was too much for Joe."

Of course it was. Sweet old man stopped caring about anything except beer these last two years, and to then find out he didn't have to go through that agony? That his wife chose to leave him? No matter what her reasoning, that's a pill not a lot of people could swallow without choking.

"Why?" I ask. "Why'd she have to leave, or pretend to die?"

My mother looks into the distance, searching for the words that might make me understand. Open-minded as I'm trying to be, I doubt she'll find them.

"It's too much to explain in one conversation, Sunshine. That might sound like a cop-out, but there's a long history of witches that makes everything--"

"Yeah, I know the history," I interrupt.

"Well," she says, doubt heavy in her voice, "you know the history as told by the races that have been killing us for generations."

It's a fair point, though it's not like Darius, Zev and Rune minced words. None of them painted the treatment of witches in a flattering light. God, how is it that it feels like everyone on both sides of this argument is telling the truth and lying to me at the same time?

I want to ask more questions, about Betty, Alex, Mom--shit, I haven't even thought to ask about the father I never met, who was almost undoubtedly a minotaur or talking fish. However, all questions will have to wait, as a deep red glow ignites in the sky above us, accompanied by a low, bone-rattling hum.

Every member of The Order is on guard, and my mom is out of her chair the moment it happens.

"Where's the breach?" she yells to no one in particular. "Are they inside the field?"

A younger woman who I don't recognize runs over, her fiery red hair flying behind as her hood falls to her back. She speaks with some sort of accent, one I can't place except to say the girl ain't from Mass.

"Someone crossed the river basin," she explains, her words rushed and breath short. "Non human. Three."

My hopes rise as I realize all three Sexies are coming for me, but they fall just as quickly. Are they coming for me *and* my baby, or just my baby?

"Arm yourselves and take your posts!" my mother yells, transitioning from chill witch mom to intimidating general in an instant. "There's a vampire in the woods, so don't show any hesitation."

She turns on me, suspicion clouding her eyes. "Bernie, what's your relationship with these men?"

"What? You know more about them than I do, you've been--"

"No," she cuts me off, searching for specifics. "I

know they've stolen your trust, but have they taken your heart? Have you slept with them?"

This feels way too much like I'm a teenager coming home from the drive-in movies, and I don't really know what to make of it.

"No," I answer defensively but truthfully.

"Any acts of passion? Any connection that's more than skin deep?"

Her insistence seems strange, but the pointed questioning does make me think more clearly.

"I… there was a car crash, with Dar--with the vampire, and to keep me conscious, to help me recover…"

I don't finish the sentence because it's clear my mom has already heard enough.

"Oh, Sunshine," she says, with a mix of pity and scorn. "He gave you his blood. And now he owns you."

Before I can respond, she sprints off into the night, leaving me and Rain alone by the fire.

The Order is preparing for battle with the Sexies. The Sexies have come for me and Rain and will probably kill any member of the Order that gets in their way. Including my mother.

I'm caught in the middle and don't know which way to turn.

A howl in the distance lets me know that Zev is near. It'll be an interesting twist if he can convince the wolves of New England to join the fight.

I stay by the fire, as it's my only source of light in these unfamiliar surroundings. I know both sides of this skirmish say they want to keep me safe, but I still feel the need to duck and take cover. That need only gets stronger when the sky lights up again in a bright crimson, and a shrill siren wakes Rain. I cover her ears, trying to protect her. She probably wants to feed, but the poor thing will have to wait a bit longer.

"They're on the last ridge!" a man calls from the darkness.

"Ready yourselves!" my mother responds. "Stun, confuse, or kill, whatever you need to do to stay alive and protect the child!"

Moments later, clusters of light burst out of the trees and into the clearing. I can't tell where the Order's assault is targeted, but I know it's unending. I fear for the men who have come to save me, though I still wonder how much it's them I should be fearing.

Suddenly, I see the shadow of a tree uproot, and the sound of branches cracking echoes through the woods.

"To the East!" a voice screams. "Target the fae!"

More fire and lighting bolts erupt from the witches stationed in the trees, now all directed nearer to where Rain and I sit. If this fight moves any closer to us, we're liable to get barbecued by an errant blast of fire.

Another tree tears from the ground, and I hear the sound of a man screaming as he falls from his perch in the branches, then a sickening thud as his body hits the snow. Seconds later, a beam of white light scorches the ground beneath the tree, and I hear Rune cry out in agony.

I'm compelled to move towards him, to see if I can help, to offer some sort of protection, but I know that's a fool's errand. I have my baby. I can't walk blindly into a firefight. Instead, I take the only action I can think of.

"STOP!"

I scream at the top of my lungs, clutching Rain to my chest, trying to top the sound of the magical powers clashing around me. I don't expect my cry to be heard, but it's all I've got.

A few more shots are fired, but then the chaos seems to settle. A trace of quiet enters the night. Either everyone died, or my plea worked. Neither seems likely, so I keep Rain hugged against me, waiting for another outburst.

Instead of fire, the next thing I see flying through the air is my pet wolf. Zev lands at my feet, then quickly begins circling me, staring and sniffing in every direction.

Around us, I hear the sound of bodies scurrying down trees, swinging from branch to branch as they head towards the ground. Footsteps come from every direction as the Order surrounds us. Zev looks more like a frightened animal than I've ever seen him, moving around me in a low crouch, a constant growl humming in his throat.

The Order members begin closing in on us, but there's still no sign of Rune or Darius. I don't understand what could have happened to them. They're both too strong, too powerful, too cunning. What are we up against? And of course, I'm once again torn by the lingering question in my mind… which of them is truly my enemy?

Darius, are you here? I think, hoping for an answer but afraid of what he'll say. Silence is the only answer I get.

"Get away from the baby, Wolf," my mother orders. Zev makes no move to obey.

"You're outnumbered and up against a magic

your teeth can't cut through," she says savagely. "Move away and die quickly, or stay put and I'll make the pain linger much longer."

Zev only growls and continues his guard of me and Rain. I don't like where this is headed, and I'm terrified of how it might end.

"Mom," I say, fighting past the lump in my throat so I can speak clearly. "Please don't."

"I'm sorry, this isn't your conversation." Her response is quick and firm, putting me in my place like I'm a child and, in the process, pissing me the hell off.

"Of course it's my conversation!"

"Sunshine--"

"Don't 'Sunshine' me, Lauren." Her name escapes my lips before I even know what I'm saying.

"I'm late to the party, but I'm also the one holding the Last Witch," I say, glancing down at my baby. "If I'm going to bear this cross, I get a seat at the table."

My mom--Lauren--takes a few steps closer, seeming to accept that she won't win this argument with her I'm-in-charge attitude.

"Sweetheart, you're at the table. I won't keep anything from you..." she pauses, looking from my face down to the wolf. "...As soon as you're safe."

No sooner have the words left her lips than her wand is in the air, pointed at Zev, a golden light bursting from it. He's quick enough to move his head out of the way, but the blast catches him in the shoulder, sending him flailing away into the snow. The yelp he lets out as he crashes and falls still breaks my heart.

"No!" I shout, whirling back to face my mother.

"Baby," she starts, ready to dish out another lie, or tell me the truth. I get the feeling I may not know who I should actually trust until it's too late.

She takes another step toward me, but before her foot can settle, a blur of darkness streaks through my vision, toppling my mother and sending other members of the Order scrambling. Before my eyes can follow the movement, the shadow appears behind a hooded member and knocks them uncon-scious with a blow to the head before they can even turn around.

The vampire has arrived.

Fire starts to fly again and I duck down, hunching over my shrieking baby to keep her out of harm's way. I look behind me to see if I can spot

Zev. I can only make out what might be the outline of a rock, or perhaps a motionless wolf.

Suddenly, I feel a body at my side.

"We need to flee, Bernie."

Order members are scattered about, some heading our way but ceasing the onslaught for fear of hitting Rain. This is as good a time as any to escape, but…

"Not without Zev and Rune."

"Bernie, they may not survive--"

"It's a three-way pledge, Darius," I say firmly. "We're not leaving if they're still alive."

Darius stands his ground, his face conflicted. He's trying to respect my wishes, but it's clear his chief concern is keeping me alive. I can't imagine a world in which this man would hurt me, no matter what consequences he may face. If I had to choose between my mom and the vampire this instant…

"Bernie, you need to trust me!"

My mother's voice comes from the ground near the fire. She's slowly getting to her feet, obviously hurt from the blow she took.

"No matter how charmed you are, or protected you feel, each of these men is trying to save his own race! The stakes are too high to be blinded by their powers--or your feelings! Don't you think they would snap your neck in an instant if it meant saving everything and everyone they care about? Do you really think you and your child matter to them more than their entire realm? More than their own lives?"

She limps toward me, looking hurt and afraid, and speaking words that ring true. It would be foolish to think about how each man has treated me without remembering why they came in the first place.

"Matilda's daughter, I presume," Darius says calmly.

"Don't say her name like you know her," my mom says.

Interesting. It looks like I know something my mother doesn't. What to do with this information, I'm not sure.

"You don't know of what you speak, woman," the vampire spits back, sounding much more like the Darius I was first introduced to. "None of you know the first thing about this child, its powers, or the prophecy."

While Darius gives my mother a verbal lashing, the other members of the Order fall in behind her. It's me, my baby, and a vampire against a much larger, seemingly more powerful group. My baby might have magic one day, but that day is not today, and I already know I don't have any--thanks to Nanny. So really, it's Darius against the Order, which doesn't seem like great odds, even for a super powerful vampire.

I look back toward the clearing, vaguely making out the movements of a body slumped against a tree. I know in my heart it's Rune. He's alive at least, though it's hard to say for how long.

"Is that why you've killed so many of us, you monster?" my mom fires back. "Just racing to get to the last one so you could feast on the innocent for eternity?"

I throw another glance back toward Zev, and see that he's starting to rise. I may not know who to trust, but I know I'm not ready to see any of these strange, beautiful men die.

When I turn back, I see my mom slowly raising her wand.

"Mother," I say in my most admonishing voice. "Do not."

I expect her to ignore me, but instead she looks at the ground and starts to cry.

"Oh, Sunshine,' she whispers between sobs. "Why won't you let me save you?""

Her words strike a chord, and I see how painful

this is for her. She knows she hasn't earned my trust, and yet I think she truly believes that I'll die without her help. But then, her expression shifts, a new malice in her eyes and a harsher tone in her voice.

"Don't you see what this magic becomes?" she wails, gesturing to the fire and devastation all around us. "There's no end to this, Sunshine. Everyone will always want to achieve the greatest power, to live forever, to rule over the others. There's only one way to end this."

She lowers her wand and reaches out to me with her other hand. "Give me the baby, Bernadette. She is the sacrifice that will save us all. Her death will end the wars forever."

A collective gasp comes from the Order members behind my mother. A figure steps forward and removes her hood--it's Joe's wife, Betty. She hovers over my mother's shoulder and speaks while keeping her eyes on me and the vampire.

"What are you talking about?" Betty asks. "The objective was always to save the child, Lauren."

"No," my mom says firmly. "It was always to save our families, our husbands and brothers, our sisters and mothers… our daughters."

She turns her attention back to me. "I'm asking

you to do something impossible, Sunshine. No mother could ever willingly harm her child."

Except you, I think to myself. *By trying to take my baby from me.*

"But this goes beyond your pain, or mine, or my mother's. You have a chance to end so much suffering. If we don't do the right thing, these cursed magic creatures will haunt the world for another million years."

This whole time, my mom has been trying to convince me of the evil forces conspiring against me. I know she believes what she says, but she's lost sight of who the real monster is.

I look down at Rain--cold, hungry, and crying. I need to get her away from here. Away from the witches who are supposed to be her family.

I turn to Darius, whose eyes have been locked on my mother this whole time, every muscle in his body ready to spring into action and save the baby he pledged to protect.

That's it. The pledge.

He takes his eyes off my mother to look at me, a hesitant expression on his face. I know he heard my thoughts. "Bernie…"

"Darius," I say, not giving him a chance to stop me. "Take the child."

"What are you doing?" my mother yells, her wand hand raised again.

"I'm taking your advice, mother," I say, with every ounce of sass I can muster. "I'm doing the right thing."

I hold Rain out toward the vampire. He's the only one who can keep her safe right now, and that's all I care about. "Take the child."

He looks at the baby so tenderly, a sort of compassion on his face I never thought could have existed. And then he raises his gaze to me.

"No."

I don't understand. Neither does my mother or any member of the Order, who all seem dumbstruck at the scene unfolding before them.

"Darius, I've broken the pledge," I say. "All I want is for her to be safe, away from all this, and you're the only one I trust to make that happen. Please, Darius, take my baby."

He pushes Rain back into the nook of my arm, then reaches up and touches my cheek.

"She's safest with you. Your love for her is as strong as any magic, and has already kept her alive against all odds. I refuse to take her from her mother, no matter what."

When I open my mouth to object, he inches

closer, wrapping an arm around me while keeping his other hand on Rain.

"I can't allow any harm to come to the child," he says softly, his dark eyes penetrating all the defenses I had built up around my heart. "But I can't allow any harm to come to you either. I followed the star that night expecting to find a savior for my people. Instead, I found a savior for my own soul, and I will not let her go now."

For the briefest moment, all the fear drifts out of me as I lose myself in Darius' eyes, feeling secure in the midst of this madness.

"All right," I say, knowing I can't change his mind and realizing how much I need him by my side. I linger on his eyes for a second longer, finding strength in them that I know I'll need for the fight ahead.

And then, before I can turn away, Darius and I are hit with a blast of magic that sends me flying back several feet and crashing into the snow. My grip on Rain tightens as I hold her close to my chest and pray she isn't hurt. The wind is knocked out of me and my head spins from the impact.

I look around frantically for Darius and scream when I see him.

He is on fire. Blue flames licking at his flesh,

burning him from the inside out. I try to crawl to him, but every part of my body flares with pain and I fall back when I realize my right leg is broken. Darius crashes to the ground flailing wildly as flames engulf his entire body. His cries are excruciating and echo through the forest as the trees themselves seem to absorb his pain.

"What have you done?" I scream as my mother stands over him, wand pointed down, smoke still curling from the tip. Then she turns, her face a mask void of any emotion, as she locks her gaze with mine and takes a step toward Rain and me.

Chapter Twenty-One

"**Y**ou stupid girl." My mother's voice is cold, harsh, absent any warmth it once held. She moves toward me slowly, wand still raised. I push my heels into the earth below, trying to put as much distance as possible between us and this murderous lunatic who is my mother. My heart is hammering in my chest, cold sweat slicking my skin, tears burning my eyes as I glance over to Darius, his body now still and smoldering in the snow.

"After all the horrors you've been through in the last few days," my mother says, taking another step forward. "After watching your grandmother lose her mind and live the rest of her life in agony, destroying her husband's life in the process. After growing up without a mother, you still can't see where all the trouble stems from."

I stop scooting along the ground, knowing I won't get away. Hopefully, I'll have better luck hurling words.

"You're blaming all those things on *my child*? Every problem for the last fifty generations can be pinned on this tiny, defenseless girl?"

"It's what she represents, Bernie," my mother says, a little exasperated with my defiance. Not sure what else she expected.

"You won't understand now, you'll probably hate me until I'm dead and gone, but this is the only choice." My mom softens her voice, toning it down so she sounds more like the woman who almost won me over just moments ago. "Please, Sunshine. Hand her over. Don't make me hurt you as well."

It's a sweet attempt at saying the most hateful thing ever, and I'm not buying it.

"Oh, mom." I'm overrun with emotions, but my voice is calm and clear. "All these years wishing I had one more minute with you, could see you one last time. And now I just wish you really were dead."

Her face twists with anger, then she stands tall,

composes herself, and aims her wand at me. "Me too, Sunshine. *Szünet.*"

There's a flash, and then I feel nothing. No pain, but also no cold, no touch. I know Rain is pressed against me, but I can't even feel her. My thoughts still tumble around in my mind, my eyes still see, but it's like my head has no body. Every effort to move a leg or an arm fails. As my mother reaches down and extracts my baby from my arms, all I can do is watch through blurry, tear-filled eyes.

"Please don't," I mouth, my lips barely moving while the sound stays trapped in my throat.

She lifts Rain and tucks her under her chin, gently cooing as she walks away from me, toward the fire. "What a sweet girl you are. What a sweet, beautiful girl."

What a goddamn psychopath.

I fight to move again, but it's all for not. Whatever connection there used to be between my brain and body has gone offline. I've still got control over my eyes, and I look as far as I can in every direction.

I can barely make out Zev in my periphery, and I've got no clue if he's breathing or not. Rune's too far away, hidden amongst the trees, at least that's where I hope he is.

Darius is much easier to spot. Not twenty feet away, I see smoke rising off his motionless body. Fear hits me in the gut at the sight. I know vampires are hard to kill, but a witch's fireball seems like it would be deadly to just about anyone.

I shift my eyes back towards my mother, helpless to do anything but watch as she waves her wand and summons a platform of blue fire under her feet. It lifts her into the air, hovering above the open flame. Along with my baby.

"Gather round," she announces to her followers. The forest has fallen silent, save for the sound of footsteps shuffling across the snow-covered earth. Rain doesn't even cry. She seems to be in some kind of trance. The eerie quiet is much worse than the cacophony of battle from earlier. Paralyzed from the neck down, my baby dangling above a sprawling fire, and all I hear is pounding, merciless silence.

"I know you've fought to save the Last Witch," my mother says as the Order members circle around the fire. "But as you've seen here tonight, it's an impossible task. It took everything we had, every spell we could muster, to fend off just three attackers, and more will come." She gestures to the woods, as if enemies lurk there even now. "The vampires, the werewolves and the fae will have armies at their backs. Kingdoms to come against us, if we do not end this now. Who amongst us wants to die at the hands, teeth, or claws of these abominations?"

There are murmurs from the circle, voices offering both agreement and protest.

"Remember that this was never about a single child," my wretched mother continues. "This was about all of our futures, and the future of humanity. This is about righting centuries of wrongs that our ancestors had to endure at the mercy of those monsters!"

She's talking about my princes, men who risked so much for me and for Rain. How could this be my reality? The three sent to steal my child, once the most frightening of foes, now lay around me dying, because they chose to defend me and my baby from the mother I thought to be long dead. So many twists of fate, and all so cruel.

I hear muffled whines coming from Rain, still under my mom's control. I choke on my sobs, wishing more than anything that it was my body hanging above that fire. If only Tilly had sacrificed me after I was born, shattering my mother and putting an end to these magical tragedies. So many lives could have been saved, and I'd have never experienced the greatest loss of all.

But Nanny would have never done that. She broke herself trying to bring her daughter back. I feel that connection to her now, stronger than ever before. I recognize the love she felt, and the sacrifices she made because her heart told her to. God, I wish Nanny was here. To comfort me, and to talk some sense into her craven daughter.

My chest burns, and I feel like it's the actual sensation of my heart giving out. Rain is about to die and I have nothing left to live for, so why should my heart keep beating?

"The Order should vote," a woman yells, interrupting my mother's tirade. "It's how we've always addressed issues in the past. We've thwarted the attack and we're safely convened at the coven fire. Let us vote, Lauren."

"There isn't time for a vote!" my mother shouts back. "You think the attack is over? That we're safe? Each and every one of us will die if we don't act swiftly."

The threat of death seems to quiet her dissenters, yielding control back to my mother.

"We stand before the First Fire, ignited by the Fates, the sacred flames that have burned even as our numbers dwindled. We now have the chance to restore the order they once sought to create, by letting the flames consume the Last Witch, bringing an end to the powers that have long been a source of death and destruction among ours and all races. This child's sacrifice will quench these eternal flames, allowing the great magic to consume itself, and thus end these powers forever."

As she lifts my baby into the air, the burning in my soul becomes almost unbearable. I want to move so badly, to break free of this pain, but my body won't allow it.

I want to scream, to rage against what is happening. And then, just as I think I'm about to succumb to the heat building in my chest, a soft amber glow shines in the sky. Perhaps my heart did burst, and this is my journey to the other side. Or maybe Rain has been fed to the fire, and the world is twinkling with the magical brightness that existed in that beautiful, perfect baby.

Bernie, my dear.

I hear the voice in the same way I hear Darius when he speaks to my mind, but it is not the vampire who speaks to me now.

It's Tilly.

Nanny?

A shimmering form appears before me, clarifying within the amber glow, a silver wisp that takes on the form of my grandmother. She steps forward, her translucent arms outstretched, her body an effervescent figure pulled straight from a dream, hovering just about the snow. The glow from her being washes the whole forest in a warm, golden light.

My eyes snap from her back to the fire, to the scene I'd looked away from because I thought it might kill me to watch. My mother is frozen, holding Rain above the fire. Everyone is frozen.

Everyone but Nanny and me.

What did you do? I ask the figure before me.

I have slowed time, but only for a moment. I've come to give you back what I took from you so long ago. Nanny approaches me, kneeling to touch my cheek with her ghostly finger. Warmth infuses my skin, and I feel tears slide down my cheeks as sensation in my body slowly returns.

I have to go now, Nanny says, stroking my cheek like she did when I was scared as a child.

Where? I ask, still feeling stuck in something between a dream and a nightmare.

No one knows. She smiles gently. *That is the great adventure, to discover what life looks like on the other side of the door we call death. Thank you for bringing me. For releasing me.*

What's she talking about? What did I do? *Nanny, what do you mean?*

You called out to me, your voice a source of pure love. When I heard you, I knew it was okay to let go, she says, her tone so calm and sweet as she delivers this crushing news.

No! I feel my heart crack open, emotions too big to bottle up spilling out of it even as my body refuses to feel it all. *I need you. Rain needs you. Don't leave us.*

Oh child, I'm not leaving you. I'm leaving an old body in a hospital bed. I'll always be in here. She removes her hand from my cheek and places it over my heart, and I watch in awe as a blinding light flashes in her soul and pushes through her hand and into me, filling the cracks that have formed at my core. As I fill with that light, that magic, my body comes to life again, pulsing with every sensation. My broken leg mends itself and my very skin begins to glow with the kind of power I have never felt or even imagined in my life.

Nanny's eyes are full of light even as the rest of her begins to fade. *I commited a great act of evil that was inspired by the greatest love when I stole your magic to bring your mother back. It is not for witches to interfere with the destinies of others. My beautiful granddaughter, I am giving you back your destiny. I will be here, watching over you. Watching over Rain.*

My body burns, but this time it is a welcome fire that sparks my soul to life, a part of me I didn't even know was dead until now.

But at what cost? My Nanny has almost entirely disappeared. The outlines of her body are fading like smoke dissipating on the wind. Only her face remains clear. Her eyes, still full of so much love.

But girl, know this, she says, her voice becoming faint even in my mind. *It was always you.*

And then, she is gone. I feel it the moment her soul departs this world, as all the power she released slams into me.

I scream.

The sound of my voice rings through the forest, waking up all the creatures who live here, driving magic into each leaf, each blade of grass, each stray rock.

Time--which was at a standstill--now snaps into motion, my mother moving to sacrifice my child over the fire. The whole interlude with Nanny happened in the blink of an eye, so my mom never saw Tilly. She doesn't see what has changed in me.

With instinct born of desperation and fear, I push it all out of me, every drop of magic I feel swelling within. I can't tell if I'm reigning power in from the natural world or if it's all emanating from my own being. I'm acting without thinking, and the result is a tsunami of electricity.

Light crashes over the Order, my mother, everyone near me.

While the world bends and shakes around me, I set my intention to one thing only.

Save Rain.

I must save Rain.

My eyes stay focused squarely on my baby as wave after wave of brilliant light crashes through the others. They scatter and fall to the ground, stunned or unconscious. If a fallen witch tries to stand back up, she's immediately struck down again. Meanwhile, Rain floats gently on a soft, glowing cloud, safely above the fire.

My gaze never leaves her as I walk to the fire's edge. She's hovering just above the flames, the same ones that were meant to consume her life, and yet I feel no fear. She'll wait for me. She is safe.

I pull her from the floating stasis and move away from the blaze, squeezing her in my arms. "Oh sweetheart, are you okay?" I check her little body for any injury, the light from my fingertips soaking into her soft skin. She coos, grasping at the glowing streaks my magic leaves.

I stand amidst the chaos my power has created, but my feet do not sink into the snow. Instead, I find myself floating above the earth, moving toward my mother, who was blasted to the ground and now struggles to right herself.

She stares at me, slack jawed. While the other Order members lay motionless, my mother is still alert. Whether that's because she's the stronger witch or my subconscious intention was to leave her standing I cannot say.

"How did... where did you get such power?" she asks, fear in her eyes for the first time tonight.

"It is mine by blood," I say. "And you are done here."

My mother's lips curl like a rabid dog and she reaches for her wand and pulls at the blue fire still burning between us.

"I didn't want it to be this way," she says. "I wanted to spare you. But you've made that impossible."

With a flick of her wrist, she casts the fire at Rain and me, intent on completing what she started, even if it means I die with my daughter.

Without thought, without knowing what I'm doing, I call my magic to me on instinct. My intent is enough. A golden shield forms around my child and myself, and when the blue fire comes for us, it is repelled backward by the vibrant light.

My mother's eyes widen. Before she can manage a scream, the fire wraps around her body, her own flames consuming her.

As relieved as I am to be alive, I can't help but feel the pain of losing her all over again.

I hold Rain so she can't see her grandmother die, but I watch. I bear witness to the consequences of messing with dark magic. Of bringing back the dead. And trying to kill the innocent.

When her screams die to nothing, the fire flashes. I blink, and when I open my eyes again, my mother is gone. Nothing remains of her body but a dim blue light fading out into the night.

Around the eternal witch's fire lay the remains of the Order, all unconscious but alive.

But they are not my concern.

I look around, seeking out the three men who have turned my life--and my heart--upside down in such a short time.

I find Zev first, in wolf form. Laying a hand on

him, I press my magic into his fur and close my eyes, willing him to heal, to live.

His body twitches, then jerks and he shifts to human under my hand, his green eyes opening. I exhale in relief as he pulls me into a hug, careful not to crush the baby between us.

My tears fall on his shoulder, and he pulls away to wipe them. "I guess it's not so bad," he says with a smirk.

"What's not so bad?" I ask.

"Being mated to a witch. It could be worse."

If his words are a shock, the kiss that comes next nearly undoes me. My body is already raw, exposed from the inside out, so when he takes my lips with his, cupping the back of my head with one hand as the other wraps around my waist, I feel everything. Every sensation, every emotion, every shift in his body against mine. I feel him under my skin, in my heart, in some primal part of me I've been denying my whole life, and if I were a wolf, I would howl right now. But, alas, I am human.

Or rather, I am witch. And so I kiss him back, deeply, passionately, with nips at his bottom lip as my fingers dig into his back.

I pull away, painful as it is to do so, but I can't go on knowing there are two of our pack still missing. "We will talk more later," I say. "About this mate business."

His eyes are filled with need, but he nods, nuzzling my neck once more before pulling away. "I'll go to Rune. I can hear him in the clearing. He is alive. You find Darius. He will need your blood."

I hand him Rain. "Take her," I say. "If I have to feed Darius my blood, it's best if she's somewhere else."

He nods, accepting the child, his face softening as it always does when he looks at her.

Before I can leave, Zev cups my face with his palm. "It was always you," he says softly.

The very same words Tilly spoke to me before she died.

I kiss him once more, then turn to find Darius. Around me, the night fills with the scents and sounds of the forest. With a heightened sense, I experience every shift of the trees groaning deep in their roots, every tiny movement of each animal and insect, every shimmering moonbeam lighting my way. It's heady, intoxicating and dizzying. I have to stop and lean over to catch my bearings again. The world around me is too bright, too noisy, too filled with wonder. I feel as if my head will explode.

But Darius. I need to find him. He could be almost dead, meaning I have no seconds to spare.

I push through the discombobulation, but I can't remain upright. Instead, I crawl through the snow, my ability to hover now gone as I struggle to settle my mind and stabilize this new power surge I'm having. If not for Darius' blood flowing in my veins, increasing our connection, sending me a guiding ribbon of light to follow, I'm not sure I would have been able to find him through the snow now falling once more. It's as if nature is trying to reclaim the forest we have defiled with fighting and death.

I choke back emotion as my mind wanders to Tilly and my mom. To everything that has happened here.

I blink against tears, and against the memory of Darius bursting into flames.

Feeling through the snow with hands that are becoming numb from cold, I hit on what I know is the vampire's body. Relief surges through me as I sense the smallest speck of life still present in him.

I pull myself up to where he lays, my head swimming as I study his too perfect face, which is now covered in charred burn marks. Rage swells up again at my mother and the suffering she caused, but I push it back. I can't afford anger right now.

I need healing. Love. Peace. I need to bring this man back to me.

I search his cloak for the knife I know he keeps there, and hold it to my wrist. Praying it's sharp enough but not too sharp, I swipe at my vein, releasing a crimson ribbon across my arm that glows with the same golden light as my skin. I squeeze my eyes against the pain that follows the swell of blood, then I hold it over my vampire's mouth.

I hope the magic in my bloodstream will be an extra healing elixir for Darius.

It takes a moment, but as my blood drips into his mouth, his body comes back to life, the burn marks on his face healing first to pink puckered scars, and then to smooth, clear skin.

When his eyes open, revealing the dark orbs that always pull me in, my heart skips a beat in relief.

When he pulls me into him, replacing my wrist with my neck as he continues to feed, my heart skips a beat in desperate desire. The pain of his teeth sinking into my flesh is turned to pleasure as his lips caress my neck, as his hands grip my body laying on top of his. As his strength returns to all parts of him.

And when he continues to feed, to consume my blood, and my reality dips and spins and closes into darkness, my heart skips several beats. And then is silent.

Chapter Twenty-Two

"Bernie?" A voice calls my name, but he sounds so far away. Like a dream through mist and clouds.

"I think she's coming to," another voice says.

It isn't until I hear a heart-rending cry that I find my way out of the fog I feel I've been lost in for ages.

When I open my eyes, three beautiful faces stare down at me. Silver eyes that glow with an inner light. Forest green eyes that take me into the wilds of the woods. And eyes so black I am lost in their eternal darkness.

"Welcome back," Rune says, his voice filled with worry. "You've given us quite a scare."

"Rune used every potion and herb on you," Zev says. "I've never seen his magic so useless."

Rune glares at the werewolf who just shrugs.

"Even my blood did nothing to revive you," Darius says, his voice choking on more emotion than I've ever heard from him. "I nearly killed you. You should never have offered yourself that way to me. I had no control."

Zev, much to my surprise, puts a comforting hand on the distraught vampire. "But you did stop. You stopped in time. Because you love her and would never hurt her."

It's the first time I've truly seen a glimpse of who they might have been had they not turned on one other so many eons ago, and it makes me hopeful for what might yet be. But also… *love?* That's a big word. One I'll have to unpack later.

I try to lift myself, to get a sense of where I am, of what happened, but the room is spinning.

Strong hands support my back. "Easy there. You've been out a long while."

"Rain?" I whisper, my throat dry as sandpaper.

Someone hands me a glass of water. "Drink," Zev says.

I do. And someone else hands me a bundle that squirms in my arms. "Rain." Tears fall as I hold her close to me. As my vision clears, I realize I'm in my bedroom. The Sexies are all here. I've got my baby. And AJ is sitting in the chair in the corner, her head lolled to the side in sleep.

"Is she okay?"

Rune nods. "She hasn't left your side. We didn't want to wake her."

"What happened?" I ask, instinctively pulling out a breast to feed my daughter.

Before they can answer, I notice my skin and pull Rain away, handing her to whichever Prince is closest. "What's wrong with me?"

It takes me a moment for memories to return. The power I inherited from my grandmother. The surge of energy I felt when my mother died. The glowing skin and glowing blood.

I stand, pushing away the hands that try to stop me, and stumble to the full-length mirror on my closet door. I can't believe what I'm seeing.

"I'm still glowing. How… why?" From head to toe. My skin shines like diamond dust, my eyes shimmering like living sapphire and even my hair is streaked with gold and silver glitter. I didn't expect it to last past that night. It'll be real hard to live a normal life if I… sparkle. Oh Jesus, I can already imagine the jokes at the bar.

"The power you possess is too much for a single body," Darius says, the worry clear in his tone. "When your grandmother returned your magic, she also gave you what was left of her own. And then, when your mother died by her own flame, the magic in her blood flowed into yours."

"So, what are you saying?" I ask. "I'm three witches in one?"

Darius nods. "Essentially." The vampire comes up behind me and slips his arms around my waist. "You have more magic than your body knows what to do with, which is why you can't control the glow of your skin."

I cling to him and lean my head against his chest, feeling suddenly unstable, nearly blinded by my own reflection. My head is spinning and I twist away to vomit, but there's nothing in my stomach, so it's a painfully dry heave.

"You're being poisoned by the magic in you," the vampire whispers, laying a cool hand over my fevered forehead.

I turn to face him, gripping his biceps. "What does that mean? What do I do to stop it?"

"I can bleed some off of you by drinking your blood," he says. "That seemed to help. But it's only a temporary solution."

Rune approaches. "Darius is correct. That won't keep you alive long term. We need a more permanent solution, and soon."

"The Council has reconvened," Zev says, approaching us. "All of our kind have united in one purpose."

My stomach tightens and my pulse races. "What purpose is that?"

"Rain," he says simply. "They all want your child. They've decided they will share her, to try and save everyone."

"Share her," I say, my brain coming to life slowly. "You mean kill her?"

They each nod solemnly.

"And you're going to help them?" I ask, pulling away, my voice full of hurt and accusation. As I do a blast of light rips out of me and slams into Darius, pushing him across the room and into my wall, where he makes a man-sized cut out.

"What the hell?" I run over to him. "Are you okay? I'm so sorry."

Darius steps out of my wall and dusts himself off. "I will be fine. Your blood still flows in my veins, and it's very powerful. It's you we need to worry about right now."

I'm shaking as I look again at my hands, which

seem to have a mind of their own. I pull away from all of them, retreating into a corner of the room like a scared animal. "What if I hurt one of you?" I ask, then my gaze lands on the bundle in Rune's arms. "What if I hurt my child?"

"You'd never," AJ says, sitting up and stretching. "That's bullshit and you know it."

"But how can we be sure," I ask. "Maybe my mother was right about one thing. This power is dangerous. Unnatural." I've never feared myself, what I'm capable of, and it's not a good feeling.

Darius clears his throat. "I have an idea. Wait just a moment."

With vampire speed he disappears from the room and reappears a moment later holding something I'd entirely forgotten about.

It's the star that brought these men to me. The rock I pulled from the wall just before Rain arrived. I inch forward to look at it, wondering if my magic is causing my eyes to play tricks on me. "It's glowing the same color as my skin."

Darius nods. "It's been glowing since you got your powers back. Maybe it can help you control them until we think of something more permanent."

He offers the rock to me and I reach out

nervously to take it. I don't know what to expect, but the moment I wrap my hand around it, I feel a shift inside myself, a settling. Light from my skin pours into the star until my body stops glowing and I return to normal.

"How do you feel?" Rune asks, passing Rain to Zev to come kneel before me. He peers into my eyes, studies my palm, takes my pulse.

"A bit better," I say with relief. "Not so dizzy or out of control."

"Try setting the star aside," Rune suggests.

My eyes widen. "What if I hurt you?"

"I'll be alright and Zev won't let anything happen to Rain. But we need to see what we're dealing with."

I nod and carefully set the star on the ground and then release my hand from it. The moment I do, power rushes back into me like a tidal wave. My hands blaze with lightning and the dresser near me explodes in shards of wood.

Quickly, I grab the star and hold it to my chest, my breathing rapid, my body practically buzzing.

Once again the star absorbs the excess power and I feel myself stabilize.

Rune reaches for my hand to help me stand.

With one hand clutching the star, I give my other to him and let him pull me up.

"It would appear she needs to be in physical contact--"

"With the star to control her magic, yeah," AJ cuts Rune off, not needing the play by play. "We were literally all here watching, Elfie."

Before the two can get into one of their sibling spats, I interrupt. "Okay, so I'm a magical bomb about to explode and all of your kingdoms are coming for my kid. What about you three?" I ask, looking at each of them. "The pledge you made is broken. I broke it." I glance at Darius who holds my gaze with his. "Will you go home? Take your rightful places and help them?"

"We are not working with our kingdoms," Zev says.

Rune nods. "We have taken a new pledge."

"What kind of pledge?" I ask.

Darius takes my hand in his, speaking directly into my mind. *We are yours, Bernie. Yours and Rain's. We will each lay down our lives for you if we must. Forever.*

I suck in a breath, unsure what to believe. But then he pulls up his sleeve and shows me a tattoo he didn't have before. A triangle with a star in the middle. Rune and Zev have the same marking on their arms. And then I notice my own arm--it has a matching symbol.

"We are bound to you," Rune says. "And we will do whatever we must to protect you."

So many emotions flood me. After nearly losing my child, watching my grandmother die, watching my mother die, worrying the men I've come to care for would betray me, and now being filled with so much magic I can't control, I don't know what to do or think, but I know what I feel.

For the first time in a long time. I feel hope.

Darius caresses my cheek. "We will find a way to keep both you and Rain safe. You have my oathe."

I STARE into the glowing full moon that casts its silver light over the water, breaking through the surrounding fog and giving a soft glow to the night sky. It's peaceful. A peace I don't think I've ever felt before.

"Shall we?" Rune says, extending his hand to guide me.

I turn and look at the handsome fae, his expression genuine and understanding. Zev and Darius stand behind him, both wearing tailored black suits, as is Rune. Dashing as ever, but now in a more formal, earthly way.

Darius' mind brushes mine lightly, and I feel his emotions. A steady calm mingled with great tenderness. This is a new thing between us that started after he fed on me. I can't say that I mind. Now, it's as if we can touch each other even when we aren't together. It's a comfort I never imagined I would find so valuable.

Darius stays with me as I extend my hand and give it to Rune. Under the light of the moon, my skin is glowing, and not in the way people said it glowed while I was pregnant, which I still think was bullshit since I was red and sweaty through most of it. No, my skin very literally glows these days, a soft amber hue flowing through my pores, even when I'm holding the star. Darius will need to feed on me again soon, or I'll never be able to leave the house.

And just as intimately, I feel the wave of a wild, primal connection when I look at Zev. We still haven't talked about what he meant when he called me his mate, though I have ideas. And the thought of it, while slightly terrifying, also heals something in my heart I didn't know was broken.

I look forward to exploring these complex

emotions with each of the men in my life, once things get back to normal.

Or whatever normal now looks like for me.

I finally take Rune's hand and we join the others, then move as a group to the cliff's edge. Below us waves crash against the rocky coast, spraying sea mist into the air and creating a steady rhythm with the intervals of the break.

It's been a little over a week since I saved Rain from my mother. Since I became overwhelmed with magical powers that cause my skin to glow and silver streaks to run through my hair. Since I brought Darius back to life with my blood. Since my Nanny died. We've kept the bar closed in mourning, just as we did after my grandfather passed. But patrons have taken to slipping envelopes of cash under our door, with notes and cards. I've also found a casserole or dessert on the porch leading to my apartment nearly every day. My community has come together to take care of me and Morgan's Pub while I process my Nanny's death.

Now we stand at the cliff my mother leapt from, back when she was still good, before dark magic warped her perception of right and wrong. A tear rolls down my cheek as I think of how much her heart must have hurt, how broken she must have been to decide that the best thing for her child would be for her to take her own life.

But we're here for Tilly. As much as I hated losing my mother twice, saying goodbye to my Nanny is just as hard. I plant a kiss on the top of Rain's head, her cute little body strapped tightly against mine in her carrier. She won't have any memories of her great grandmother, but I'll see Nanny in everything my baby girl does, and Rain will have no question about where she inherited her greatness.

We stand a few feet back from the precipice, wind whipping through our hair, a steady stream of light coming from the moon. Hard to call this a funeral, but I feel it's the right service to honor Tilly and everything she meant to me.

Darius and Zev flank me and Rune stands just behind, his hands resting on my waist. Supported on all sides. It's so strange to stand with these princes and have an aura of calm about us. The Order members who posed a threat not that long ago are now just grateful the baby is alive and that I'm protected. Betty came to see me after I regained consciousness and made clear the misguided intentions were my mother's alone. After my final moments with Tilly and the magical stand off with my mom, I know she's telling the truth.

So now I have a moment to reflect and feel safe. And yet there's still an anxious knot in my stomach. I can't place the cause, but the feeling won't go away.

"I'm here! I got it!"

Our little ceremony has been waiting on one last guest, and we all turn to watch AJ bounding through the grass.

"I had to look through like six boxes before I found it," she says, handing me the final item we needed before this ceremony could get underway.

"That's fine, thank you so much for going back," I say. "I can't believe I forgot it."

"Yeah, it's not like you've got anything else on your mind," AJ jokes. "Vampire wound, killed your mom, skin freaking glows all the time."

I stifle a laugh. The "killed your mom" thing is almost off color, but that's how AJ rolls. Also, when you break it down, I did kill my mother, and I'd do it again if I had to.

I look down at the keepsake she brought, and my lip immediately starts to quiver and tears bubble up.

Nanny's old Red Sox hat.

Before she lost her mind, we'd watch baseball together all the time, going down to Boston to watch the Red Sox and even driving up to Portland for minor league games. Nanny was a fanatic, though she wouldn't shout or cheer at the games; she'd just watch, her eyes wide, a constant smile on her face. It was like a kind of magic she couldn't understand, these men batting around and chasing after this tiny orb.

After the incident, which I now see in a *very* different light, baseball was the one thing that could pull her through an episode. I always thought it was the boring commentary from the announcers, but it was something deeper. It was a peace she found in the skill and strategy, and watching the little ball take flight.

I don't have many other trinkets of Nanny's, and I don't really feel a connection to her possessions. I truly do feel her inside my heart, a piece of her soul living inside mine, flowing through the magic she returned to my veins. So I'm going to throw this hat off the cliff and into the waters below, saying goodbye to the hardships Tilly endured while in her physical form, and turning the page on this chapter of her magical existence.

The princes each bring their own element to

this goodbye ritual. I said they didn't need to make any grand gestures, but they clearly feel a sense of gratitude for Tilly, as they should. Darius squeezes a drop of blood into the hat, Zev adds a tuft of hair, and Rune places a single leaf, one from a tree in his homeland, he says.

AJ pours in a shot of Powers Irish Whiskey, which was the first thing she got drunk on, stolen from our bar during a sleepover when she was 14. Tilly helped her through the hangover and never told her parents, something AJ has never forgotten.

When everyone finishes their moment with the hat, I take it back and add one more thing. Her ashes. Finally, she will be free.

I walk it to the cliff's edge and conjure an image of my grandmother, of times I spent with her growing up. Of her smile. Of the love in her eyes. "Thanks for saving me, Nanny. Me and Rain."

I feel a slight ripple in my stomach, like the sensation when you're on a rollercoaster. It's just a little tickle from my Nanny and it makes me smile.

I throw the hat off the edge and watch as her ashes begin to glow as they are carried to sea by the wind. In the distance, I could swear I hear Nanny's laughter, like she's on a great adventure and enjoying every minute of it.

After a long moment of silence, I turn back to this utterly bizarre and beautiful little family I now have.

"Okay," I say, forcefully wiping tears away from my eyes. "Now we have to head back to the bar so the community can say their goodbyes to Tilly and Joe the Irish way."

"Here, here," AJ says, taking a swig from the bottle of Powers.

I pass Zev the baby and walk over to Darius, who's still standing at the cliff's edge, his gaze lost in the horizon.

I slip a hand into his and he squeezes it. "She was an incredible woman," he says, referring to Nanny.

"Yes, she was."

He looks down at me. "She was so proud of you."

That means more than he'll ever know, or maybe he does know, I realize, as I feel a swell of love for him.

"It's time to go," I say softly. "But I can't show up to the bar glowing."

His nostrils flare and eyes dilate as I tilt my neck.

As his teeth sink into my flesh, I close my eyes

and wrap my arms around him.

He holds me up as my legs wobble, and he takes just enough to ease the magic building up in me. The pleasure and pain spiral in me and I wish we were alone, because there's so much more I want to do with this man.

But that will have to wait.

We have time now.

We have my whole life, it would seem.

THERE'S a line outside Morgan's when we return. I keep the star tucked in my pocket, with a small hole so it can stay in contact with my skin. It's not an elegant solution, but it works well enough for now.

Zev shifts into wolf form before we enter, since that's how he's known here. Though he complains about it, I think he secretly enjoys not having to talk to anyone.

We go in through the back so I can unlock the front door from the inside.

Rune and AJ get in place behind the bar. Zev stays at my side wherever I am--a gesture that now carries added weight given our relationship, and Darius takes the baby so I have free hands to hug and greet people.

I unlock the door and folks I've known my whole life pour in. That night, everyone shares stories about my grandmother, from her younger days to more recent years. She touched so many lives. There are many toasts and many tears, but also so much laughter. And Joe's spot at the bar is kept empty, with his favorite beer in front of it. We toast to him, to the man who would wake in the middle of the night to help a friend, no questions asked.

Rain is passed around as everyone greets her. Zev sniffs each person who touches her and makes sure they know if they hurt her they will regret that choice.

For one night, I forget about the looming war with three powerful kingdoms and just focus on this moment, being surrounded by friends and family, celebrating two lives that were well-lived and will be well-remembered.

My eyes are red-rimmed and my face hurts from laughing as we close up and let the last patron out.

When I finally lock the door I'm ready to pass out for a few days straight, but Darius halts that plan as he approaches with a box.

"What's all this?" I ask.

"Some personal effects of your grandparents we found when we upgraded your living environment. I thought you might like to look through them. Maybe they can bring you some comfort."

I walk over to him and peek into the box. I've seen it before. There are pictures, letters, newspaper clippings and cards spanning almost half a century. Nanny and I spent many nights pouring over the contents.

Darius sets it on one of the tables, and I sit and begin removing items one by one to show them to the others. The Sexies all sit with me, while AJ, who has seen the box before, goes upstairs to put Rain to bed.

I smile at the picture on the top of the pile. "This was their wedding day," I say. They were just teenagers with a lifetime ahead of them. I wonder if they could have imagined what their lives became. Can anyone ever truly know what path they will ultimately end up traveling?

There are newspaper clippings from weddings, funerals and births in the family. And love letters my grandparents sent back and forth during the war. One of these days I will curl up with a glass of wine in front of the fire and read these. Nanny always said I should.

My hand drifts over another letter, and I freeze.

This one is new.

My name is scrawled across the envelope.

The handwriting is familiar.

"My grandfather must have written this… but I never received it," I say, opening the envelope and pulling out the letter within. The paper looks fairly new, and the writing seems to be scribbled hastily in black ink. My throat tightens as I read the letter, my hands shaking.

MY SWEET BERNIE. If you are reading this, then I am dead. More than that, my life was taken by forces more powerful than you can imagine, all so that you will return to Rowley. Bernie, you need to leave. Forget about Morgan's. Save yourself and my grandchild. I wish I could have been there for her birth. I know Nanny does as well.

Please heed my warning. You are not safe. Go to Budapest. There you will find a man named Timothy Trendle. Tell him I sent you. Tell him… tell him you are his daughter. He will help you.

I DROP THE LETTER, and it floats to the floor as tears begin to sting my eyes.

"What's wrong?" asks Darius, as Rune takes my hand, and Zev meets my gaze.

"My grandfather says he was murdered, and that my father…" I say, my voice cracking. "My father is alive."

THE END

Want book 2 in The Last Witch series the moment it goes live? Be sure to sign up for our newsletter. You'll also get **TWO FREE BOOKS** plus a weekly inspirational newsletter. Just let us know where to send your FREE books>> http:// thenightfirm.com/karpov-kinrade-newsletter/

Acknowledgments

Writing a book with a friend is a whole new kind of fun, especially during a global pandemic! Evan made me laugh so much during this process that I give him a 5/5 stars. Highly recommend as a co-author. (But you can't have him, he's mine.) So thank you, Evan, for not only being one of my best friends, the best theater teacher my kids have, my favorite actor on The Office, and an all around awesome human being with a really cute kid, but also for being an incredible co-writer!

Also a big thanks to our patrons for always being there for us. Our ninja beta team who help spot the typos that add themselves to our books after we are done writing and editing. BAM the

BRILLIANT, for always helping with launches, ideas, graphics and more! And of course, to our readers, for being the best in the whole world!

~Lux KK

About Karpov Kinrade

Karpov Kinrade is the pen name for the husband and wife writing duo of USA TODAY bestselling, award-winning authors Lux Karpov-Kinrade and Dmytry Karpov-Kinrade.

Together, they live in Ukiah, California and write fantasy and science fiction novels and screenplays, make music and direct movies.

Look for more from Karpov Kinrade in *The Night Firm*, *Vampire Girl*, *The Last Witch*, *Dungeon Queen*, *Mad Girl*, *Of Dreams and Dragons*, *Nightfall Academy* and *Paranormal Spy Academy*. If you're looking for their suspense and romance titles, you'll now find those under Alex Lux.

They live with their three teens who share a genius for all things creative, and seven cats who think they rule the world (spoiler, they do.)

Want their books and music before anyone else and also enjoy weekly interactive flash fiction? Join them on Patreon at Patreon.com/karpovkinrade

Find them online at KarpovKinrade.com

On Facebook /KarpovKinrade

On Twitter @KarpovKinrade

And subscribe to their newsletter at ReadKK.com for special deals and up-to-date notice of new launches.

~~~~~

If you enjoyed this book, consider supporting the author by leaving a review wherever you purchased this book. Thank you.

Also by Karpov Kinrade

A reverse harem paranormal romance with humor and good liquor. (with Evan Gaustad)

The Last Witch

A Werewolf, A Vampire, and A Fae Walk Into A Bar (The Last Witch, 1)

A reverse harem Greek Mythology adventure with a badass heroine and some serious kickass action. (with Liv Chatham)

Dungeon Queen

Warrior Queen

A reverse harem paranormal romance with mystery,

suspense and plenty of twists. (with Heather Hildenbrand)

Mad Girl: Locked Up

Mad Girl: Fights Back

The Night Firm

A reverse harem fantasy romance with mystery, suspense and depth.

I Am the Wild

I Am the Storm

I Am the Night

A standalone dark paranormal romance with mystery

Wanted

In the Vampire Girl Universe

A fantasy romance with mystery and intrigue.

Vampire Girl

Vampire Girl 2: Midnight Star

Vampire Girl 3: Silver Flame

Vampire Girl 4: Moonlight Prince

Vampire Girl 5: First Hunter

Vampire Girl 6: Unseen Lord

Vampire Girl 7: Fallen Star

Vampire Girl: Copper Snare

Vampire Girl: Crimson Cocktail

Vampire Girl: Christmas Cognac

Of Dreams and Dragons

Standalone fantasy romance novellas

The Winter Witch (with Heather Hildenbrand)

Forever Bound

Get the soundtrack for I AM THE WILD, OF DREAMS AND DRAGONS and MOONSTONE ACADEMY wherever music can be found.

Nightfall Academy

Court of Nightfall

Weeper of Blood

House of Ravens

Night of Nyx

Song of Kai

Daughter of Strife

Paranormal Spy Academy (complete academy sci fi thriller romance)

Forbidden Mind

Bella World

Maddie World

The Three Lost Kids and Cupid's Capture

The Three Lost Kids and the Death of the Sugar Fairy

The Three Lost Kids and the Christmas Curse

About Evan Gaustad

Evan grew up in Northern California before moving to Los Angeles in 2001. He worked as an actor and a writer in LA until 2015, and now splits his time between writing and running the drama department at the School of Performing Arts and Cultural Education in Ukiah, CA.

Follow him on Amazon.

Also by Evan Gaustad

It's Not the End of the World

A book about that time the world didn't end even
though it was supposed to.

by Evan Gaustad and Clint Gage

A reverse harem paranormal romance with humor and
good liquor. (with Karpov Kinrade)

The Last Witch

A Werewolf, A Vampire, and A Fae Walk Into A Bar
(The Last Witch, 1)

Made in United States
North Haven, CT
29 January 2023

31826017R00212